PRAISE FOR
THE PRETTY CROOKED SERIES

· ·

"Crackling-good adventure."—*Kirkus Reviews*

"A pretty twisted, modern-day Robin Hood story."
—Melissa de la Cruz, *New York Times* bestselling author
of the Blue Bloods series

"Packed with romance, humor, and adventure, *Pretty
Crooked* will steal your heart."—Sarah Mlynowski, author
of *Ten Things We Did (and Probably Shouldn't Have)*

"Tantalizing. For fans of Sara Shepard's Pretty Little
Liars books."—ALA *Booklist*

Pretty WANTED

Elisa Ludwig

KATHERINE TEGEN BOOKS
An Imprint of HarperCollins *Publishers*

Katherine Tegen Books is an imprint of HarperCollins
Publishers.

Pretty Wanted
www.epicreads.com

ISBN 978-0-06-206612-1

Typography by Joel Tippie and Laura Lyn DiSiena
15 16 17 18 19   PC/RRDH   10 9 8 7 6 5 4 3 2 1
❖
First Edition

TO RAINER, my most wanted.

PROLOGUE

"RUN!"

Aidan and I darted through the maze of bleeping machines, dodging the mindless drone-type people attached to them. Our mirrored selves moved in my peripheral vision, silver flashes amid the blinking lights and too-bright colors. To anyone else, maybe, we were just part of the shiny casino décor.

We followed the patterned carpet out into the hallway where it seemed to stretch out into infinity. Past the dimly lit bar area, smelling of ancient smoke. Past the gift shop with its decks of souvenir cards and ashtrays and fuzzy dice. Past the change station with its yellow plastic buckets of tokens.

My heartbeat egged me on, a steady drumming. Legs, arms, lungs moving together in an orchestra of fear and adrenaline.

And my brain, churning. I thought of all we had

learned so far, and what we still needed to find out. There were some clues by now, but too many unanswered questions. That was what kept me going. No matter how hard things got, I couldn't forget what I'd come here for—to uncover the truth.

"Look out! Heads up!" Aidan called out as a man wheeled a metal cart in front of him. Aidan's reflexes were quicker than mine as he lurched to the right and re-upped his speed. But I paused, feet jamming on the floor.

Big mistake.

A hand grabbed my shoulder.

I shuddered as I turned around, expecting to come face-to-face with the man who'd tried to kill us.

But when I looked up, I saw that the hand belonged to a security guard, a tall acne-faced guy in a pale blue uniform.

"Miss, can I see some ID?"

Bailey was after us. So were the police and an angry FBI agent in California, not to mention the general public, who'd seen our police sketches on the evening news. Now was not the time to stop.

"Sorry," I called back over my shoulder, ducking out of the way.

He shouted something but I hurled myself onward, ignoring him, and followed Aidan through the entrance to the Rock 'n' Steaks restaurant.

We tore past the hostess stand and the people waiting

in line. Then the waiters and tables, the giant guitars. An Elvis statue and a mannequin dressed like Katy Perry and a buffet spread of green things and brown things.

"Excuse me," I called out repeatedly to the customers, not wanting to be rude. Sure, we were interrupting their prime rib platters like the two derelicts on the lam that we were but at least we could be, you know, polite about it.

The side exit dumped us onto the dock in the middle of the river. The sky was darkening now, and I was trying to get a hold on where we were, where we would go. We had to get back on solid ground, back to where the road was.

"This way," I called to Aidan, angling us around the outside of the boat toward the front entrance.

Our feet pounded the wooden boards and we flew down the ramp toward the parking lot. I had a stitch in my side and my head throbbed, but there wasn't a fragment of a second to lose now, certainly not enough time to get our stolen car back from the valet. We'd abandon the wheels and go by foot.

The lights of the city were just flicking on, cars turning on their headlamps to forge through the purple dusk. I could make out Aidan ahead of me as we scrambled up the steps to the pedestrian walkway of an old railroad bridge. There was still shouting, sounds of running behind us. I couldn't say how close.

We kept on running while two lanes of traffic rushed

by in each direction, the Mississippi seething brown and frothy far below our feet. We were crossing back into Missouri and the Gateway Arch loomed ahead of us, lit up by strategic spotlights. Like a reassuring smile. Or a mocking one, depending on your frame of mind. Mine was, needless to say, a little bit bugged out.

I'd made mistakes. I'd taken chances. But I'd done it out of love, and that had to count for something, right? I only knew one thing and it was this fact that kept me going: We had to get there, before he got to us.

ONE

AS WE ROLLED forward, I flitted in and out of the dream. Me and Leslie, racing our bikes. In this imaginary world we were the same age—maybe eight or nine—going around and around a dead end in a suburban neighborhood. New Mexico, maybe? Or Washington State? I couldn't place it. All I could see was the pavement, sparkling through the spokes of my wheels, and Leslie's blond head bobbing in front of me. We were singing a child's taunt: *They can't catch us. They can't catch us.*

Then she stopped short.

Mom's calling, Leslie said.

I looked up and saw what could only be a bullet, metal glinting against the white sky, the body of it twisting in excruciatingly slow motion, coming for me.

Look out!

I startled awake, gasping. A scream caught in my throat.

"Willa? Are you okay?"

I nodded. It was a dream, I knew that. Yet the pain on my brow was real. The driver must have hit a bump; my head must have hit the window.

"Damn," I said, rubbing it. Sensation flooded my body as the reality came back in bits and pieces. The bus. Aidan next to me.

"You had a nasty bang-up there."

"Yeah. I startled myself," I said. What I didn't say was that the dream was worse than the hit. The dream chilled me to my bones, and I wanted it gone from my mind. "Where are we?"

"Almost to St. Louis. We just crossed the Missouri," he said.

Sure enough, the brown-and-green strips of farms had given way to office buildings and shopping centers. A little later, the city skyline appeared on the horizon, silvery and ghostlike, the famous Arch cupping it protectively. It was a welcome vision, a relief. We were here, finally.

We limped out into the fluorescent light of the Greyhound station on a Monday afternoon, the noisy, low-ceilinged den filled with people and their sprawled baggage. It was a thirty-six-hour bus ride from Bend, Oregon, or it would have been except that we got off at Boise, Idaho, and spent a few days lying low, waiting for the media firestorm to die down. This included Thanksgiving in a diner, eating open-faced turkey sandwiches.

Which, believe it or not, was not as depressing as it sounds.

Thanksgiving was rolling into Christmas as it's wont to do, and the new holiday was already here, it seemed, hanging from the green boughs strung up all over the depot. There were also cardboard strings of dreidels, even red, green, and black flags that said HAPPY KWANZAA. It was time for inflatable, lawn-sized snow globes, peppermint everything, sugar binges, and forgetting grudges.

I welcomed the cheery atmosphere, especially after this last leg of the journey, a full seventeen hours. My knees had forgotten how to straighten, and my whole body felt sore and battered. That wasn't even counting the bruises and aches we'd both acquired while running away from the cops and the thugs that were trying to kill the woman I'd always thought was my mother but who, as it turned out, was actually my sister.

Let's put it this way: It had been a rough few days. Add to that my constant fear that everyone we saw was looking at us funny, and I was in quite the jacked-up state.

Still, I couldn't help but feel a little more hopeful in a new place. On the way out, I grabbed a city map from the tourism and information desk. Neither of us had been to this city before and that added to the sense of possibility and excitement.

Then we put on our sunglasses, adjusted our hats—all

part of the disguises we'd picked up at the last stop in Denver—and stepped out into the cold air. I was already rocking the hideous dye job I'd given myself at Sam Beasley's house in Santa Barbara, California, a few days back. (Yes, *the* Hollywood star Sam Beasley, and no, we did not get to meet him, because, well, we'd broken into his house and squatted there overnight.)

Aidan pinched the thrifted, baggy, boy jeans that were hanging off my hip bones. "Anyone ever tell you that you look sexy when you're undercover?"

My heart lifted and shimmied, like one of those inflatable men outside of a car dealership. No, nobody had ever said that to me. Sure, I'd never been on the run before, but I'd also never really had a boyfriend, either.

"You don't look so bad yourself," I said, appraising his hunter-green down vest, the now-shaggy blond hair falling across the broad planes of his face and some newly acquired stubble. Even thirty-six hours on a bus and countless days on the road before that could not diminish his charms. He was a hottie. It was his essential nature, like birds and flying, or the sun and rising. Just something he did very, very well without trying.

Aidan held up a plastic-wrapped wedge we'd picked up somewhere along the way. Boise? Laramie? "We've got half a roast beef left. Want some?"

He took a few bites and handed the sandwich to me, which I gobbled gratefully as we walked, even though it was soggy and the bread was now infused with the chemical flavor of its packaging. "Can I just say that you're awesome?"

He put his arm around me. "You don't have to say it."

"I do, though. How many guys would put up with this?" By "this," I meant the life on the run, the danger, the crappy food, the questionable fashion.

His green eyes locked on mine. "Since you come along with it, I'd say it's a pretty good deal. Besides, I kind of like the excitement." That part I already knew. He outperformed everyone, even me, in the danger junkie Olympics.

I melted into the crook of his elbow. At least I had Aidan. After she'd disappeared, we'd spent days searching for my sister, Leslie—it was still weird to even think of her as my sister and to call her "Leslie" when I'd always known her as Joanne/Mom. It was when we'd finally found her that she'd dropped the bomb about who she really was. She was on the run, too, and now, with the help of FBI Agent Jeremy Corbin, we'd "killed" her off and she was on her way to Mexico. I'd probably never see her again.

I'd lost everything—I had no structure, no semblance of real life, nothing else to keep me tethered to any kind of sanity, but I had Aidan. We'd gone through some rough patches, and he still harbored secrets—namely why he'd gotten kicked out of school and why some skank named Sheila was sexting him. I'd chosen to look beyond that, though, because I couldn't have done any of this without him. And because I had a major case of the lovins.

We were salty and sweet—together a perfect combination, like a caramel, which was our inside joke. If he was still a mystery to me in some ways, well, that made him all the more alluring.

"Think Corbin knows where we are yet?"

I shrugged. Corbin was supposed to take us into FBI custody, and we should have been back in Paradise Valley awaiting trial. But we'd skipped out on him. "Maybe. I hope not."

Not that it mattered. We were going to have to proceed with our plan either way. I knew I couldn't keep running forever, but I was going to do this thing, find out who my real mom was, while I still could.

We crossed the street and a man in a knockoff Burberry overcoat passed us, holding my gaze for what felt like a long time. Panic shot through me like an electric shock. Did he see us? Did he recognize us? Was he a cop? Or was he working for Chet and Bailey?

No, I told myself. He was just some guy. Maybe he was admiring Aidan's vest or he recognized someone behind us. There was careful, and there was complete paranoia. *Get a grip, Willa.*

Besides, we were better off here than we'd been in all those small towns in California. In a big city, we could find resources more easily and duck into a crowd if we needed to. Surely, the people of St. Louis weren't looking for us when they had their own criminals to worry about. This was one of the murder capitals of the United States, wasn't it? I smiled to myself, mostly at the twisted fact that being in a murder capital could be so comforting.

Then I remembered that my real mom had been murdered. She was one of those statistics. The smile was replaced by a sudden bout of nausea.

"I see coffee," Aidan rasped, extending his arms out like a caffeine-deprived zombie in the direction of the nearest green sign.

"That's a Starbucks," I said, trying to shake off the icky feelings. "Out of our budget."

Our cash was limited—we had three hundred dollars our friend Tre and a network of supporters had given us. We'd used most of it on the bus tickets and we couldn't use credit cards, not unless we wanted to be traced. (We also had our phones from home, but we couldn't use them, either; they were secured in a GPS-free off position while we relied on a temp phone I'd bought in Tahoe.) I was pretty sure that Aidan, son of a high-tech CEO, had never heard the word *budget* in his life, let alone observed one. So it was up to me to be the guardian of spendage.

"You're killing me, Colorado," Aidan said, using the pet name he'd given me when we met at the beginning of the school year, because I'd moved to Paradise Valley from Castle Pines.

That was all before my life had spun out of control.

Where my mom was my mom, where there were no secrets (that I knew of), where I was a regular teenager without so much as a mailbox-whacking on my record.

Aidan was still looking at me like my pupils were double espressos. He showed me his shaky hands. "C'mon. Help a brother out."

What could I say? A four-dollar latte was out of the question. I scanned the blocks ahead for other options. "There's a 7-Eleven across the street. Go in there. I'll wait out here and look at the map."

He disappeared through the hot dog–decaled doors, leaving me outside as I tried to orient us to our new surroundings. I could see where we were. Olive Street. I just needed to figure out where we were going.

As I trailed over the page, scanning landmarks and unfamiliar names, a moving smear of white and blue caught in the corner of my eye. I looked up.

Cops.

My pulse skipped over itself.

Two cop cars, actually. City police. Now in the parking lot. A few feet away from where I stood.

They were probably here for donuts, right?

Except, I remembered, it was late afternoon.

I cast a tentative glance over and saw an officer sitting in the front seat of the car closest to me, talking into a radio. Looking actively involved in police business of some kind. Like he could be reporting something suspicious. Me?

No. No way. No.

When Aidan emerged, carrying a brown paper bag and two cups of coffee, I grabbed his elbow and steered him away from the store parking lot.

"We need to move," I said through gritted teeth.

"Five-oh at four o'clock," he said.

"Right."

We walked a few paces hurriedly. Then I saw a third police car, coming toward us in the opposite direction. It seemed to slow down as it neared.

Oh shiz. I was tempted to break into a run.

"Act natural," Aidan said, holding me back with his firm tone. "We're just walking."

There was nothing natural about it. We were wanted. I'd imagined the scenario too many times to count, when and how I'd be dragged back to juvie. The place I swore I'd never end up again. The place where everything seemed to veer offtrack.

If I hadn't been caught stealing stuff and trying to help the kids in my school, I wouldn't have been on TV. And if I'd never been on TV, those guys would never have found Leslie and gone after her. She and I would still be together. But then, I never would've learned about my real mom, either.

The police car was almost in line with us. We had only a minute, a minute and a half, maybe, before they caught up and dragged us away. My heartbeat raged through every artery and vein. My eyes darted around,

13

looking for an escape hatch. On our right was a big granite building fronted with marble-relief panels, the bulk of the thing taking up most of a block. On our left was just a park. No cover at all.

Think, Willa.

If I didn't find something quick, I'd never find out who my mother was. If I couldn't figure this out, it was all over, before it had even begun.

TWO

IT REGISTERED THEN, somewhere in the back of my fear-addled brain. What that big hulking building was. The Central Library. The door was within our reach. There were probably labyrinths of shelves inside to get lost in. Best of all, it was the most uncontroversial place two teenagers could go.

"In here," I said, making a quick decision.

Beyond the main entrance was an oval-shaped pavilion with a soaring, coffered, gold ceiling and marble floor. Aidan trashed our still-full coffees but stuffed our food into his bag before we stepped past the front desk, cursing under his breath.

The library was relatively empty for a weekday afternoon, but we went downstairs, headed for the farthest corner from the front door. Cautionary tactic.

We watched. We waited, breathing hard. Aidan mourned the loss of his newly found beverage. I wondered how much luck I could reliably expect to have at this point, after so many close calls. The truth was, I'd been rolling sevens for a while now. Karma was probably sneaking up to nip me in the butt.

A good fifteen minutes elapsed and we looked at each other quizzically. There was no sign of cops inside. Maybe we'd lost them. Or maybe they weren't really after us to begin with. Could I have imagined it?

"What do you think?" he asked.

"I think we need to give it more time," I said. I felt safe here, safer than I'd felt in a long time. Maybe it was the stillness, or the kind-looking people reshelving books, or just the old-fashioned idea that everyone should have access to free reading. In a library, you didn't even think of stealing, because everyone was equal.

"Well, while we're in this temple of knowledge, we may as well make use of it," Aidan said, angling across the room to a bank of computers.

He was right. We had some research to do if we wanted to learn more about my mom.

I figured it would be easy enough to look up news reports about her murder. It had taken place in 1997, I knew that much. And I knew her name: Brianna Siebert.

I typed it into the computer and hit search. But nothing came up. Nothing useful, anyway.

"It's been a long time. That info is probably not cached on Google. I think we need to try a news database," Aidan suggested.

I went back to the home screen and scrolled through

the library's options, then clicked on NewsBank. But the service required a user name and password.

"We don't have a library card," I said, sighing. I should have thought of that.

"Did you forget that I'm here, Colorado?" He nudged me aside and got to work, typing quickly. "You don't need a stinking library card when you have a hacker on your side."

He recovered cookies from a previous user and within a few minutes we were in. He made room for me again. I reentered my search terms and immediately articles from the *St. Louis Post-Dispatch* came up.

BRUTAL MURDER OF YOUNG MOTHER
SHOCKS UNIVERSITY CITY

A thirty-two-year-old woman, identified as Brianna Siebert, was found dead last night, the victim of an apparent gunshot wound to the chest. The woman was discovered by a neighbor, and police were called to the Delmar Loop apartment building at about 11:35 p.m.

Police confirmed the death as a homicide and are looking into leads.

Siebert had recently moved to the apartment on Westgate Avenue. She was working as a waitress at Blueberry Hill.

Police have been unable to locate the family of the young woman, including her sixteen-year-old daughter and newborn baby. Anyone with information is urged to contact CrimeStoppers line at 888-555-STOP.

I stared at the screen, blinking. There was a photo of her, from a three-quarters angle, shoulders up. It was reprinted in black and white in the newspaper, so it was hard to make out her coloring, but her hair, which fell in textured layers to her jawline, seemed darker than mine or Leslie's—maybe it was brown or red. She had finely plucked eyebrows and a smile that looked half formed, as if she'd been caught by the camera in midthought. Her eyes weren't smiling. They were heavy—wary, almost.

I kept looking at the photo, desperate for some connection to this person. This was the first time I'd ever seen her. I don't know what I expected to feel, but nothing about her seemed familiar to me.

"That's my *mother*," I said softly, trying it on. "How is that my mother?"

"She's pretty," Aidan said. "She looks nice."

These were not judgments I was capable of making. She was dead. She'd been *killed*. I'd never even had the chance to know her. The baby they were talking about—that was me.

And the killer, there was no word of the killer. I scanned through the rest of the articles. After five years, the case had gone cold, apparently, dipping down to little mentions farther back in the papers. Blurbs.

But there were things we knew already—things I didn't particularly want to know, that made me think the police had to be overlooking something.

We knew there was money, a lot of money—five

million dollars in total—that Leslie had accidentally taken from our apartment the day she found our mom dead. She said she'd had no idea it was there. But sensing danger and the possibility that child services would separate us, she'd run out of the place as fast as she could, taking me and a duffel bag with her. The cash was in the bag, and we'd been on the road ever since—though I'd always stupidly believed it was because she was looking for inspiration for her paintings.

We also knew that the two goons we'd run into, Chet and Bailey, had been after Leslie, hunting for the money. It didn't take a huge leap of deductive reasoning to assume that they were my mom's killers. They were certainly capable of it—we'd seen that firsthand.

So we had some idea about the who. We just didn't know the why. Or at least not completely. I still had no clue where the money came from, or how my mom was involved in any of this. Leslie said she thought our mom and Chet had some kind of thing going. That was something I didn't want to think about. In fact, the idea made me want to heave.

Aidan's breath was hot on the back of my neck as he read with me, saying out loud what I was thinking. "I don't understand how the case could be cold. Wasn't the murder on Chet's FBI rap sheet?"

I nodded and unzipped my bag to pull out the FBI file we'd nabbed from Agent Corbin's car. Flipping through it, I put my thumb on the line.

"They knew Chet was involved, yeah. According to this, he was never convicted. Not enough evidence."

Aidan cocked a shoulder. "Gotta love the justice system. They probably didn't have DNA. I don't think they even used it for most cases back then. So he's gotten away with it all this time."

I ran my hand over the bird pendant that rested between my clavicles. It was my mother's. She'd given it to Leslie, who'd given it to me when we moved to Paradise Valley. Of course, it meant even more to me now, my one physical link to that unknown past.

"We'll get those bastards," Aidan said softly but with determination. That's what I loved about him. He was always on my side. He had no fear, and he was ready to take on anything. But he was also all too happy to walk into trouble, and sometimes I had to be our voice of reason.

"I don't want to solve this case, Aidan." We weren't detectives. If the police hadn't found anything, then how could we? "I just want to know who she was. I want some closure."

"Fair enough," he said. "Then we'll get you closure. But I'd still love to see them fry."

We studied the map again and figured out our plan of attack. We would start with the apartment building, see if we could talk to anyone who knew her. Then hit the restaurant. Someone out there would have to remember. Fifteen years was a while ago—my whole life-span—but it wasn't ancient history.

For tonight, we would have to go squat somewhere. With so little money to rely on, we'd been finding fancy vacation homes to break into (à la Sam Beasley's) since we'd been on the road. I'd never attempted a break-in in a city before but we would just have to wing it.

We powered down the computer, careful to erase all of our browsing history, and went upstairs.

Our feet echoed on the floor, thin and metallic sounding in so much open space. I looked around. There was nothing else here, no carpet, no wall hangings, to absorb the noise, but it still didn't seem right, the emptiness of the place.

Aidan halted us. "Willa. Listen."

"For what? I don't hear anything."

"Exactly." He pointed to the ceiling, where most of the lights were out, then to a giant clock on the wall. It was 7:37 P.M.

In front of the computer, we'd somehow lost track. All of the doors were locked now. The library was closed for the day. Unless we wanted to risk setting off what was sure to be an elaborate alarm system, we were going to be here until it opened again.

Welcome to the Hotel Dewey Decimal.

I looked at Aidan. "Guess we know where we'll be spending the night."

When I thought about it, it wasn't so bad, really. I'd always been a fan of books, and now we were surrounded by them. It saved us the trouble of having to find and break into a new place to sleep. Not to mention that it was kind of sexy to be trapped in a deserted building with Aidan. For days on the bus, we hadn't really had any time to fool around, and the close proximity to him had been a constant low-grade torture, like a slow-burning fever. Now we were finally alone.

He clearly felt the same way as he took my hand and led me into the darkened periodicals room. He sat down on an upholstered bench and pulled me onto his lap.

"C'mon, Colorado." He reached up to cup my face, drawing my mouth to his.

I didn't think I could ever get tired of making out with him—the plush pull of his lips, the woodsy smell of his skin, the warmth of his hands traveling over me, even this new scratchy stubble. There were private, interior parts of him I'd never know, but these parts I could touch.

There was a looming question, I knew, of when and how we would take it further, but for right now he hadn't put any pressure on me and we were living in the moment. We were both good at that, it seemed. And this moment was especially irresistible.

I said a silent thank-you to all the writers of the world for giving us cover.

I lay down on top of him, so that our bodies were perfectly aligned, ran my hands under his shirt to feel his smooth skin.

I definitely didn't want to hear the footsteps out in the hallway. But there they were.

Aidan heard, too. "What was that?" he asked.

We listened as I hovered above him in non-kissing stillness. Definitely footsteps. Getting louder, too. I got up and broke away, tiptoed closer to the doorway, but shielded myself against the wall as I peeked out. Outside in the corridor, the beam of a flashlight bounced around.

Security was here, doing a check. Of course.

We should have known that they don't just close up a place like this. There were rare books in here.

I crept back toward Aidan as quietly as I could, gesturing with my arms to move. We needed to hide, and pronto.

We ducked behind the periodicals desk, a solid block of wood, and quickly arranged ourselves on the floor in fetal position. My face was pressed to the carpet and I felt its scratchy fibers imprinting themselves on my cheek as we waited.

The light swept into the room, preceding the guard who was only an arm's length behind. We could hear him whistling as he flashed and looked, the piercing gold beam moving here and there, finding the darkest corners.

Please. Don't let him see us. I no longer even attempted to pray to anyone or anything specific. With all the crap I'd pulled over the past couple of months, I knew I didn't deserve any godly intervention from any supernatural force. It was more for my own well-being that I clenched my teeth and mentally repeated the words until they became a soothing mantra. If I was going down, at least I could do so in a somewhat chillastic manner.

The sounds drew nearer. He was totally going to see us. The light was already leaking through the crack between the bottom of the desk and the floor. It was seconds before it would be on us, exposing us here in burning brightness.

There would be questions, handcuffs maybe. Our long-winded explanations. And then we'd be sent back to Arizona. Back to the cinder-block rat house they'd locked me up in before.

I couldn't even look at Aidan. I depended on him to not be afraid and I knew any glimpse of fear on his face would send me over the edge. Instead, I held my breath and squeezed my eyes shut, feeling blood fill my body, expanding every capillary. This was it.

Just then, a car screeched outside. A horn honked, belatedly but long and angry. Car doors slammed. Two people yelled at each other. A near accident, it sounded like, because both voices were full of blame. The guard went to look out the window. And then, before we even knew what happened, he was gone, taking his flashlight with him.

Somehow, by the grace of crappy drivers, we were alone again.

But the make-out mood was kinda ruined.

THREE

IN THE MORNING, we woke up to the sound of doors upstairs. We dashed toward the stacks and hid there, crouching between metal shelves filled (appropriately enough) with legal books, waiting until the library had officially been open for an hour and we could blend in with the other patrons. As we stared silently at the gold foil–lettered volumes with their white call-number stickers, I wondered if there was anything in there I needed to know. Anything that could help me make my case when it was time to make it. Probably not. In the eyes of the law, I was pretty much a deadbeat. The law didn't care whether you were looking for your mother— or whether you were doing the wrong thing in order to do the right thing.

We'd mapped her apartment building, which was almost a straight shot west, but it was miles away, too far for us to walk.

"Let's get a cab," Aidan said.

"It might be expensive," I said.

"It's more efficient. Time equals money, you know? That's what my dad always says. The sooner we do this, the better."

I thought it over. If we really got stuck we could always call our friend Tre again and get him to wire us more cash, but I was hoping not to have to do that. I knew Tre's feelings about being involved with our illegal activities were conflicted at best, and I didn't want to do anything more to compromise him.

Aidan was right, though. We had a job to do right now and we couldn't afford to stall.

"All right," I said, and Aidan stepped out into the street, raising his arm.

Within minutes, a yellow taxi pulled over and we hopped in.

"Where to?" the driver called out without turning around to look at us. Obliviousness or cynicism? Both were good in this situation. Both meant he wouldn't recognize us.

"Six eleven Westgate Avenue," I said.

The cab hurtled forward and merged onto the freeway.

"Can I have that book?" I asked Aidan. In his backpack was a notebook where I'd been keeping track of all the things we'd "borrowed" along the way, an IOU list so I could eventually send payment of some kind. I wanted to jot down the library before I forgot.

When I was done, I handed it back to him. Outside my window, I could see we were leaving the central part of the city and I began to feel nervous. Where was this cab taking us? What if we were headed to the boonies? What if I didn't like what I found out about her? Then what?

You knew what you were getting into, Willa. You just have to take what comes. Not that this internal dialogue made me feel any better.

There were lots of truths I'd learned recently that I hadn't exactly relished. Like the fact that Leslie was my sister (technically half sister, since we had different fathers), or the fact that she and our real mom were entangled with some unsavory folks. Or the fact that the money we'd lived on my whole life was most likely dirty. But I'd survived, hadn't I? I was still here. Wiser and maybe a tad more jaded, but still here.

"There's the Arch," Aidan said, pointing out the window behind us. We could see the uppermost bend of it from the backseat. I traced it with my finger. It seemed like a good sign, somehow, like it was guiding us where we needed to be. Like the North Star or a little blue GPS dot.

When we turned to face front again, the scenery on our right was changing to a huge open park. Overhead, we saw a billboard for the World Bird Sanctuary, with a cheerful illustration of an owl—it was the kind of place Leslie and I would have visited if we'd been here on vacation. She was always into the nature-type spots.

Then the cab wheeled off onto a wider boulevard. We passed a number of neat houses with red and green mansard roofs, all with well-kept lawns, and I exhaled, my spirits lifting again. I saw signs for Washington University, and we were moving closer to what looked like a busy downtown area, with people everywhere.

Finally, the cab pulled up in front of a three-story U-shaped building with a white stucco front and a circular front drive. The style was vaguely French, from an era when people seemed to care much more about detail.

"Valet parking," Aidan said, approving. "Classy."

We paid for the cab and then approached the sliding-glass front doors.

"Now what?" Aidan asked. "Should we Sly Fox our way in?"

I shook my head. "No. We go in like normal people."

I wasn't above Sly Foxing when we had to but we were here for legitimate reasons. Besides, it wasn't a high-security type of place, probably because it was in the kind of neighborhood where thieves or break-ins didn't seem to be a major concern.

Except, of course, the night she was killed. *They could have used more guards then*. I gulped down my unease.

The building was nice, though. Really nice. I could see why she would have wanted to live here. The swishing doors revealed a lobby of sorts, fronted by matching potted plants and a wall of mailboxes. Signs pointed to the gym, pool and sauna area, the courtyard garden, as well as an in-house dry cleaner. There was a front desk, but the concierge behind it was busy talking to what looked like a couple of tenants. Easy enough.

My mother's unit was 3B. The elevator opened to the third floor where the hall was laid with shiny hardwood floors and a narrow strip of fresh Persian carpeting. I'd lived here once, too, I realized. Not that I would remember anything—it was just the first few months of my life. But it was strange to think about, that I could add this to the list of places Leslie and I had called home. Leslie still remembered it, I was sure. How could she forget the place where she found our mom . . . ?

I shuddered, quickly brushing the thought away again.

We would start with some neighbors. We found 3C and knocked. A tired-looking woman in workout clothes and a ponytail came to the door, a gray cat trailing inquisitively behind her.

I smiled, trying to put on my friendliest face. "Hi. We're looking for someone—well, we want to find out about someone that used to live here a long time ago. Her name was Brianna Siebert. Do you think you can help us?"

The woman paused a moment and then shook her head. "Name doesn't ring a bell, but I haven't been here that long."

"Do you know anyone who might have lived in this building fifteen years ago?" Aidan asked.

"Actually, there is one lady, there at the end of the hall." She pointed to 3H. "Mrs. O'Leary. She's been here for a while. You could try her."

We thanked her and moved on. This time, Aidan knocked. No one answered at first but we could hear the faint drone of a TV inside.

Aidan hit the door again, a bit louder.

"Coming," we heard a voice call, and then footsteps in a lopsided rhythm. Someone with a limp, or hip problems, maybe.

The door opened to a woman with dyed red hair that capped a heavy patina of makeup and false eyelashes. She was probably in her seventies but she was clearly fighting against it.

"Can I help you?"

Aidan tipped his head at her. "Yes, ma'am. We're wondering if you might have known someone who used to live in three B. Her name was Brianna Siebert."

I glanced sidelong at him, admiring his sudden show of manners. The woman was clearly responding well to them, too, because she smiled.

"Brianna? Hmm. No, I don't think I remember anyone of that name. There was a family that used to live in that unit, with a few young boys. I don't remember a Brianna."

"When did you first move here?" I asked.

"Right after my husband died, 1999."

That wouldn't work. "She would have lived here in 1997. Anyone else here that would have been around that long?"

She shook her head. "I'm afraid not. People come and go, you know. Was this a friend of yours or something?"

She was my mother. I felt the words like a bone in my throat. *She was killed.* "Yes," I said. "A friend."

She smiled, looking genuinely sympathetic. "Sorry I can't be of more help, dear. I'd say you should try three B but that unit has been empty for the past month. The last tenants moved away."

"Should we try people on the other floors?" Aidan asked after she'd shut the door.

It was freaking me out to be in this building, so close to where the murder took place. It was impossible not to be acutely aware of that haunting history. I paused in front of 3B, staring at the little brass number, as if standing there could tell me something, but of course it couldn't. Not unless I was a TV psychic.

We were wasting our time here.

"No. Let's move on. We can always come back if we need to. Can I see that map?"

He pulled it out of his bag and handed it to me. I'd marked Blueberry Hill on there. It was only a couple of blocks from the apartment building. She'd had an easy commute. She must have been a practical type of person.

As we stepped back outside, I tried to look around

and see what she must have seen every day on her way to work, tried to process it through her eyes. Bars with neon signs, a bookstore, a butcher shop with a green awning, a hamburger joint. It was a funky neighborhood. Had it looked like this then? What had she liked about it? What did she want to change? What had she daydreamed about? Had she taken me with her, ever, to work? Or to stroll around the neighborhood? Did I check out the little dogs on the street, like the two dachshunds in matching Christmas sweaters crossing in front of us?

Blueberry Hill was right where it was supposed to be, an azure marquee out front with light-up figures of a man and woman dancing on its uppermost edge. It looked like a relic from another time. Maybe some things *didn't* change, not even after fifteen years.

We walked in through the front door, but the place didn't seem to be open to customers just yet. Inside were wooden booths, surrounded by old records and funky displays of PEZ Dispensers and Simpsons figurines. Opposite them was an old, elaborately carved bar capped with taxidermied animals, a giant swordfish. A huge 1950s jukebox glowed yellow and red from the adjoining room.

A portly guy with a goatee and a stained apron approached us. "Can I help you with something?"

"We're looking for anyone who remembers a woman named Brianna Siebert. She worked here in 1997?"

"Hang on," he said. "You'll want to talk to Rich, the manager."

He disappeared behind a swinging door. We stood by the bar and looked up at the television while we waited. A sports program recapping a Rams game was replaced by a man with a long, sun-pinkened face and blond hair that was thinning on top. He was handsome, in an older-politician sort of way.

"I'm State Senator David Granger. I've lived in St. Louis my whole life. I've dedicated my career to making this city a better place. But some people have sent our jobs overseas and now our state is hurting. I know what it's like to watch your friends and families struggle while someone else makes the big decisions. That's why I'm running for U.S. Senate: to bring back the American dream. And you can help me."

Your typical political ad. I tuned out the TV as I was more interested in looking at all of the memorabilia around me. This was quite a place.

When I turned back at the screen, pictures flashed of the man shaking hands with factory workers, cutting ribbons, posing with his arm around senior citizens.

On top of the images were the words DAVID GRANGER FOR U.S. SENATE. VOTE IN THE RUNOFF DECEMBER 12.

The guy who had to be Rich came out from the back room. He was taller and more slender than the first guy, and he wore a red baseball cap over his gray hair.

"I'm so sick of hearing about this runoff. I just want

34

Granger to win already. Hermann's a joker." He flicked his chin in our direction. "You kids were asking about someone?"

"That's right," I said. "Brianna Siebert. We think she probably worked here in 1997."

Rich nodded, tucking his hands in his armpits. "I was a server back then. The name doesn't sound familiar, though."

I sucked in a breath, feeling my hopes falter. So he didn't know her. Then who would? "Did anyone else you know work here at that time?"

He shook his head. "I'm old. Most people, they come here as Wash U students, stay for a few years to supplement their books or beer allowance, and move on. Sorry. Wish I could help you out."

"Do you mind if we look around a little bit? Is there an employee room or anything?" Not that I expected there would be any trace of her from fifteen years ago. At the very least I could see more of what she might have seen. Maybe it would fill out the picture of her a little bit more.

"Sure, the break room's right back here." Rich led us through the swinging doors through another doorway.

Not very inspiring. I looked around at the row of small lockers, a white fridge, and a table with a few dinky chairs. I didn't know what I was expecting to find, but there was nothing much here.

I turned toward the door. That's when I noticed a

series of photos on the front wall, documenting what looked like an annual softball game, each dated with a little plaque. I scanned through them and found 1997 on the second row. There were twenty-five or so people lined up, all wearing Blueberry Hill T-shirts with their first names embroidered on the front pocket.

I studied the image, going face to face. It took me a moment, but I found her. She was resting her head on the shoulder of the woman next to her, smiling broadly, giving the camera a thumbs-up. Her hair was pulled back and she had a baseball cap on, but there was no mistaking it—she looked exactly like the newspaper image we'd seen yesterday.

"Aidan!" I cried. "I think this is her."

"It does look like her. But her shirt says Angie," he pointed out.

Rich closed in on where we were standing and looked over our shoulders. "Oh, Angie Chambers. She was the one who was killed."

I felt air drain from my chest. Why was she using another name? "So you remember her? Her name was Angie? Not Brianna?"

"I never knew her. I think I started a couple months after that all went down. But it was tragic. Everyone knew about the murder. Now that you mention it, I do remember the cops saying she'd been living under some kind of alias."

She'd changed her name. Just like Leslie had. Why?

My mind was going in a million directions.

"And who's this?" I pointed to the woman next to her, squinting to make out the name on her shirt. "Toni?"

"Yeah, I knew Toni. Those two were pretty tight, supposedly. I think Toni was a student at Wash U."

A friend. Toni. A student at Wash U. I committed the information to my mental contacts list. I motioned to Aidan that I was ready to leave. "Thanks so much for your help," I said.

"Like I said, it was a while ago." Rich shrugged.

"This is something, though," I said. It wasn't much, but it was the first real piece of information I had about the mysterious Brianna Siebert aka Angie Chambers aka my mother.

FOUR

THANKS TO RICH, we had a next step: finding Toni Whateverherlastnamewas.

We needed access to another computer. As we walked around and looked for one, I pulled my hat lower and scanned the people on the street, waiting for buses, walking strollers, slumped on benches. Did anyone recognize us? I couldn't be sure. Was this how someone like Sam Beasley felt? Fame was kinda like a fabric softener sheet no one told you was clinging to your ass.

"You think maybe Toni knows more about Chet?" Aidan asked. "Especially if he was your mom's boyfriend?"

"It's possible," I said. "I don't know if I buy that my mom could have been involved with a criminal."

"Hey, I'm with *you*, aren't I? And vice versa?" He gave me a lopsided grin.

It wasn't the same thing and he knew it. "He's just

such a creeper. And dangerous. Who could be attracted to that guy?"

He shrugged. "You never know what he was like fifteen years ago. People change over time. Maybe he was better looking and nicer back then. Or who knows what she was really like? Maybe she had issues."

I tipped my head in concession. It was possible. If you considered all of the information I had so far, it was even probable.

Still, I knew I was biased, but I couldn't imagine that anyone related to me could be an evil person and especially not Chet-level evil. "There must be other possibilities. I mean, we still don't know what the relationship was."

"Something went wrong. We know that. She changed her name, right? Maybe she got mixed up in bad stuff without realizing it, whether it was romantic or not." Aidan stared up at the gray sky as he thought through potential scenarios, playing detective. "Maybe he used her to hide the money in her house or something. She found out what he was doing and questioned him about it and he killed her."

"Maybe," I said doubtfully. "But she changed her name before she was killed. If we're going on the theory that she changed her name because she knew she was in danger and was trying to escape him and his shady money, that wouldn't explain why the money was in her house that night." That led me to the other possibility, which neither of us was saying out loud: that she was fully culpable, that she knew exactly what Chet was doing and had even participated in it in some way. People changed their names when they were avoiding the law all the time. Hadn't my sister done that very thing? She'd changed my name, too, from Maggie Siebert to Willa Fox.

This was all beside the point, though. "Look, like I said before: We're not here to solve the case. I want to know who she was."

As we crossed the street, Aidan's face grew taut with seriousness. "I'm not sure we can separate out who she was from what happened."

Maybe he was right, but I didn't need him to protect me from it, either. "Can you just help me find a computer?"

He held up his hands. "As you wish."

I'd led us toward the Washington University campus. We were now walking through the gate and moving along a tree-lined path. The wide lawns on either side were frost tinged and covered with patches of snow.

"Why don't we try one of these buildings?" I pointed to an arrangement of brick-fronted buildings around a clock tower ahead of us.

His eyes widened. "That looks like dorms. You're suggesting we use the computer in there?"

"Unless you have a better idea," I said, feeling the giddy spark I always felt when I was about to pull a maneuver. Of course, breaking in was wrong—I knew that—but we had a purpose. As long as I could say that to myself, I could justify what we were doing. Unlike the apartment building, this situation called for Sly Foxing.

He grinned, accepting the challenge. "All right. Let's see your magic."

We circled around the building, doing our reconnaissance, looking for doors, peering through windows. We could see that the front entrance was flanked by a desk with a receptionist-type person. Even if it was a student, and it probably was, we couldn't take a risk going in that way. The windows were tightly sealed, I could tell without trying. There were fire escapes leading to the second floor, but that seemed a little too dramatic for the circumstances.

Finally, we traversed a parking lot and came around to a back door by the loading dock. A row of bikes was chained up to a rack and I instantly felt a pang. I still missed my poor vintage bike that I'd abandoned back in Paradise Valley during a scuffle with the cops. Tre had rescued it and kept it waiting for me, but even so, bikes were a painful memory of how this all started and what I'd had to leave behind.

"That's a magstripe device," Aidan said, pointing to a black card reader mounted outside the door. "Old school. I can't believe they don't use RFID here yet. We can try to crack the programming code and reprogram

41

the magnetic stripe, or we can break the wiring on the reader—"

"That won't be necessary," I said, nodding toward the two girls coming down the pathway behind us.

I was thinking of one of Tre's lessons, which was that in a lot of cases human error was the simplest way in. Besides, we didn't have time for Aidan's schemes, not when two human-shaped keys were right in front of us.

The girls were deep in conversation: "So, you know, the other night at Jasper's? How he totally blew me off when Lara was there?"

"Yeah?"

"Well, he did it again yesterday in the dining hall."

"I can't believe it."

"I know."

I removed my sunglasses and hat, and Aidan did, too, as we stepped right up behind them. Girl A removed her ID card and swiped it through the scanner. Girl B opened the door, barely looking over her shoulder as she held it open for us.

In we went, like it was our business to be in the dorm building, which was basically a maze of white-painted concrete walls. To our left was a deserted laundry room. We ducked in there and let the girls get some distance ahead of us.

"If you were a computer, where would you be?"

Before he'd gotten kicked out of Valley Prep, Aidan

was a typical college-bound senior. "Everywhere," he said.

That didn't exactly help. My pulse was speeding, skittering along as I led us toward the stairwell.

I had to remind myself that it was only trespassing. Not nearly as dangerous as breaking into a house, stealing money from the bitchy girls at school . . . or ripping off the FBI, for that matter. This was Pee Wee League. The worst that could happen was someone yelling at us. But then, of course, that would give them time to recognize us, which would actually be pretty bad.

I held my breath as we opened a door to the first-floor hall and thought of everything I'd learned from Tre. *Act like you know.*

There were a few storage rooms, a mail room, and then a small room that was left undecorated, except for a long table and—booyah!—three Macs. Only there was another card reader by the door. We peered in through the little window and saw that two guys were sitting in the corner, working on their laptops.

I knocked gently on the door. One of the guys, the taller one with long stoner sideburns, got up and let us in.

"Thanks," Aidan said. "We forgot our cards."

The guys nodded. We were in. Simple as that.

We each settled down at a station and I got to Googling: Toni Washington University alum . . .

I would have preferred better, more specific search

terms, but this was all I had to work with. Business profiles came up, a Twitter account, something called Prison Inmates Online. The last one definitely sparked my interest. But most of these women were much older or much younger. If Toni'd been a student or recently graduated when she knew my mom, that would mean she was still in her late thirties or early forties now.

I Googled the alumni directory, but that was password protected. Of course. She was probably in there.

C'mon, Toni baby. Work with me.

Another search: Toni Washington University alum 1990s St. Louis . . .

I pulled up a page about a fifteenth college reunion with a comment from someone named TCumberland.

Hey, guys, can't wait to see you! It's been way too long. Toni (Patterson)

This was something. Toni Cumberland. That must be her married name. The date added up, too. I searched Toni Patterson and confirmed that she'd graduated from the university in 1996. So she wasn't a student when she worked at Blueberry Hill, but close.

Aidan, meanwhile, was typing furiously, slamming on the enter key, and typing more.

"Ack," he said, pulling at his hair.

"What's up?"

"I can't get in."

"To what?"

"The police database."

I pinched his arm.

"Ow!" he yelped.

Aidan and I exchanged looks. What mine said: *We can't have these two randoms lurking around while we look up sensitive intel.*

What his said: *They don't care who we are. Chill out.*

But the sideburns guy seemed to be looking at me for an extra-long time. I saw him give his friend an elbow.

"What was the date again?" Aidan asked.

"What?" I was distracted by Sideburns. He was grinning at us now. Or mostly at me. Maybe I was being paranoid again. I hoped.

"The date? Of the . . . event?"

"October 22, 1997."

After another pause, Aidan groaned. "Aagh. This is so frustrating. I'm close, I think. I just can't figure out the right string. . . ."

"Need some help with something?" Sideburns asked.

"No," I answered for both of us. We most certainly did not. I didn't trust most people right now, especially strange, scruffy boys who smelled like goat and eavesdropped and had the potential to rat us out. Even if they'd let us into a computer lab.

"I ask 'cause I'm good at tech stuff." He was up on his feet now and he edged closer. "I'm actually tutoring my friend over here. I can help you, too."

45

"I doubt you could help us with what he's doing," I said, trying to brush him off. "It's very high level."

"I'm on an accelerated track to get my PhD. No disrespect, but I know my stuff more than most people. And I'd like to help you." He raised his eyebrows and smiled. Flirty-like. He saw I was here with Aidan, right? "I'm on your side, you know."

There was no doubt now. It was obvious. He knew exactly who we were.

Aidan slid his chair away from the computer. "Actually, dude, I could use some help."

"What are you doing?" I stood up and tried to block the screen from Sideburns.

"Trying to help *you*," he said softly. "You want more information, right? Well, I want what you want."

When he said stuff like that, how was I supposed to argue with him? Still, this was a bad idea. It was one thing to hack into the police database and quite another to do it with witnesses.

I inched away reluctantly, allowing a view of the screen.

"So there's a database I want to hack into," Aidan said.

"Aha," Sideburns asked, pulling over a chair. "I knew you were doing something fun. SQL?"

"Yeah. I tried to query for an emailed password with a quote. I got the five hundred error message but when I tried to manipulate the query again I got a server error."

"And you schema mapped the fields?"

"It's not letting me."

"You're not asking the right questions. What about log-in underscore ID? Full underscore name? Try those."

Great. Now they were deep in conversation, yammering away in Nerd. The other guy, who had the physique of a gnome and wore a knit skullcap, moved closer to watch over their shoulders. He glanced at me and I broke the eye contact quickly, not wanting to encourage either of them. They looked extra young, like they could be high school kids themselves but they were probably just malnourished from spending all their time in front of screens.

Sideburns leaned over and typed something into the keyboard.

Aidan's face was knotted in concentration. "Right. Okay."

"Try it now," Sideburns said. Then he looked at me and winked. This guy was unbelievable. In another situation I might have found his boldness intriguing—he almost reminded me of Aidan, actually—but right now I couldn't handle it.

Aidan keyed more in, then hit enter again. "This is it," he said excitedly. "The complete case file. We're in."

Sideburns grinned. "Cha-ching. Told you."

"You're a genius," Aidan said to Sideburns.

He did a little corny bowing gesture. "I like to help out my brethren where I can. Especially if there's a cute girl among them."

Brethren? And now he was calling me cute in front of Aidan? He couldn't be serious.

But he was. The guy totally knew who we were and he was Team Sly Fox. A few weeks ago I would have been happy to meet him, happy to know there were people out there who were rooting for us, but I now was filled with unease. Everything about this situation felt wrong and out of my control.

I looked over at Aidan and saw he was getting uncomfortable. He put a protective—or was that jealous?—hand on my shoulder. "Right," he said. "Well, we've kind of got a thing going already."

I was mortified.

"My bad," Sideburns said. "Didn't mean to overstep."

I leaned in to look at the screen, desperate to change the subject and finish our job here. "So what's in there?"

"Looks like some photos." Sideburns clicked on the mouse and brought them up, a blur of red and white.

Aidan scrambled to quickly click away from the images. "We shouldn't look at those."

"What was it?" I asked.

"Crime scene photos," he said, barely meeting my eye. He didn't want me to be hurt.

I felt my stomach turn, although some small part of me was curious. Maybe there would be something useful in there. Not that I wanted to look at any of this stuff with Sideburns hovering around.

Sideburns must have finally gotten the hint because

he was backing off and he and his friend returned to their spot on the couch. "Seems like this is personal. We'll be right over here if you need us."

Aidan clicked on another tab. "Here's the inventory of the evidence that was found in her apartment."

I read through.

Master Bedroom
  - (1) clear drinking glass with 9 ounces brown liquid, tested and shown to be Diet Coke
  - (1) television remote
  - (3) DVDs
  - (1) 24-inch-screen TV
  - (1) DVD player
  - (4) pillows and pillowcases
  - (1) jar of change and loose bills, totaling $430
  - (1) poetry book, with a receipt from St. Louis Books, dated 10/22/97
  - (3) .380 spent shell casings

My shoulders seized as a chill skimmed over them. Bullets. From the gun that killed her.

Master Bedroom Closet
  - (8) trash bags of women's clothing
  - (4) cardboard boxes of household items, labeled
  - (1) apron embroidered with the name McLaughlin's Pub

Bedroom 1

    (3) sweaters, size 10

    (5) T-shirts, size M

    (1) American history textbook

    (3) loose-leaf notebooks

The clothes and books had to have been Leslie's.

    (1) Graco Pack 'n Play

    (1) box Huggies diapers

Those were mine, I assumed.

Living Room

    (1) handbag, blue leather

    Contents:

    (1) wallet, red leather

        Contents:

        $25 cash

    (1) Missouri driver's license issued to Brianna
        Siebert

    (1) library ID card issued to Brianna Siebert

    (1) Blue Cross insurance card issued to Brianna
        Siebert

So she'd changed her name, but not legally.

    (1) ticket stub to Smashing Pumpkins concert

    (1) business card for Psychic Services

(3) sheets from a Guest Services pad containing personal notes

(2) photographs of victim with two children

(1) ball-point pen, blue, with the name Blueberry Hill imprinted on the casing

(1) Turkish evil eye keychain

(1) Maybelline lip gloss, Bistro Red

(1) CoverGirl powder compact, Beige

(1) unopened package of Certs mints

A weird sense of recognition settled over me as I looked at this list of things that belonged to my mother, like I was filling out the picture of her in my mind, and she wasn't that different from me. She used makeup. She liked to read. She ate mints—the fact that there were still uneaten mints left in her bag when she died filled me with sadness.

She'd bought a poetry book that day, too. She hadn't planned for this. She'd had a future ahead of her. She had fully expected to live. She'd even thought about seeing a psychic. Maybe that would have changed things, if she could have possibly known what lay ahead.

At the same time, these little details felt so paltry. Was that all that was left of a person when they went, a few measly personal belongings, a couple of random clues? If this was the sum total of what I had, how could I ever understand who she was?

The more I knew, the more I wanted to know. I wished I could at least see the notes she scrawled on her waitressing pad. Or even the photographs they had of us. Maybe they could tell me more.

"Are you getting all of this?" Aidan asked.

I looked around. Unfortunately, there were no printers in here, so I had to write down what we saw the old-school way. He handed me a pen and a piece of paper from his bag.

"There's some stuff about the witnesses," he said. "Jot these names down, okay?"

My eyes trailed down the list. A few neighbors, the woman who ran my day care. I noticed Toni's name wasn't on the list.

"So is it true what they say?" Sideburns's friend called out from his side of the room. "That your friends got out of a police roadblock by impersonating an FBI agent?"

"What are you talking about?" I snapped.

"Your friends. In California? There was something on the Facebook page about it. That's, like, a felony offense. Bananas. How'd they pull that off?"

I stared at him blankly. All I knew is that the four of us, me, Aidan, Tre, and Cherise, had hijacked a Betelman's snack truck in Tahoe. Aidan and I jumped out of the back when Tre texted us to say they saw a roadblock ahead. Tre and Cherise had gone on without us and somehow made it through but I never did find out how they escaped.

Impersonating FBI? I hoped that wasn't it. That didn't sound like either of them, and even if it was, it wasn't something Tre would want going around online. But I certainly didn't want to sit here and speculate with these two randoms.

"Don't believe everything you read," I said finally, and looked at the clock. We'd been in here for almost twenty minutes. "We should get going. We can come back to this site, right?"

"Assuming no one realizes it's been hacked and changes the passwords, yes. That's a big if," Sideburns said.

Aidan closed out of the database and typed something else in.

"What are you doing?" I asked Aidan.

"Checking my email really quickly."

I thought about checking mine but decided against it—there could be more mean messages from the Glitterati, taunting me, or even worse, nothing at all. After helping us out in Tahoe, Tre and Cherise were back home in Paradise Valley and they were probably waiting for us to get in touch. Talking to them would only raise questions, questions I didn't have the answers to yet. Besides that, I had the growing sense that they were hooking up and as much as I hated to admit it, that bugged me a little. Not that I had any right to complain. It just made me feel left out, kind of, to think of them getting on with their lives without me.

And now that Leslie was gone, that was the sum total of people I had in the world. Sure, we had a bunch of stranger fans on Facebook who had glorified the legend of Sly Fox, people like Sideburns and his friend, but that wasn't the same as actual loved ones. They would never really know me—they only knew Sly Fox.

I went back to my station and looked up Toni Cumberland. There was no direct match, but there was a T. Cumberland on Manderleigh Woods Drive. I wrote that down, along with the phone number. It was worth a shot.

Beside me, Aidan kicked at the table leg.

"What?"

"Another email from my folks. My dad is resorting to bribery now. He says if I come home, he'll buy me a motorcycle or whatever else I want."

"And . . . ?" I looked at him, wondering if he was going to fall for it. Aidan's relationship with his dad was strained before we went on the run, but now that the police and media were involved in tracking us down, things had gotten worse between them. Still, it would be so easy for him to just give up and go home now. Who could blame him?

"And he's full of it. No way can he buy me back." His jaw tightened. "Screw that guy. He didn't even ask if I was okay. We all know he only wants me home so I don't ruin his precious reputation or his stock valuation. I mean, all he had to do was show some genuine concern. But he can't. He's incapable of human emotion."

I saw why he was angry. I'd never even met his

parents, and they sounded like rich jerks. At the same time, I couldn't help feeling the tiniest stab of envy. At least his jerk parents were in his life. He had a dad, when I didn't have the faintest clue who mine was. Even if we found out the truth about my real mother, that couldn't change the fact that she was dead and I would never get to know her.

"Parent problems?" Sideburns chimed in. "I've got a guy who's a wiz with day-trading—we could really mess with the old man if you want."

Could he learn to mind his own business?

"No thank you," I said firmly. "We're done. Ready, Aidan?"

Sideburns's friend stood up. "Wait. Before you guys leave, do you mind if we get some photos with you?"

"I really don't think—" I started.

"Sure," Aidan interrupted. "Let us put on our disguises, though."

He slipped on his hat and sunglasses. Both of the kids already had their camera phones out.

"No way." I stepped away, folding my arms. Even with disguises it was a terrible idea. "Aidan, come on. Don't be stupid."

"Please, Sly Fox," Sideburns urged. "One photo . . . We won't post them on the Facebook page."

"It won't kill us," Aidan said. His green eyes glinted with rebellion. He didn't seem the least bit worried.

I'd seen that look before and I didn't like it. It was his

father. His father had brought out the devil-may-care streak in him.

He was only posing a danger to us when he was like this. I had to put a stop to it, get him back on track.

"Yes, it could. Anyone could see it."

"It's just for fun," Sideburns argued.

"Photos are encoded with info, and how do we know they won't post it?" My voice was raised now. "The cops could trace us within hours."

"Trust us. We're fans," Sideburns's friend said. "We're not gonna turn you in or anything."

"Yeah, Willa, they're fans," Aidan echoed. "It's the least we can do."

I cringed. He'd used my real name. That did it. I was up in his face. "Is that all you care about? Being famous? We can't keep acting like this is a game. We're in real trouble here!"

"You need to calm down," Aidan said, holding out his hands, looking like a counselor talking someone off a bridge.

That infuriated me more, his talking as if he had cornered the market on rationality and I was the wacked-out one. "Don't tell me to calm down!"

Now he had his hands on my shoulders. "You're being way too dramatic about it—"

I shrugged him away. "I'm not being dramatic. I'm being practical and safe. Unlike you."

A burly man in a navy-blue security uniform appeared

in the doorway. He had a shiny bald head and a few extra rings of flesh around his neck. "Something going on in here, folks? I heard a racket out in the hall."

We fell silent then, watching as he stepped closer.

"Are you guys all Wash U students?"

We nodded.

"Can I see some ID, please?"

Think quickly. "Mine's in my room," I said. "I don't live in this dorm."

He turned to Aidan. "You?"

Aidan made a show of searching his pockets and of course came up with nothing.

"They're our friends," Sideburns said, and for once I wanted to thank him for being so ballsy. "We're just hanging out."

"I still need to see some ID. Why don't you come upstairs and sign in at the front desk?"

We followed him up the stairs. So okay, we'd sign some book with fake names and that would be the end of it, I told myself.

When we got to the desk we saw the girl who was sitting there earlier. She had a messy blond bun and a Victoria's Secret PINK sweatshirt on.

"These two need to sign in. They don't have IDs on them," the guard said to her.

She looked at us, her eyes slowly narrowing. Then she gestured for the guard to come closer to her. "Can I have a word?"

Aidan and I watched as they whispered, her eyes flicking over in our direction. She knew, too, and she was definitely telling him who we were. I had no question this time, judging from the furrowed expressions on their faces. A minute longer here and we'd be cornered.

Aidan saw all of this happening as I did. In synchronicity, we bolted out of there, bursting through the double front doors. Outside, the cold air sliced us in the face like broken glass. We broke into a run.

The security guy was close behind us, shouting, "Hang on!"

He could radio for backup within seconds. We needed a faster way to get out of here. I made a beeline for the bike rack, quickly found two frames that weren't locked up.

Sorry, bike owners, wherever you may be. But your no-chain is our gain.

I threw one at Aidan and he caught it against his chest. I got on mine, pedaling as fast as I could.

After a few minutes, I snuck a look back. Not good. The guard was almost parallel with Aidan. His arms were outstretched like he could grab on to the bike.

I tried not to have flashbacks to the night in Paradise Valley where the cops had chased me on my bike until my tire gave out. Then I was toast. We would be now, too, if we couldn't move fast.

C'mon, Aidan.

When I turned back again, he had pushed ahead by

a few lengths, and the guard was a blue-uniformed blur. *Whew.*

As Aidan pulled up next to me, we rode furiously down the path, moving side by side, looking for the street exit. We wove around students in between classes, passed through one quad and then another, the huge campus buildings hulking on either side of the lawn.

"Is he still with us?" I called to Aidan.

He looked back for me this time. Then nodded. Of course we had to pick the Lance Armstrong of bike cops to race away from. Of course it was weeks since I'd last been biking, and my quads burned with the effort. Of course there was snow and ice everywhere. Of course my brain was battling with my heart, yet again.

We couldn't give up, though, not now. We just had to outride him.

A crowd spilled out on the pavement ahead. As we got closer, I could see it was an outdoor Christmas bazaar, with tables of crafts and things, bundled-up people standing around, examining the items for sale. Too busy to notice us.

"Look out!" I called as we careened toward the throng. A few shoppers reacted quickly, scattering out of the way.

One was slower than the others, though. He fell backward onto a table, arms flailing, sending all of the glass ornaments on display crashing. This was *not* what I had in mind.

"Oh my God! I'm so sorry!" I yelled. Damn. I wanted to stop, to see if he was okay. It wasn't his fault he just happened to be in the middle of our getaway chase.

"Forget about it. Keep going," Aidan yelled from my left side, reading my mind. "We don't have time."

Because the security guard was inching closer, moving through the path we'd cleared.

Make that *guards*.

There were three of them, riding in a triangular formation, one of them clutching a radio to his ear. Was he calling for more backup?

"You there. Stop where you are!" one called to us. "Stop or we'll have to take you by force."

Force. This was not good. I had to get us out of here.

The rush of air froze my ears and nose despite the hat. My eyes were filled with wind-stung tears. If either of us slowed down at all, for even a few seconds, they'd be on us. I didn't know what sort of force they intended to use, and I didn't want to find out, either.

Through blurred vision, I made out a gate up in front of us, where the quad path gave way to an actual road. This was the exit we needed. At least then we'd be off this campus and out into the world where we could get ourselves properly "lost."

There was one problem, though: a staircase between the gate and the street. And the only way beyond it was down down down to the bottom where patches of ice were spread across the cracked concrete.

Bodily safety or freedom?

I glanced at Aidan, and with a shrug he gave me the go-ahead.

It wasn't much of a choice. I held my breath and let the bike roll forward, hitting each step with a violent jump.

Dunkdunkdunkdunkdunk.

My whole body shook with each drop, the angle frighteningly steep. If I skidded, so much as rotated the handles by a fraction, I would lose the bike. My back would become plural.

I clenched the handles, gritted my teeth, and rode it out, feeling my bones thud and crunch, feeling my brain crawl into its cave of blank terror until the tire rubber hit the flat ground again.

Please let me get through this.

But when the landing came, it was anything but smooth—the bike frame wavered as I struggled for balance, the handles swerving out of my grasp. I had to stop for a second, throwing my weight forward and planting both feet on the ground to steady my body.

I had it, finally. Control. Until I remembered.

Oh God. Aidan was still up there.

"Careful," I called back to him, but my voice was lost in the sounds of traffic.

I was in the middle of the street, I realized then, because a pickup truck came by, honking loudly and cutting me off, its mirror just grazing against the sleeve of my jacket.

"Get out of the road!" the driver yelled.

In another situation I might have yelled back, but now I was just too stunned to do much of anything except push off the ground with the sole of my sneaker, attempting to regain some momentum and cross the road, silently praying Aidan made it down in one piece.

There was no red light, and no time to wait. My sweaty hands barely gripped the bike as I wove in and out of three lanes of traffic, hoping no one would speed up and pin me between bumpers.

I heard a scream behind me, a scared-but-not-staring-death-in-the-eye scream.

Phew. He'd made it. Freaked out, yes, but alive. I turned to see that his face was spread into a grin of pure relief.

When I turned back, a bus pulled into the far right lane, blocking me. With only milliseconds to spare, I braked, hard, just missing it by inches.

My bike flew up onto the curb, dragging me with it. I did a donut and paused, straddling the bike and waiting for Aidan to cross so we could figure out where to go from here.

"Willa, they went another way!" Aidan called, dodging a VW and then an SUV.

"Which way?" I yelled back.

"I don't know. But they didn't take the stairs."

Another bus was coming.

I called out to warn Aidan. He sped up—and it must have been *too* quick, he must have hit a slick of ice—the bike spun out from under him and he went flying, catching himself on the winter-gouged asphalt with his hands. The bike landed with a clang a few feet away.

He cursed. It was a killer spill. It hurt just watching. I rushed to his side as traffic continued to flow around us. "Are you okay? Can you get up?"

He did, wincing.

"Is anything broken?"

"I don't think so." He reached for the bike, nervously looking behind him. No sign of the cops but we were less than a block away from campus. They could pop out anywhere.

"Leave it," I shouted. I dumped mine, too, and we ran, huffing in the frigid air as the pavement underneath us became a gray-and-silver haze. We ran until our lungs burned and our legs gave out and we were sure that the security guys were no longer behind us. Soon we were away from Delmar Loop, out of University City, and closing in on an area with a large park.

"What the hell were you thinking?" I said, finally. "Photos, Aidan?"

If I expected remorse, I wasn't getting it. "Meeting us was the highlight of their day. Didja see how bored those guys were?"

"It doesn't matter. We shouldn't have been in that

situation. Security never would have come if we weren't fighting."

"You were the one yelling." His palms were hoisted up to his armpits. "You have to learn how to trust people, Willa."

No, I didn't. Not after everything that had happened to me. "And why should I?"

I was furious at him, so mad I could barely speak. How could he just put us in jeopardy like that, over something so stupid? Did he care about what we were doing? Did he care about our freedom at all? I was getting the feeling I'd had back in California, that Aidan's "charms" were the exact qualities that threatened our well-being.

"Because some people deserve to be trusted."

Maybe so. But how could you tell who fit into that category? For the first time in a few days, I felt despair bleed through the numbness and exhilaration. It was an impossible task to get to know my dead mom. And as soon as we learned anything, I was going back to juvie or I'd have to live the rest of my life as a fugitive. Either way, I was an orphan. Either way, the future for me was bleak.

He, of course, couldn't see that. "It's so easy for you," I said, spite creeping into my voice. "You have parents waiting at home. Anytime you feel like it, you can just give up and go home to Mommy and Daddy."

"That's not true," he said angrily. "You don't

understand what it's like with them."

"You're right. I don't. Because I don't have any family anymore, Aidan. This is all I have. And I can't go taking risks like this because you're feeling pissed off or rebellious."

He was rubbing his hand, not saying anything. I saw that it was inflamed, embedded with gravel. Road rash. I'd been there before and it was the worst.

And then my fury subsided some. He was injured. His feelings were clearly hurt. Snapping at him didn't help matters.

"Do you need a bathroom?" I asked. "Should we get some cold water on your hands?"

"We can stop if we see one," he muttered into his collar.

After a few more minutes, he spoke again. "Don't be mad, Colorado. It's going to be fine."

I looked up and gave him a weak smile—not because everything felt fine, but because I wanted it to be.

He took this as encouragement. "God, the look on that security guy's face." He laughed as he mocked the guard running with his arms out. "The way he was trying to grab the bike? Priceless."

It *did* seem funny in retrospect.

And just a few short weeks ago, I might have laughed with him. I might have seen lots of humor in the situation. But this time I couldn't.

I was mad, and it wasn't only at him. I was mad at

myself. How had this whole thing become a game? When did I stop knowing the difference between right and wrong? When did I start letting us take such crazy risks? It was becoming clear to me that being lawless and free, as exciting as it once seemed, wasn't everything it was cracked up to be.

FIVE

THE AFTERNOON SUN was hanging low, a pale imitation of itself, and the air was frigid. I hadn't lived in Arizona too long, but I'd already forgotten how cold winter could be anywhere else. I thanked the thrifting gods for my parka and hat, which were doing double duty as disguises and necessary layers.

We ducked out of the stinging air and into a CVS to get some antiseptic cream and a bandage for Aidan's hand. We were halfway down the first aid aisle when our temporary phone rang.

It was Tre. "Willz." He'd picked up Cherise's nickname for me. Ergo, they were probably doing it. Or something along the lines of "it." "Where are you?"

"St. Louis. Home of the Arch and the World's Fair and 7UP." I tried to keep the mood light. "How are you?"

"Me? I'm all right. So what's going on?"

I took a breath and decided to tell him the truth. I'd

left out a few key details the last time we talked, which was at the Bend bus station. "Look, things are a tiny bit more urgent than I let on. Those guys Chet and Bailey? They found us in the Painted Hills, and they kind of tried to kill us. We managed to escape and we found Leslie and she told us that she was my sister. Then we had our FBI contact Corbin help us fake her death so she could go underground. On the condition we'd go into custody. Only we sort of dodged him and came here."

The words flew out in one long, breathless string. Maybe I was hoping he wouldn't pick up on the scarier parts.

No such luck. "They tried to kill you? Jesus." His familiar voice took on more than an edge of concern. "And then you escaped? From the *FBI*?"

"It sounds worse than it is," I countered. Aidan gave me a look.

"It sounds pretty damn bad," Tre said. "Why didn't you tell me?"

I saw an opportunity to deflect attention. "Well, why didn't you tell me how you got away that day in the truck? I heard something about impersonating FBI, from Facebook?"

"Don't be ridiculous and don't change the subject. Go on, tell me the rest. Just tell me everything now."

"We got some other information." I stepped away, leaving Aidan to pick out his goods, and moved to the dental hygiene aisle, lowering my voice. "You know how we thought it was my grandmother who was murdered? It turns out that was my real mom. We think those guys who were after Leslie did it. But we don't know all of the specifics."

"So what are you doing in St. Louis? Playing Sherlock? You should leave this to the cops."

A woman with a plastic shopping basket stuffed with makeup and maxi pads pushed past me to look at the floss selection. I moved away, turning my back to her and lowering my voice to a whisper. "No, no, no. I'm not trying to solve the case."

"What then?"

Somehow, it was getting harder to explain this when it should have been easier. "I just want to know who she was. And I can only find that out here."

He was silent for a beat. "Either way, I wish you'd give it up. You're putting yourself in serious danger, you know that?"

"I know. But this is something I have to do."

"Look, all I'm saying is there are people who care about you, who don't want to see you hurt." His voice wavered a bit. "Don't forget about those people."

I was taken aback by this sudden display of emotion from him. He'd always been the strong, silent type. "I appreciate that, and I won't, but—"

"—but you need money."

"Yeah," I said, feeling guilty suddenly that this was what our relationship was reduced to.

"Okay. I'll talk to Cherise. We'll get back with you about the details." He sighed. "Listen, I want to support you, I really do."

"But?"

"But it's gotten out of hand. I think—I'll get you the money, but then I might need to take a break."

"I get it." I stared down at the floor. "I know you're putting yourself on the line and I understand if you need to keep your nose clean."

"It's not just that, Willa. I have other reasons, too. It's . . . harder than I thought. Worse than I thought."

On that point I agreed with him. "Okay," I said uncertainly. "If that's what you want."

"Stay safe, all right? I'll text you."

I hung up, powering off the phone, and with it, my fragile connection to Paradise Valley.

"What'd he say? He sending more cash?" Aidan asked when we were back outside. A gauze bandage was now wrapped around his hand.

"He said—he said he needs a break." I don't know why I felt the need to use his euphemism. Maybe it was easier than saying the truth, which was that Tre was probably abandoning us—like almost everyone else in my life. "He said they'll text us about wiring more money."

"A break." He nodded. "Well, that sucks. But I guess he can't be the Sly Fox fan club president forever."

Like that was all I cared about. Didn't he see it went far beyond that? Didn't he see how much of a loss this was? Without Tre behind us, our mission suddenly seemed that much more daunting. Tre had always given me solid advice from the first time he showed me the thieving techniques he'd picked up from the other guys at his boot camp to just a few days ago, when he'd helped Aidan and me formulate a plan to get to Oregon with the stolen truck (even if I still didn't know exactly how he pulled it off). More than that, he was someone I could truly depend on. He'd always kept me on track and held me accountable.

But he had his own freedom to protect. And that was his choice.

"No," I said finally. "I suppose he can't. How's your hand?"

"It's bumpy but I think I'll live. Look, don't be upset. So we've had a few setbacks. We're still going to do this thing."

"Yeah?" I looked into his face.

His eyes were bright and serious, and I felt my anxieties ebbing. He was unpredictable and rough around the edges but there was no fighting against the Aidan Murphy dreaminess. He could sell a fire extinguisher to a pyromaniac. The guy had serious moves.

"*I'm* not giving up, Colorado. But we can't work on an empty stomach. Let's go get some lunch. I'm starving. My treat."

"So you're treating me with *our* Facebook money?" I nudged him in the side.

"Order anything you want." He waved his bandaged hand. "I'm feeling generous."

"So what next?" Aidan asked me, licking barbecue sauce off the back of his thumb. We were sitting in Bubba's Smokehouse restaurant, back in downtown St. Louis. Aidan had insisted that since we'd skipped breakfast we could afford to splurge on this slab of ribs for our late lunch, that in fact we actually needed the calories if we were going to survive. I thought that was a little bit dramatic.

"We talk to Toni Patterson slash Cumberland." That was the plan, at least. I took a bite of the smoky meat with sweet, spicy sauce. "These are pretty good, I have to admit."

"Best in the city," he said, pointing to a ribbon on the wall. "Don't say I never take you anywhere, Colorado."

A couple of college-aged guys and their girlfriends were watching highlights from last night's football game on the mounted TV over the bar. My eye traveled upward and saw that the show had broken for an SUV commercial. The group was sparring about their predictions for the rest of the season.

"Football," Aidan said, looking over that way. "Never my favorite sport."

"I always took you for more of a rugby guy," I said. "Or is it lacrosse?"

"Neither. Soccer all the way, man. My dad's supposed

to fly me to the World Cup in Brazil." He paused over his rib. "Well, I guess I blew that one, didn't I?"

The game ended and another political ad came on. David Granger again.

"Enough of this guy," someone at the bar said. "I'm so sick of this election already."

He changed the channel to a cable news show, where two girls were being interviewed. I squinted. Was that . . . ?

"Kellie and Nikki," Aidan said, taking a sip of his soda. "This has gotta be about us. It's a bad scene when the Glitterati are on TV. That's all they need, more reasons to act like divas."

"Shhh," I said, trying to listen.

They were sitting in two armchairs in what looked like someone's living room. Probably Kellie's, but if so, it would have been only one of the three separate living rooms in her gigantic mansion. A caption flashed underneath their made-up-for-TV faces: FORMER CLASSMATES OF TEEN OUTLAWS "SLY FOX" AND AIDAN MURPHY.

"I wish they'd give me a nickname already," Aidan said. "It's completely unfair that you get such a cool one and I'm stuck with what's on my birth certificate."

Kellie was staring into the camera, the tears in her big blue eyes threatening to drip mascara down her cheeks. "She's my friend. Or she used to be."

"And you're still hurt about it?" the interviewer asked gently. She was softballing them. Of course. Their

73

parents probably had lawyers write up some agreement about what questions they could and could not ask ahead of time.

Kellie pulled on her diamond-studded earlobe. "Yes. One minute she's here, and the next she's gone. I feel . . . I don't know. Violated, I guess. It's really a trust thing."

"Oh, come on," I muttered. Those were the most obviously fake tears I'd ever seen. Now she was acting like her feelings were hurt? The girl had viciously bullied Mary, Sierra, and Alicia. She had threatened me and Cherise on numerous occasions. She maintained a rotating stable of hookups that she picked up and put down at her convenience. She didn't know the first thing about trust or real relationships.

"This whole thing has gotten way out of control," Nikki was saying. "I mean, this girl has stolen from us. Doesn't anyone *care* about that? It's, like, she's become this hero or something, when we're the real victims here. I'm still traumatized. I can't sleep at night. My parents have had to get me therapy to deal with my anxiety."

"That rich chick needs a reality check," one of the guys near us said. "Victim? Give me a break. Next thing you know, she's going to sue someone for damages."

"I don't blame her for being mad," his girlfriend piped up. "The criminal kids are celebrities, crisscrossing the country. These girls are stuck in their boring little hometown, baking brownies on Friday night. Hell, I'd sue, too."

Baking brownies. If only. They had no idea what the Glitterati were capable of, or why I'd stolen from them to try to help the scholarship kids. In a way I felt nostalgic, looking at their perfectly dewy eyes. They reminded me of a simpler time, when stealing from rich jerks was the biggest challenge in my life. Now things were much more complex.

"What I want to know is how come they haven't caught those kids yet? Seems like they're on the news every day," the other guy said.

I gulped for air. Did they even know that we were sitting right behind them? Aidan tugged his hat lower.

The camera flashed back to the announcer who was standing at the gate of Valley Prep, the little white sign framed to his left. "For days now, members of the media have been camped out at this elite school, trying to make sense of the story, and how the actions of its two lawbreaking students have impacted an ordinarily sleepy and affluent community. Most of the teachers and staff at the school refused comment, but we did manage to speak to Latin instructor Sheila Clemons, who offered her thoughts."

The camera flashed to an attractive thirtysomething woman with satiny black hair and long legs emerging from a slim gray skirt. I vaguely recognized her from the halls of VP, but I'd never taken Latin.

"Did you know these students?" the interviewer asked, frowning with faux concern.

"I knew Aidan Murphy, yes. He was my student."

I looked over at Aidan. His face was slack.

"How does it feel to see kids you've nurtured and trained on the run like criminals?"

Ugh. Could the question be any more leading? I was starting to really hate the media.

She paused and tossed her mane of hair. "For most of us here, it's very strange. We're trying to do the best we can to keep the school running as usual so that those students who are following the rules and doing what they're supposed to be doing don't get shortchanged. But it's a distraction, I'll say that much."

The interviewer nodded sympathetically. "What would you like to see happen to them? Do you think they should be put in jail?"

"I just hope their immature behavior isn't rewarded with a reality show or something. They're already getting way more attention than they deserve. No, I hope the cops find them and justice is served."

"What a bitch," Aidan said.

I looked at him, surprised at how strong his reaction was. I'd never heard him use that word before.

Then it hit me: *Sheila*.

Sheila was the name of the woman who had been sending him text messages. I'd caught them on his Droid and tried to confront him back in California, but he'd told me that it was a long story, that he couldn't explain it because he was trying to protect me.

Miss you, baby. That was what one of them had said. My stomach roiled, all the greasy food we'd eaten minutes before threatening to revolt. Did he have some kind of fling with *his teacher?*

His secret—all this time I'd been trying to give him the benefit of the doubt, but I realized with sinking dread that it was something much bigger than I'd ever guessed. He promised me he never lied. Secrets or lies, what was the difference? Aidan had been dishonest with me all along. Just like everyone else.

I'd thought I could deal with whatever he was hiding, that true love was stronger than anything, but now I was starting to think differently. In the situation we were in, with so many people against us, I needed complete trust. And, bottom line, Aidan still hadn't proved that he deserved mine.

I looked up again. Cops were standing in front of the dorm at the university.

This time, I only needed to see the infographic: Fox and Murphy Sighting in St. Louis. The screen flashed to footage—it had to have been cell phone footage—of us racing across the campus on stolen bikes.

"Ohshhhh—" I put down my fork, unable to even complete the curse.

Aidan and looked at each other, eyes widened in terror. It was just as I'd feared. The cops now knew we were in the area, our time was marked, and we'd barely scratched the surface in terms of doing what we came here to do.

We didn't have to say anything else. What was there to say? We dropped a fistful of dollars on the table and walked out.

SIX

"I COULD KILL you right now," I said to Aidan through my stress-wound jaw.

We were run-walking, hats lowered, sunglasses back on, not wanting to call more attention to ourselves by fully sprinting, yet trying to get away from Bubba's as quickly as possible. Not like it really mattered much. At this point, I felt like I might as well have been wearing one of those house-arrest anklets, blaring an alarm for everyone to hear.

Aidan, to his credit, was working hard to keep my rising panic at bay. "So they saw us. Big deal. We're not murderers. We're hardly on the Most Wanted list."

Not that I was letting him off the hook. "The big deal is that they know we're in St. Louis. And that narrows down the field considerably. You were careless, Aidan, and selfish. You were showing off with those computer guys."

"I wasn't being selfish when I found your mom's police report, was I? Or when I gave up my life to come with you on this trip. Besides you loved the attention from those guys. Or should I say *guy*. It was obvious he had a thing for you."

That made me furious. "Are you kidding me? All I could think about was how weird the whole thing was. I did *not* want the attention, from him or anyone else, Aidan. You were the one encouraging them."

"Well, without him we'd never have gotten into the police database. I thought it was only fair that we let them take one harmless photo. . . ." He threw out his hands. "Okay, maybe I made a mistake."

"A mistake is leaving the house without your sunglasses. A mistake is texting the wrong person. This is way more than a mistake."

"But we know how to hide. We'll dye your hair again. I'll dye mine, too. We can find new clothes."

Yes, we could do those things. But that wasn't the point. Didn't he get it? We shouldn't have been in this situation, and now that we were, time was of the essence. "We can't waste any more time playing dress-up. I just want to find out about my mom so we can get out of here."

"We will. Trust me. But you have to stop blaming me—"

"I want to know about Sheila," I said quietly.

His eyes flickered so that he was looking everywhere

at once. Everywhere but at me. Aidan Murphy, always too cool for school, was finally losing his calm. "Sheila? I don't—"

I broke in. "It was her, wasn't it? On your phone? Don't tell me you're protecting me, okay? I deserve to know." He owed me that much, didn't he?

He sighed, letting his eyes close. When he opened them again, he began talking. "Okay. You want to know? Fine. Here it is. She only came to Prep last year. I signed up for Latin because I'd heard it was a blowoff. I liked the class in the beginning. I thought she was really friendly and nice, and I actually liked all the conjugations and things."

"Yeah, okay," I said, urging him to cut to the chase.

"Anyway, Sheila started inviting me to her classroom after school to do these"—and here he curled his fingers up in air quotes—"special projects."

"What kind of special projects?" I asked cautiously.

"They were stupid at first, like watching *Clash of the Titans*. And there were a few of us showing up, like a Latin club. But then I noticed that I was the only one she was inviting. And she started sending me these emails and texts, flirting."

"Flirting how?" I countered. "Did you flirt back?"

He looked down at his shoelaces, pressed his lips together. "I guess . . . I guess I thought it was sort of cool in the beginning that this teacher was paying all this attention to me." He glanced up quickly, gauging my reaction. "I didn't think she actually liked me in that way—just that she was extra friendly."

Ew. I don't know what I'd been expecting but this story was creeping me out. Sure, I knew he was a player. Everyone had told me about him back when I started school. I'd imagined him messing around with some typical VP girls. But with an older woman? A teacher? It was the kind of thing you read about in tabloids. And here he was, my boyfriend. . . . Everything I thought I knew about me and Aidan floated above us in a little balloon, about to be punctured.

"So then?"

"So then, one day she actually kind of put the moves on me. She tried to give me a massage and then she tried to kiss me. It was so weird. I didn't know what to do."

"Jesus, Aidan. Did you kiss her back?" I asked, my heart dragging painfully in my chest. Was he really that stupid? Or that much of a horndog?

"No!" he exclaimed, practically yelling in my face. "This is why I didn't want to tell you. You're freaking out. And you have no need to freak out. It's not what it sounds like."

"Then what is it?" My voice croaked. I felt like I could barely talk over the sob that was mounting. His telling me I was overreacting was only bringing it closer to the surface. How could this not be freak-out-worthy information?

"I actually pulled away and told her she was

overstepping. And that's when it got really strange. She grabbed my wrists and started to threaten me. She said if I didn't kiss her she was going to tell the school officials that I'd forced myself on her. She got straight-up psycho."

"Oh my God," I said, covering my mouth with my hand. Teachers were supposed to teach things. Set a good example. Remind you that the adult world was kind of boring. They were not supposed to act like slutty Cylons from *Battlestar Galactica*.

"Then she started to send me messages, asking for money. Like if I sent her fifty thousand bucks, she'd keep quiet." He looked up, his mouth half open, eyes wounded. "I think that's what she was after all along. Isn't that effed up?"

"Um, *yeah*." It was one of the most effed-up things I'd ever heard, and lately I'd been hitting the jackpot on effed-up things.

"I tried to go to the school administration and explain what was going on but she'd gotten there first and had already filed charges. Assault charges. She had a whole story worked out. They had a disciplinary hearing and they expelled me."

"Is that why you got kicked out?" That was the other great mystery, the other big secret Aidan had been keeping from me. Well, now we were putting everything on the table.

"The crazy thing was that I had been trying to get

expelled for so long—I'd done so many things that Mr. Page had overlooked because my dad was on the board of trustees—that this was kind of the last straw."

I remembered that the very first day I'd met Aidan, in fact, he'd set off a fire alarm in the school and told me he was hoping they'd catch him. All along he was trying to prove some point, make his dad angry. Which, the more I thought about it, was lame. No matter how bad his relationship was with his parents, acting out in this way seemed completely juvenile and unproductive. I felt the family-envy rising up inside me again like a toxic gas. He didn't even know how good he had it, did he?

"But no one would believe me. She had this way of making everything I said seem like a lie. I mean, it was brilliant in a totally twisted sort of way."

"And you got arrested for that, too?" I asked. "For assault?"

"No," he said. "There would never have been any evidence. Because it didn't happen! But the arrest part was my fault. I was so mad after all this went down that I went to her house and spray-painted 'Liar' on it, and that's when the actual cops got involved. That's when I got stuck on probation. Anyway, my parents' lawyers made me sign an agreement that I would never talk about it."

I could only stare at him. "That's an awful story."

And yet I was relieved. As far as crimes went, spray-painting wasn't too deep. He hadn't been cheating on me and he hadn't had an affair with a teacher, both of which would have been more serious, possibly unforgiveable offenses. And hearing what this lady did to him, I could hardly blame him for wanting revenge. I probably would have done the same thing.

"Even now she keeps taunting me, sending me these text messages, like the one you saw. It's like she wants me to mess up again. Or maybe she still wants me to send her that money."

"Can't you get her arrested for harassment?"

"I'm not a minor. And who would believe a woman was harassing a guy? She has all the power in her favor. She's the teacher and I'm the son of a rich guy. It's always going to make me look bad, like a spoiled brat. No matter what, people are going to side with her."

"What about blackmail? That's a real offense."

He sighed. "I just want to get away from her."

"She sounds truly sick," I said, softening. "I'm so sorry you had to go through all of that."

"Yeah, well, I'd been wanting a reason to leave for a while. This gave me a way to get out from underneath my dad's thumb. Ironic, huh? I finally ended up getting kicked out—but it was for something I didn't even do." He kicked at a flattened soda can on the street. "It's really hard, you know, when no one will believe you and you're telling the truth."

We walked in silence for a while, watching our shadows elongate on the pavement. The Arch came into view up ahead, the uppermost part of it peeking behind the tallest buildings. So far it had been a good-luck charm, and when I saw it I took comfort in knowing it was out there, watching over us.

I guess I was relieved to know the full story, finally. It was creepy, but it explained everything.

Even so, I was still uncomfortable with his whole family situation and the way he was just throwing it all away, like it was no big deal. As if the people who raised you were disposable or replaceable. That was something about Aidan I would never understand, one way we'd never be connected.

In the meantime, though, we had enough problems. Bigger ones. Like cops.

"Where are we going to sleep tonight?" I asked.

"I guess we can't go back to the library," he said. I'd thought the same thing, even though we were only a few blocks away from there. It was tempting.

I nodded agreement. "I don't think, under the circumstances, we should be squatting in a private home, either. That's what they're expecting us to do."

It was now four o'clock, according to the time on our phone. I searched through the files of my mind for possibilities. We certainly didn't have enough money for a hotel room. Sleep out on the street? That seemed like a bad idea. We could look for a hostel or a Y, or something, but we wouldn't have any privacy. We kept walking, passing a postal center and some other office buildings. We turned down Washington Avenue and up 16th Street where red ribbons were tied onto each light post. Even if I wanted to forget about Christmas it was impossible with them jamming holiday cheer down your throat at every turn.

"Cool," Aidan said, pointing to two serpent sculptures meeting fang to fang at the edge of a parking lot. "And look up there."

On the roof of the building behind the lot was a Ferris wheel. Next to that was a school bus and a gigantic praying mantis, and an airplane hull. We looked down to the ground level, where there was a large complex of monkey bars from which several kids were swinging delightedly. Every time I was ready to hate St. Louis, it went and gave me a beautiful landmark or a plate of delicious ribs or some crazy-looking joint like this.

"What is this place?" I asked.

"The City Museum and World Aquarium," he said, reading the sign on the side of what looked like an old factory building. "So what about this?"

"This what? Sleep here?"

"Why not? If we pay admission now and stay with the crowds we can hide until after it closes. It'll be like the library. You said yourself we can't break into a house."

He had a point. The library had worked out well for us. And this place looked just huge and busy enough that we could purposely get lost in it.

"All right," I said, after weighing the nonexistent

options. "But no screwing around."

He saluted me. "Aye, matey."

"I think you're mixing pirate and military metaphors," I said.

"Always a stickler, Colorado." Our eyes met, his crinkling. That was our tentative attempt at a peace treaty.

We entered, waited in line, and paid our admission like normal people, though my heart was pounding the entire time. One person. All it would take was one person to recognize us, call us out. Crowds were equal parts danger and safety.

But we made it through, clipping the little square aluminum museum tags onto our collars, and here we were on the other side of the atrium.

"Amazing," I said, looking around and taking it all in.

The floor was covered in a mosaic of bugs and other creatures. Discarded industrial parts had been fashioned into stairways and slides, with cement supports in the shape of dinosaurs. The walls of the lobby were lined with metallic tile like zippers. Above us, people scampered around, yelping with delight. We crossed into another room where the ceiling was hung with crystalline icicles. Kids explored the inside of a beached white cement whale. Columns glittered with imagery of waving squid and dancing octopi. It was like a Dr. Seuss book come to life.

I'd never seen anything like it.

Inside, Aidan and I slipped into bathrooms to change

our clothes. Then we tried as best as we could to disappear. We started on the upper floors. On the fourth floor there was a humongous thrift store. I didn't even know they had thrift stores in museums.

Through the window, I spotted a red 1980s dress with a sweetheart neckline and a flouncy skirt. It would have been perfect—you know, had I not been on the run and stuff.

Aidan was behind me. "Do you want it? I'll buy it for you."

"You can't buy it for me," I said. "We can't spend the money right now."

"I'll steal it for you then."

Was he crazy?

"Absolutely not." I grabbed his elbow and led him out of there, away from the temptation.

We went down a floor and wandered through the Granger Pavilion, a wing of the Architecture Museum, named, I could only assume, for the very same State Senator Granger we kept seeing on TV. The guy got around.

We crossed through rows of antique busts, statuary, columns, all pieces of masonry that had been taken from real buildings in the city. They also had the cement cross that was used in the movie *The Exorcist*.

Next to the cross, a large sculptural frieze caught my eye. It was the type of thing that would have been on top of a temple or government building. Inside the triangular frame were two figures huddled together. What struck me was the bird they were holding, which was the same shape as the one on my necklace. Words etched into the bottom read THE WELFARE OF THE PEOPLE SHALL BE THE SUPREME LAW.

A little placard beneath it explained that the frieze had once been part of the city's original courthouse building that was built in 1910, in the neoclassic style. The bird was supposed to represent love and fairness for the "least" among us. And the words were Missouri's state motto.

Remembering, I touched my own little bird pendant, making sure it was still with me.

"Can we go? I want to see what else is in here." Aidan was like a little kid, bouncing on the balls of his feet. I told him no screwing around, but who was I to deny him? This place, with its colors and textures and unexpected treasures at every turn, was completely awesomesauce.

We passed into an indoor "skateless" area, a skate-board park where you could run around.

"Tre would love this," I said out loud, and the thought of him brought on a pang of homesickness. I missed him, and I worried that he wasn't in our corner anymore.

"Forget that guy," Aidan said, like it was that easy. "He dissed us."

"He didn't diss us," I said. "He's just doing what's best for him."

"Well, I'm doing what's best for you," Aidan said.

Was he, though? Or was he using me to get back at his parents?

With that thought, I felt my mood darken again. Aidan, however, was too busy pulling me onward to the next room, which was filled with carnival memorabilia from the twentieth century. We walked through a neon-lit area called the Shrine of Shameless Hucksterism.

To our right was an old-school machine with a gypsy lady hovering over a crystal ball pulsing light. She beckoned us over with jerky robotic movements. Aidan pressed the button on the front of the console. Her glittering head rotated back and forth, her manicured hands opening over the ball as she "looked" into our future. A ticket popped out of the machine.

BEHIND EVERY STORY IS A CHAPTER UNTOLD. KEEP AN EYE ON THE THINGS YOU CARE ABOUT. PASSION IS THE ENEMY OF GOOD JUDGMENT.

"Generic," Aidan said, handing the thick card to me.

Reading it again, I couldn't be so sure. I put the fortune in my pocket, just in case. Anything right now could be a sign, good or bad. Was she talking about me and Aidan? Or something else?

I turned around and Aidan was gone. Completely out of sight. Where did he go? I turned around a full three hundred and sixty degrees. Suddenly, my head was spinning. It was too much, the lights, the people, the action.

I was overstimulated, underrested. Everything was hitting at once.

I turned and then pivoted again. Still no Aidan. Had he left me here? Without him, I was really lost.

I passed by pinball machines, blinking arcade games, clattering hockey tables. People's faces loomed large in front of me. Colors blurred together. My legs felt unsteady. I thought I might faint so I closed my eyes and counted to ten, told myself this wasn't really happening.

When I opened them again, he was right in front of me, carrying a paper bag. Almost like I conjured him up. "There you are," he said.

There *I was*?

"I think—I think I need to sit," I said.

He grasped my shoulder. "Okay. But let's find our hiding spot first."

It was close to five P.M. and the museum was shutting down and the crowds began to disperse. There were innumerable places to choose from, really—the whole place was like a jungle. We ducked into a supply closet on the second floor, behind the snack bar. Our backs were pressed up against shelves of paper goods, ketchup bottles, and sugar packets. It was dark and uncomfortable, but even so, I was glad to be out of the chaos and into the quiet. Here, I could at least regain control over my senses.

On the other side of the door, we could hear chairs being propped on tables, brooms sweeping, the voices of gossiping employees.

Eventually, all of that died down, the lights outside the door flicked off, and footsteps echoed away. We waited for what felt like another hour, not daring to speak to each other, just to be sure. Sweat dampened my hairline and my palms. I felt Aidan next to me all the while, his muscles as tense as mine. All it would take was one security guard, one unlucky stroke of timing.

Finally, we opened the door and looked around. The space was darkened. Where there had been people were now shadows. An eerie blue light flooded the space out in the hallway ahead. Tiny red lights flickered on and off in the distance—smoke detectors, I assumed. I hoped they were not alarms. Disarming a system in a house was one thing; doing it in a big building like this one was another. I didn't know the first thing about museum security and had none of the acrobatic skills needed to dodge a laser grid if there was one. I thought of Tre again, and his love of *Ocean's Eleven*. I wished he were here.

When we were sure the coast was clear, we walked downstairs to the Enchanted Caves area, a cement labyrinth of hulking rocky forms with hidden tunnels and hanging stalactites.

"We should sleep down here," Aidan said. "Nice and cozy."

We crossed into a small passageway under an arching roof into an even more enclosed space, the rock striated with markings.

I paused, feeling my heart race.

Why am I tripping right now?

Then my mind caught up to my body and I realized what was bugging me: This was all a little too much like the night we'd spent hiding out in a cave in the Painted Hills, after we'd barely escaped being shot by Chet and Bailey. We were looking for Leslie and they were, too, but when we wouldn't tell them anything, they threatened to kill us. If we hadn't escaped . . .

A shiver ran through me, as I remembered that dark and terrifying night, the hours Aidan and I spent cramped up and waiting, not sure if we'd make it to see another day.

"I don't think I can," I said.

Aidan was feeling it, too. "Good call. We don't need to relive that stuff," he said. "Let's go back upstairs."

I followed him up away from the caves, wishing I could climb away from the dread and anxiety I felt, but it seemed to cling to us like a stubborn fog. Underneath, it was a harder, starker reality: There was still a murderer out there—and the longer we were out here, the more we were risking our lives.

Aidan paused on the stairwell. "Listen, I was going to wait to give this to you, but you should have it now." He handed me the paper bag. I stopped to unfold the top and peek inside. It was the red dress.

"Are you kidding?" I asked. "You *bought it* bought it?"

"I did."

I blinked a few times, to make sure it was real. It

meant so much to me, that he'd gone out of his way to get it. And most of all that he was still trying to show me he cared.

He moved closer. "I want you to know how serious I am. About us. About making this work. We have to let go of the past. And you have to believe me, Willa."

I didn't know what to say. Here we were in the darkened, abandoned museum. Cops were looking for us. As were dangerous criminals. We were perpetual trespassers, always on someone else's turf. The thing was, we only had each other. We couldn't let anything get in the way of that. I was done fighting.

I reached over and took Aidan's hand, stroking the back of it with my thumb. "I believe you."

"You're probably the only one in the world right now who does," he said. "You—you're the only one I care about, anyway."

He leaned into me and we kissed, his lips pulling on mine. His hands encircled my waist, his hair was soft in between my fingers, and I felt anticipation quicken inside me. If I closed my eyes and let myself drift away, I could make the rest of the world, all of our fears and problems, disappear. Maybe not forever, but for right now, and this minute was the only one I could control. This minute, however fleeting, was the one we desperately needed.

SEVEN

THE SOUND SEEMED to be coming from somewhere by my feet. A high-pitched tone, and then a buzzing. My dreams gathered around the sensation, trying to make sense of it, rippling and then scattering like a school of minnows.

There it was again.

Panic coursed through me in an electrical current, my body shuddering awake. Where was I?

I opened my eyes.

Right. The museum.

We'd fallen asleep on the aquarium floor, the ghostly pale light of the fish tanks a strange comfort in the open, spooky dark. In front of me, a pair of bumbling sea turtles moved silently through their own dream world.

"Willa." Aidan, who'd been curled up beside me, was now sitting up. "We have a text."

Oh God. I swallowed. "From Corbin?"

Was he on our trail again? Last I knew he didn't have the number for the temporary phone, but that didn't mean much. He was FBI. He could find it out. He'd done it before.

Reality broke through—all of the problems we'd tried to kiss away the night before were still very much with us in the cold light of day.

"No." He handed me the phone. "Tre."

Tre? I blinked the blurriness from my eyes and looked at the screen.

I'M ON A BUS TO ST. LOUIS. MEET ME AT THE STATION AT 9:30.

"He must have left right after we got off the phone yesterday," I said in disbelief. Phoenix to St. Louis was at least a day's worth of driving. "He'd told me that he was giving up."

Aidan shrugged, and he looked slightly annoyed. At what I couldn't tell. That Tre was coming? They were friends, though I'd noticed tensions between them cropping up back in Tahoe. "Guess he changed his mind. Guess he decided he still wanted in on the action."

That wasn't like Tre. I didn't know what to think. I had to admit, though, the fact that he was traveling all this way to find us made me smile. He still cared. He wasn't abandoning me after all.

Aidan was fully standing now and flipping his bag

on his shoulders. "His timing is good. We have to get up anyway. It's nearly seven. People will be here soon."

I summoned whatever coordination and balance I could muster and went to find a bathroom to wash up. In the too-bright light over the mirror, my complexion looked sallow, my hair excessively dark.

So not cute.

I splashed water and hand soap on my face and under my arms, then used some paper towels to dry off. I may have mastered half-assed hygiene, but after the last few days I was more than ready for a proper shower. We would have to figure out a way to get one in, and if that meant a little B&E, then so be it.

The good news was that Tre would be here soon, and if he was back on our team, we could finish up what we needed to do more quickly. Maybe even in a day or two. Not that I necessarily wanted to think about what lay beyond that.

The bus station was crowded for a Wednesday morning, though not quite as hectic as it had been the other day when we first arrived. We were early, so we parked ourselves on a row of molded plastic chairs and waited, watching a woman leaning over a stroller, tickling her baby in the folds of his chubby neck. Another couple was standing at the ticket counter, arguing with the clerk.

Our twenty-three minutes sitting there felt twice as long. I updated my IOU list. I examined my fingernails.

I counted all of the big-as-Texas hairdos and all of the comb-overs I could see. I hadn't realized my foot was jackhammering against the floor until Aidan slapped a palm down on my knee.

"Do you have to do that?"

"Sorry. I'm just nervous, I guess." But I couldn't exactly put my finger on why. There was no good reason. Tre was our buddy, and we'd seen him a few days ago.

Maybe it was the idea of having another part of Paradise Valley back with us again. Maybe it was the fact that Tre had seemed to change his mind so quickly—what made him come here? Or maybe it was Aidan's seeming irritability all morning, which buzzed and nipped at me like a wayward fly. Try as I might, I couldn't be at ease.

"You might want to take your museum tag off," Aidan said, pointing to the little red button that was still clipped on my parka collar.

"Oh, right," I said, slipping it off and putting it in my pocket as a souvenir. "Thanks."

Finally, Tre's bus arrived, the passengers disembarking and coming through the glass doors into the terminal in a shaggy line, all the men and women loaded up with stuff: shoulder bags, purses, shopping bags filled with purchases, paper bags filled with snacks, rolling suitcases trailing behind them. They looked weary and beaten down by their burdens and by the journey. We'd probably looked the same way when we'd gotten here. After two days of roaming the streets of St. Louis, I was sure we looked even worse now. I self-consciously ran my hands over my hair again.

And here was Tre—we couldn't miss him in the moving queue, given that his head loomed over everyone else's. He was wearing a baseball cap over his close-clipped hair and a light-blue ski jacket that contrasted with his brown skin. At the sight of him, my breath stirred and the nervousness bubbled over into excitement.

I knew that we lived in a high-tech era, but sometimes it felt like a miracle that you could reconnect with someone in a different space and time, that all your cells and atoms or whatever could rearrange themselves and meet up in a whole other city, and that the person you'd left behind could look just the way you remembered.

We'd done it. He was really here.

At first, he didn't see us—he was heading in the wrong direction—so I called out his name. He turned and I caught his dimpled grin as he made eye contact and changed course.

As soon as he was in grabbable proximity, I was up on my tiptoes, throwing my arms around him. And that's when I noticed he was only carrying a small backpack, which should have been my first sign that he didn't intend to stay for any period of time. That's when I realized he was nervous, too.

I breathed in the familiar smell of his soap. "How was your trip?"

"Fine . . ." He pulled away and looked at me. "Listen, now don't flip about this but I'm here to take you home."

"I'm not going back there," Aidan said.

Tre waved a hand. "I wasn't talking about you. You can do whatever you want, Murphy. I was talking about Willa."

"Thanks, man," Aidan said, wiping away a fake tear. "And here I thought you really cared."

He came all this way to try to convince me to leave? "I thought you gave up on us," I said.

"Naw, I just gave up helping you with your plan. I can't stand by and watch anymore." The concern on his face, the way it stitched up his brow and burned in his eyes, was very real.

He was cautious—I knew that. He'd had his own troubles with the law, and who could blame him if he didn't want to be sent back to boot camp? He'd been trying to toe the line, watch out for himself, and he'd been warning me all along that I was taking too many risks. He didn't want to see me make the same mistakes that he had made.

So I got it. And it was sweet that he was so protective of me. Moving, even. But that still didn't change the fact that I wasn't ready to leave.

I tried to reason with him. "I'm looking at serious time in juvie now, and if I can't figure this out before I go, it will be that much harder when I get out."

"Do you even realize what you're up against, Willa?

You don't know what kind of snakes are hiding under this rock you're messing with. What if this guy Chet is part of a gang, or something much bigger? Do you really think that the two of you, unarmed, can step to someone like that? Do you know what they're capable of?"

We'd come this far on our own, hadn't we? I didn't need the lecture now.

"Actually, we do realize," I said, my voice rising with indignation. "We've seen them up close."

"And the police," he was saying over me. "They're onto you, too. Did you know that one in three police shootings involve unarmed people? One wrong move and you're part of that statistic."

"We're being careful," I said.

"Not careful enough," he barked but his voice broke a little. He took a breath and started over. "All I'm saying is it's not cool anymore. This Sly Fox stuff is just not cool."

Well. It's not like I thought it was cool, either. What had started out as a plan to help the scholarship kids in my school had spiraled into something much more serious. What we were doing here was bigger than stealing from the Glitterati. This was about blood, my family blood. Secrets that had caused years of pain. Secrets I had to finally put to rest. Because if I didn't do it, no one else would.

Aidan stepped in so that now he was in the middle, his shoulder cutting an angle between us. "And all I'm saying is you don't get to show up all of a sudden and tell us what to do. We have a plan here."

"What's that? Ducking more FBI? Or messing with the CIA this time?" Tre leaned in. He wasn't having it. "Back in the day, I asked you to escort Willa on this journey because I thought you would help keep her safe. But all you've done is put her in some risky situations. And it's gotta stop."

Why was he blaming Aidan for everything? It was my fault. "California was my decision, and this trip was, too. I never needed Aidan."

"Never needed me. Wow." Aidan shrank back. As soon as he did, I knew my words came out wrong.

"That wasn't what I meant," I said, closing my eyes, feeling the dizziness from the museum come back to me. Everything was happening too fast. This conversation was all wrong. I couldn't even make sense of it.

But Aidan had already turned to walk away from us. I jumped up to follow him. Tre did, too, grabbing the back of his shirt to stop him.

"A, wait."

"Get your hands off me." Aidan whipped around, his arms swinging to free himself from Tre's grasp. Only I was there between them and his hand struck my chest, his fingers tangling up in my necklace. The silk cord snapped and the cloisonné bird pendant went flying, clattering on the floor and landing underneath another plastic chair.

"My necklace!" I scurried across the room, fell to my hands and knees, and felt around for the bird until my fingers brushed against it. When it was back in my hand I saw that there was a small chip on the end, near the tail. I looked around for the missing piece, but it was nowhere to be found.

"Oh my God, Willa, I'm so sorry." Aidan rushed over to me.

"She gave me this," I murmured, feeling the room around us blank out into bright nothingness. "It's not replaceable."

My eyes brimmed with tears, a whole fountain of mixed-up emotions churning up inside me: despair, fear, loneliness, anger. It crashed and surged, threatening to spill over, wash me away with it.

Tre wanted me to give up. I could have done that, maybe—but only if I were a different kind of person.

"We can get it fixed," Aidan said. "I promise you. I'll make it up to you. This was my fault."

"I don't want to get it fixed," I yelled. "I just want it to be whole."

Of course, it wasn't only the necklace. I wanted my family whole, too.

They were standing on either side of me now, both looking somewhat cowed by my reaction. And I knew that I had to lay down the law. My own law.

I cupped the little broken bird in my hand and held it out for them to see. "This necklace is all I have. Do either of you understand what that's like?"

They didn't say anything. Because they couldn't understand. How could they? They had families—maybe not perfect ones, but families nonetheless.

"I need to reclaim my past now, whatever's left of it." My voice was hoarse but steady. In fact, of all the decisions I'd made over the past few weeks, this one felt the most certain to me. Now more so than ever. "I had to go to California because I had to find Leslie. And now I have to find out about my real mom. It's as simple as that. No one can tell me not to do it. If they want me in custody, then they'll have to drag me out of here."

I saw Tre's lower lip drop a little, as if he was going to say something, but I kept on.

"Tre, I really do appreciate you coming out here. I appreciate all of your help over these past few weeks. And yours, too, Aidan." My eyes swept up to meet his, and I could see how intently he was watching me. "But I'm staying here. I can't turn back now. If either or both of you want to stay, you're welcome to. Just don't ask me to leave, because I won't. Not until I find out the truth."

They exchanged a glance, and I saw something that looked like agreement.

"She's a tough girl," Aidan said to Tre.

"Sly Fox don't play," Tre replied. Then he held out a hand to me as a peace offering. "Okay, Willz. We'll do it your way. I'll stay. But I'm still going to keep an eye on you until this thing is done and we can go back and you can turn yourself in. If you pull any crazy stunts between now and then, I'm going to call you on it."

I took his hand and went in for the hug. "Deal."

EIGHT

OUR TENTATIVE PEACE and goodwill lasted for precisely
ten minutes—until we started discussing how we were
going to get to (the woman we suspected was) Toni's
house. That's when I realized that the last time we were
all together, back in California, we had Cherise and her
cousin Rain helping us out, and the two of them were
critical in buffering the tension between our three very
strong wills.

I looked up the address again, on Tre's phone this
time, and found out it was a good twenty miles away,
at least a thirty-minute drive. Aidan suggested we jack
a car as we'd done all through our California trip. His
argument was that it was the most convenient way of
getting there.

"No way," Tre said firmly. "Not this time."

"But it's going to take us three times as long on public
transportation," Aidan said.

"I'm not stealing a car." Tre gave each word emphasis, then let them hang with a starey pause so we knew he meant business. "You're not stealing a car with me in it, and I will not ride in a stolen car. I'm not here to break laws or to encourage you to break more laws. Get over yourself and get a damn bus pass."

Aidan knew how to hot-wire now, so it's not like he needed Tre's permission or guidance. But I guess deep down we both knew Tre was right. More stealing was more bread crumbs for our trail, which was already too closely watched for our comfort. I didn't need to remind Aidan of what happened at the dorm.

It was decided then. We were going to have to catch the number 10 to the Central West End Station and transfer to the 57X, which we would take to Toni's suburb, Town and Country.

"What kind of name is Town and Country, anyway?" Aidan asked. "Isn't it kind of redundant and/or contradictory?"

"It's definitely posh," I said. It made me think of horseback riding and crystal chandeliers and debutante balls. Children in matching outfits, live-in staff, and family trees with long traceable lineages. All stuff I would never have. And after seeing that kind of lifestyle up close in Paradise Valley and the way people who had it usually acted, I was okay with that.

"Guess they want it both ways," Tre said. "Rich people always do."

"I'd say you're pretty rich, my friend," Aidan retorted. "So no need for the third person."

"My pops is," Tre said. "There's a difference. I didn't grow up that way. All this stuff is still new to me."

Tre's father was a coach for the Phoenix Suns and had been a pro baller before that, but Tre only recently reunited with him and moved to Paradise Valley after years of living in Detroit with his mom. He'd started at Prep around the same time I did, which was one of the things that had brought us together. But we both always felt a little like outsiders. Well, Tre got it before I did—he was the first to see the absurdity of the Valley Prep social ecosystem when I was still caught up in the glamour of the Glitterati.

We got on the first bus, and Tre insisted we sit separately to avoid attention. I moved toward the back, so I could watch them from behind: Tre by the side door squeezed in between a couple of senior citizens, Aidan on the front left side, sitting next to an Hispanic woman in hospital scrubs who was immersed in her Kindle. There were two little kids next to me, bickering over the fact that one of them didn't want to be touched—the other one kept sneakily moving in, letting her leg press against her sister's, just to bug her. I thought of Leslie, how we never even had the chance to grow up like that together. How she'd always had to act like a grown-up even when she wasn't one. Sure, we'd been super close, but she'd been shouldering that responsibility of taking care of me the whole time. And I felt sorry, then, in a new way, for all she'd gone through, the tough decisions she'd had to make.

It was another cold day, and the snow hung like delicate lacy handkerchiefs from the long fingers of the trees. They were old trees, grander ones than I'd seen since I'd moved to Arizona where most of the plant life was squat and low. Along the street sides, they were strewn with ball-shaped clusters of Christmas lights, now unlit. Black ravens circled overhead, apparently preferring this scene to Florida heat. I didn't blame them. It was a regular winter wonderland.

I wrapped my arms closer to my chest. The parka had the faint smell of mothballs, still, from the thrift store, but that comforted me in a weird way, thinking of how someone else had loved and taken care of this jacket before it found its new home with me.

We entered the Central West End, and the street thickened with stores and restaurants and galleries. At the station, we transferred onto the second bus and took our seats there. Soon we were on the highway.

Aidan was right, this bus trip wasn't exactly the most convenient, but I tried to use the time to plan out what I wanted to ask Toni when we saw her. What she might be able to tell me. I rehearsed some lines in my head. Maybe it was silly but I knew I might only get this one opportunity to talk to the single-known friend of my mother's and I couldn't afford to mess it up.

The bus finally pulled to a stop at the intersection we'd mapped, but we were not at our destination yet. There was still a one-mile-and-change walk to Manderleigh Woods Drive.

"You want us to walk separately, too?" Aidan asked when the bus had roared onward.

Tre nodded. "Willa, you take the other side of the street."

"This is ridiculous," I muttered as cars rushed past us. It was a busy road with no sidewalk, dangerous for pedestrians. It reminded me of Paradise Valley, where I was the only person on a bike, where I always felt small yet brave, going against the flow. But now I didn't particularly want to get clipped by a passing SUV, not when we were so close to finding Toni. "No offense, Tre, but I don't see the point. We'd be the only three people walking down the street. I think anyone watching would deduce that we were together."

Tre tipped his head. "Fine. You two can walk together. I'll just act like I don't know you."

We passed a series of election signs on the side of the road. "There's that guy Granger again," I said.

"He's everywhere," Aidan said.

The sky was whiter than before. It had that heavy look to it that I remembered from living in Colorado. And then, as if on cue, it started to snow, fat flakes spinning and floating from above.

"Great," Tre mumbled from behind us.

"I think it's pretty awesome," Aidan said, holding his face up to let the snow catch on his skin.

"That's because you didn't grow up in Michigan," Tre said.

"I grew up skiing every winter. And I still love it."

Tre laughed, though not his usual gleeful, full-throated laugh. "Just so you know: Detroit and the Alps, not quite the same thing."

They were joking, I knew that, but a small alarm went off inside my head. This bickering was bad for all of us. No doubt it was a difficult situation we were in, one that could bring out the worst in anyone, but we couldn't let any more bad blood tear us apart now.

No, I needed them to be on the same page. Mediating was going to have to be my job, I realized.

"It's probably right around this bend," I said, trying to call their attention back to the matter at hand.

The road wound around into a traffic rotary with a turnoff on the left-hand side for Manderleigh. Finally. The snow was falling faster and thicker now, a soft carpet of it muffling our footsteps.

When I saw what was ahead of us, I drew in a breath. Impossibly large, sprawling houses emerged on both sides of the pavement, colonial mansions and black-shuttered Federal-style homes. It was a neighborhood, but the homes were set back behind long driveways and there was at least a half mile of snow-covered lawn between them.

"We're looking for 11208," I said.

"Do you think we should have maybe called first?" Aidan asked.

I didn't. I'd thought about this and decided it would be harder to explain the whole situation over the phone. If we showed up at her door, she'd have a tougher time pushing us away.

"What if she's not there?" Tre said.

I could not even entertain that possibility. "Then we wait."

"She better be there and she better have cocoa," he said. "The good kind. None of that Swiss Miss BS."

"I'll put in an order as soon as we get there," I muttered.

We found the house, an ochre three-story structure with French-style wrought-iron balconies and plantation shutters. A mailbox that was an amazingly detailed miniature version of the house stood guard at the end of the driveway. Out front, the walls of hedges on either side of the driveway were spun with Christmas lights and a dusting of snow.

"Whoa," Tre said. "Pretty sick."

"C'mon," I said, urging them up the walk. I thought it was nice, too, but we weren't here to shoot an episode of *Cribs*.

"Can't we wait here?" Aidan asked. "Seems kind of shady for the three of us to show up at her door. We might intimidate her."

"No," I said. "Waiting and lurking around would be infinitely more shady."

Also, I couldn't admit it out loud, but I wanted their backup.

Hand trembling, I reached up and rapped on the brass pineapple-shaped knocker.

"Pineapple's good. It stands for hospitality, right?" Aidan said, clearly rattled.

"Why are *you* so nervous?" I asked. "We just did this."

"I know. But this time, it's a bigger deal, don't you think?"

It was. I was plenty nervous myself, and Aidan's nervousness was not canceling it out. It was kind of amplifying it.

I didn't have time to answer before the door opened to a petite woman with frosted hair, coiffed into a wedge shape. She looked like a mom. A real mom, I mean. Not like Leslie. She had wrinkles around her eyes, a teal-colored, blousy, tunic-y type of top, and the kind of sensible shoes I'd seen at the walking store at the mall. But she also had a gigantic round rock on her left ring finger, a diamond set in platinum. Maybe it was the thief in me, but I couldn't help noticing that.

"Are you Toni?" I asked.

She frowned, eyeing the three of us. "Are you with Greenpeace or something?"

"No," I said, noticing the coffered ceiling and long gallery hallway framing her. The place looked like an art gallery, with rows of original paintings lit by tiny brass lamps. I thought of Leslie, how much she would love it. "We're here for something else. I think you knew my mother? Her name was Brianna Siebert."

"Doesn't ring a bell." Her head turned a few degrees away from us, as she prepared to walk away.

No, no, no. Don't shut the door on us. Not when we've come this far.

"You might have known her as Angela Chambers," I added quickly, remembering.

Then it must have clicked, because she took in a sudden gasp of breath.

She looked at me again and I could practically feel her scanning the image in her mind and computing the information. Her eyes filled with recognition. Her voice, though, was flat, almost disbelieving. "Angela's daughter."

"We wanted to ask you a few questions and find out a little about her."

I leaned in slightly and glimpsed a curving, carved wooden staircase and Persian carpet behind her. Two large urns sat on either side of the stairs, each filled with gigantic bunches of orchids. A Christmas tree towered over the room to our left, filling the air with its piney scent. Whoever she was, this Toni Cumberland lived the sweet life.

"I'm sorry, but I can't help you. That was a long time ago."

"But you knew her," I said quickly, sensing she was about to turn away.

She put her palm on the door frame. "Look, I didn't want to get involved in whatever trouble she was mixed up in then, and I certainly don't want to now. Talk to the police."

"But *you* never did, did you?" I tried. Her name hadn't been on the witness list.

"I'm sorry," she repeated. "I'm very busy and I need to be somewhere."

She shut the door, then. Leaving us on the step.

I turned back to Aidan and Tre.

"Now what?" Tre asked.

Aidan put his hand on the pineapple. "We could try again."

"No," I said, walking down the driveway and they followed me. I circled back behind the large hedge wall as I made my way to the left side of the house. I crouched down into a squat, making a place for myself on the frost-crunchy lawn.

"Seriously, Willa. What are you doing?" Aidan hissed.

"Waiting for her to go do whatever she's supposed to do," I whispered. There was no way I was leaving now, not when we'd finally found somebody who knew her. Maybe Toni wasn't going to talk to us but that didn't mean we couldn't get some more information. The thought occurred to me then. What if Toni somehow knew more than she was letting on? She'd definitely blown us off.

They looked at each other, exchanging what were probably skeptical glances, but they knelt down next to me, anyway. We watched through the window as Toni's receding back disappeared across the hallway into what looked like her living room, though it had to be the size of half of a football field. Then she came into view again, right in front of us in an office of sorts, with a massive mahogany desk. Tre threw an arm across our bodies, signaling for us to get lower. But she seemed to be too preoccupied to notice us.

From the ground, I craned my neck up to keep watching. She sat down at the desk chair and leaned over to open a drawer on her right. She fished out a small black book, set it down on the desk, and flipped through the pages, shaking her head.

What was she looking for?

She picked up the book again, hugged it close to her chest, and then left the room.

"Where's she going with that?" I asked. I could no longer see her.

Aidan was up on his feet, following her along the length of the house.

"Looks like she went upstairs," he whisper-called to us. "I can't see up there."

We stayed where we were, the snowflakes dampening our skin and clothes. I put my hand in my pocket and nervously stroked the little museum tag. That book. The way she was holding it. It had to be something important. I knew there was more we could get here.

"You're planning on going in, aren't you?" Tre asked.

I nodded. He looked away, shaking his head. But he knew he couldn't stop me or make me feel guilty. A couple of locks stood between me and my mom. If I had to break them, then so be it.

A few moments later, we heard the garage door sliding up with a creak. A white Beamer pulled out with Toni behind the wheel. She reversed down the driveway, pivoted left, and then drove down to the end of her street, signaling a right turn.

Time for us to get in there. I got up and circled around the back of the house. There was a long, covered pool out back surrounded by a maze of hedges, marble sculptures, and a stone patio—and even better, I saw sliding glass doors. That was something I'd never tried in any of my previous break-ins, but it was a useful method—Tre had told me about it himself. I leaned up against the glass to check for bars or rods. None.

I took a quick look behind me—the fresh snow was already filling in my footprints. Nature's own forensic foe.

I grasped the handle with my right hand and used my left to apply pressure to the frame. Aidan came behind me and added his weight. We leaned forward, pushing. Nothing.

"If we do it your way, we'll never get in." Tre quickly looked in both directions behind us. Then he pushed up to the door. "Did you learn anything? Look. Let me just show you."

He stretched out his arms along the length of the glass and grunted. Within seconds, the door was off its track. He was able to lift it up completely, making an opening, and we stepped into what looked like a morning room, a little seating area with a leather banquette, lush plants, and a wall of stocked bookshelves filled with cookbooks. A chandelier dripped its crystals from the ceiling overhead and there were oil paintings of fruit on the walls, a built-in espresso machine, and a juice bar. This is where they had their Cheerios or whatever? Jeez.

"That was too easy," Aidan said.

"When you know what you're doing," Tre said, breathing hard. He set the door back on the track, popping it into place.

"Thanks," I said to Tre. Obviously, we were better off with his help.

"Let's make this quick, a'ight?" he said. He found a kitchen towel and wiped our prints off the door. "We have no idea when she'll be back. And since she didn't set the alarm, I'm assuming it'll be soon."

"I don't want to spend a lot of time here," I said, taking off my shoes, and motioning for them to do the same. We couldn't go leaving a bunch of tracks in her house. "I just want to find that book."

"I'm giving you ten minutes," Tre said. "Starting now."

I walked through the kitchen and into the hallway, carrying my sneakers in my hand, crossing over to the office where Toni had been sitting. There were several photos on the wall of weddings and parties, awards for the Belles Nuits catering company. That must have been Toni's business. No pictures of my mom or anything that I could see, not that I was expecting that. But there was the still-ajar file drawer. I knelt down and thumbed through some of the hanging folders. Looked like bills, some tax paperwork, receipts. Actual work stuff. Nothing of interest to us.

"I'll look around here," Aidan said. "You can go upstairs."

Careful to leave everything the way it was, I crept back out into the hallway and found the stairway. There were a few smaller bedrooms at the top—and by smaller, I mean about fifteen times the size of the one I had in Paradise Valley—their doors open to reveal perfectly neat and tidy beds, carpets, shelving. If Toni had any kids, none of them was living here now.

The master bedroom was at the end of the landing. I made my way in there. The beige carpet was endless and plush and soothing underneath my socks. Here, too, the bed was tightly made with a taupe satiny bedspread pulled smooth across it, tempting me with its jumpability. I tried her night table first, looking into the drawers. An e-reader, some glasses, cough drops, spare pens. No black book.

A giant, gilt-framed, probably antique mirror hung from the wall across the bed. I caught my reflection, thin and stealthy as a shadow, as I crossed the room toward the master bath with its white porcelain stand-alone tub and marble floor. Next to it was a huge shower stall, the kind that could fit more than one person, with spa jets and tiny blue-glass mosaic tiles. A vanity table was covered with enough fancy perfumes and creams to stock a Sephora store. Toni definitely had good taste.

The closet doors were on either side of the bathroom. I tried the handle of the one on the right. Closed but not locked. I walked down the center aisle between enormous spans of shelving that would have made even Kellie jealous. Judging by the dresses and scarves and the wall of heels, this was definitely a hers and not a his.

I knelt down on the floor, where there was a row of matching white fabric bins, the kind Leslie used to store things that didn't fit anywhere else. Same thing here. A pair of Rollerblades. A wooden box. I reached over to dig it out. Inside was a collection of random keepsakes: a few kid's drawings, pressed flowers, a wartime medal. Also, tucked in the middle—a small black book.

My breath pumped hot and fast in my lungs. On closer inspection, I saw that it was a day planner, with a spiral binding and calendar pages for putting in appointments.

The year, stamped in gold on the front, was 1997.

I started flipping though. The first few pages, the first few days of January, appeared to be empty. On the fourth page was written *Leslie—back to school. Shift at BH 5* P.M.

Blueberry Hill. Leslie. Could this really be my mom's

book? Why did Toni have it? I got up and hurried downstairs, taking my discovery with me.

"I think I have what I need," I called to Tre and Aidan who were assembled in the office. I looked at the clock on the wall. I'd made it in eight minutes.

How you like me now?

Just then, a distant rumbling. Couldn't be thunder. . . . It took a few seconds to register and then we knew. The garage door was opening. She was back already. She must have gone out for milk or a paper. Or maybe she'd forgotten something. Or—and I didn't want to think about this possibility—she was testing us all along. What if she was in cahoots with Chet and Bailey?

When you Sly Foxed enough, you started to see everyone as a sneak, every action as a scheme, the whole world as a conspiracy theory.

"Perfect timing," Tre said, though of course he was being sarcastic.

We looked around, quickly assessing our options. Tre's rule of thumb had always been to leave the way you came. That put us in a bind now. We were closer to the front door than the slider, but the front door was only feet away from the garage and we risked running into her in the hall before we got there. I could hear a car door echoing shut. Wherever we were going, we had about thirty seconds to get there.

No, we had to stay on this side of the house. I turned around and my eye caught on the window through which we'd been watching Toni earlier. That was going to have to be our way out.

"You've gotta be kidding me," Tre said, reading my mind.

"Trust me, okay?" I whispered, slipping on my shoes. And it occurred to me that Tre was not just a voice in my head as he had been during so many jobs. He was here with us.

In a few strides I was over there, attempting to wedge the pane open. I checked the locks but they were in the open position. Tried again. No give. It was like no one had opened the window in *years*. Was it painted shut? By now, I was hyperventilating and my hands were sweating.

"C'mon," Aidan said. "Just do it."

"I'm *trying*."

I wiped my hands on my pants and tried again, applying more pressure to the pads of my fingers. The window slid up a bit—then stuck again. I gave it another heave until it was as open as it could get, a gap of about ten inches or so. Cold air rushed in.

I reached through and worked the screen up. I stuck one leg through and then balled up my torso, making it as small as possible until I was out, landing awkwardly on the lawn. It made a loud sound but it was nothing you could hear unless you were standing near the window.

Of the three of us, I was clearly the smallest. Aidan had to work harder to fit himself through, practically straddling the sill in a way that made me uncomfortable to watch. Soon he was on the grass next to me.

It was Tre's turn. He had his upper body through, but then he seemed to freeze. His frame was too broad—he was caught halfway. We watched in horror as he struggled, unable to move forward or back. He bit his lip, wriggling. It made me think of when you got a ring stuck on a finger—sometimes the wriggling made it worse. You had to wait until the swelling went down. But of course in this case there was no time to wait.

The look on his face was awful. Even if he managed to get out, he would never forgive me.

There was a pause and then the garage door sounded again, signaling its descent.

That meant she was at the door. Maybe even through it by now. Steps away. It wouldn't take her long to hear Tre in the office. And then call the cops on us.

"Crap," Aidan whispered next to me.

Not like I needed him to point that out.

NINE

WE STOOD THERE, still as the statues in the backyard, watching as Tre strained in the small space of the open window. Then, suddenly, he seemed to jerk himself upward, using the angle of his shoulder to unstick the pane. It inched up, giving him enough room to push all the way through.

By the time he was free, Aidan and I were already sprinting for the neighbor's backyard. Now that we knew he'd made it, there was no time to stand around and watch Tre close the window and screen. We had to move.

We ran silently behind Toni's house, our feet crunching and chewing up the snow. Aidan jumped a stone wall and I followed so that we crossed onto a neighbor's property. Double your trespassing, double your fun.

Another long stretch of flat land and then we had to hop a smaller picket fence, grabbing its splintery wooden slats in our bare hands. This yard had a tennis court and a series of gazebos, all snowed over. A guesthouse. I could see inside French doors into some kind of bedroom.

It was remarkably quiet out here but the noises inside my head were loud enough.

Running. I was always running.

Oh, the irony: I'd avoided running all those times in gym and now I was practically an Olympic sprinter. Criminal living could do that to a girl.

Tre caught up to me, running and shaking his head.

"Damn, that was close," he said. "You owe me one."

I would always, perpetually, forever more owe him one—and it had started long before today. We both knew that.

Up ahead was the main road. A getaway car would've been real nice in this situation. But the bus was all we had. We caught sight of it just as it was starting to pull away from the stop and we tripled our pace.

We had to catch it. Who knew when the next one would arrive?

"Wait! Wait!" I called out, waving my arms maniacally so the driver could see us.

It stopped. We ran the rest of the way and hopped on, breathless, reeling, Aidan next to me and Tre in the seat in front of us. We were too frazzled to worry about anyone else, and this time Tre didn't say anything about where we were sitting.

As the bus lumbered back toward central St. Louis,

I gripped the journal tightly. Then I noticed a yellowing strip of paper sticking out from the top edge of the pages. I opened the book and slipped it out. It was an old newspaper clipping.

POLITICAL RALLY IN FOREST PARK DRAWS HUNDREDS
November 8, 1996
A group of concerned activists including local clergy, community groups, and business owners labeling themselves The Equal Minority gathered in the Forest Park neighborhood today to protest the city's adoption of riverboat gambling. Police were called to the scene but the demonstration appeared to be a peaceful one. "They weren't bothering us," said MaryBeth Drummond, a neighbor. "They just seemed to want our attention."

But the rally took a more passionate turn when an anonymous young man got on the microphone and drew the crowd into a frenzy with his rhetoric, saying that city managers were mortgaging the future of its citizens, exploiting the poor, encouraging crime, and filling the coffers of wealthy casino owners. Organizers claimed they didn't know who the man was. "He certainly seemed to understand our cause," says Michael Peskin, pastor of United Church on Beacon Street and a co-organizer of the rally. "Whoever he is, I'd love to make him our spokesman."

I turned it over. On the back was a handwritten note: *We did it, baby. D.*

D. Who was this D? Someone my mom knew well enough, apparently, for him to call her "baby."

I wondered why my mom was interested in this rally. Maybe there was more information out there. "Tre, can you look up this date on your phone and search for a rally in Forest Park?"

He did as I asked, holding out his phone for me and Aidan to see. "Looks like there's a video here."

"Let me see," I said, practically jumping out of my seat.

He opened up the link to YouTube and handed me the phone. I pressed on the little play arrow.

Sure enough, he was right. It wasn't news footage—the camera seemed too unsteady. More like someone's home video. A shaky hand panned over the crowd. They were standing in an abandoned parking lot holding signs that said *No Boats!*, *Keep St. Louis Clean*, *CasiNO*, and *Don't Roll the Dice on Our Future*. A blond-haired man stood in front, talking into a microphone. He looked extremely familiar—but I couldn't place him. There was snow, too, just as there was today. But that didn't seem to stop the people from standing there, listening intently, clapping every so often in the pauses in between his sentences. Was this the mystery man the article was talking about?

The sound was mostly garbled by the wind. I could make out the words like *transformation*, *new ideas*, *forging ahead*, and *better leadership*. "The time is now," he said. "If we want to save this city we have to take matters into our own hands. The powers that be will keep the status quo, and keep you and me out of the decision making as long as they can. They'll give our tax money away to special interests and give breaks to corporations that prey on the gullible. This is our moment, and our world." The crowd went nuts.

"Isn't that the senator dude we saw on TV?" Aidan asked.

David Granger. That's why he looked familiar. "Good call."

To the right of the podium was a woman with layered brown hair, holding her own sign: *Welfare for All.* It was a reference to the state motto, clearly.

She looked as cheerful and attentive as the rest of the protesters. She looked a lot like Leslie, actually. I hadn't seen the resemblance in the still photos but here I could see it in her posture, the way she idly swept her hair off her shoulder with her fingertips.

My mom.

I rewound the video and paused on her. My hand shook as I drew my finger over her face, no bigger than the tip of my nail. She was moving ever so slightly, nodding her head in time to the words, like it was a favorite song.

I swallowed hard, feeling an ache inside. It shouldn't have been all that different from seeing a photo, but it was. She was a living person, here, in this clip. It might even be the only video footage of her out there in the world. And somehow, just by seeing it, I could understand her better.

My mom was an activist. Was this what had freaked Toni out? That she was involved with the antigambling folks? Because it didn't seem like that big of a deal. In fact, it made me proud that she had something she believed in.

I turned toward the window, resting the skin of my forehead against the cool glass. The snow was still falling, transforming the world into whiteness. Inside the bus, I only had this book, and a few clues to work with, but they were as powerful as the snow, giving shape to some things, covering others. The picture was filling in some more.

Thank God for the book. I'd stolen it, sure, but I realized I couldn't write an IOU, because deep down I felt it belonged to me. She was my mother. I paged onward, past the calendar to a section of lined paper for notes. She'd used this part of the book, too. It was all in her handwriting, which was tight and controlled, running across each blue line with occasional flourishes like a scooping curl after an *r* or *y*. A few pages had been ripped out here and there.

In the center of the book was a list of what looked like the names of birds:

SPARROW
DOVE

CROW
BLUEBONNET
BROADBILL

I had to smile. Leslie was a huge list maker—she must have inherited that from our mom. But why birds? Maybe she was an Audubon type? Why was *sparrow* underlined? There was also a doodle of a bird in black ink in the right margin.

A few pages later, I came across what looked like a poem.

You were waiting for me, that day,
on the steps of the museum. From a distance,
I watched you scratching in your book, making
    calculations,
drawing maps
while the wings, spiraling overhead,
reminded me that our time was only a distance
    between two points.
A way of seeing that we'd agreed on until we
    stopped agreeing to see.
We couldn't help ourselves but we could help others,
    you said.
And I knew the others would always be more
    important,
and besides, I could no longer follow your maps.
So we gave it up: the scratchings, the wings,
the us.

She was a poet. Who knew? That must have been where Leslie got her creative streak. Maybe the list of bird names was some kind of sketch, notes for this poem.

I read it again. It was a love poem, wasn't it? The words were beautiful but they made me sad.

My eyes scanned up to the date at the top of the page: 4/1/97. My birthday was in July, so it had been before she'd had me. She must have been thinking about him, this man, though it wasn't clear whether this was before or after she'd moved and changed her name. Either way, she *had* loved him, and she hadn't really wanted to leave him. Or at least, she'd only done so because she had to, for some reason.

And this man, whoever he was, was most likely my father.

Could it be D? And could D be David Granger? As soon as it clicked into my consciousness, the idea startled me.

I don't know how I'd pictured my father all these years—some guy, someone younger, I guess, a guy who'd made a mistake as a kid and who'd gone on to do other things. Granger, if it was him, was an improvement over that. He wasn't just some guy. He was on the right side of the law, and he seemed to care about the same things I cared about: evening out the playing field and getting justice for everyone. Somewhere along the way, he'd become a bona fide politician, and he was still working for good.

I traced my index finger across the condensation on the window and made a G. My last name could be Granger. Willa Granger. Actually, if I was going to get technical, it was Maggie Willa Siebert Fox Granger. Hey, I thought, another week on the road and I might acquire a few more add-ons. Nothing would surprise me at this point.

I thought back to Leslie. She'd had her reasons for doing what she'd done, and my mom probably did, too—if she had, in fact, done anything wrong. But was it possible that the thing with Chet was a fluke, a random crime? Maybe she'd never even met him before that day.

The money, though . . . what about the money? Where had it come from?

No, I needed to brush those questions aside. I didn't want to waste time dwelling on all of the possible negatives when we were closing in on some real facts. What I had to do was to keep digging.

Toward the back of a book, I noticed she had an appointment scrawled in: October 25. That was after she died, a meeting she'd never made it to. The address was written in the little box: 14 Benton Place. Who was she planning to meet?

"What's up?" Tre asked me from over the seat.

I showed them both what I'd found but it was too complicated to explain how I was really feeling right then, the kaleidoscope of emotions and questions layering minute by minute. The Granger thing, the poem, the meeting. I couldn't put it all together in a logical story.

We got off the bus at 16th Street, and ducked into a café to warm ourselves.

"Are you buying?" Aidan asked Tre with a friendly elbow as we got into line in front of the counter.

He rolled his eyes. "Okay, but consider it your last meal on me and the Friends of Fox. We're going to get the afternoon bus."

"What are you talking about?" I asked.

He stared me down, wary. "You found out about your mom, right? So time's up. Now we have to go. That Toni lady has probably already called the cops now."

Not if she was involved, though. "We didn't, though. We found out something—a few more clues, but . . ."

"But that's not enough?" Tre asked. "Willz, I have a feeling it's *never* going to be enough for you."

His words cut through me. I realized, then, that he was right. That what I really wanted was to know what happened to her, why she was murdered. Anything less than that would feel incomplete.

It was our turn at the counter. I ordered my drink, and let them order theirs. Then we moved to wait by the copper-colored espresso machines.

Tre flicked his chin at me, challenging. "So, assuming we stay, now what? What's the next step in your big plan?"

"We go to Granger," I said, like it was obvious, because

it was to me. "If he really knew my mom and they were involved, then he probably knows some other stuff, too. Maybe he even knows something about Chet."

"Assuming he's D," Aidan said.

I was already assuming that, and more. "I know this sounds crazy, but I think he could be my father. The poem in the book and his note seem to point in that direction."

Tre twisted his mouth in skepticism. "That's a big if. And how do you propose meeting up with him?"

"I think we can show up there, and tactfully explain the situation. . . ."

"No." He stirred his cocoa and forcefully pitched the wooden stick into the trash. "It's way too dangerous."

I slid a cardboard cozy around my cup. "Dangerous? He's a politician. He'll be surrounded by aides and body-guards."

"So? Being a politician doesn't mean he's safe. Most of them are pretty shystie." Tre went to sit down at a table and we followed.

"I don't know, Willa. I think I side with Tre on this one," Aidan said, sitting down across from me. "As much as I want to go check it out, politicians are pretty much the worst people on earth."

Since when did Aidan become the voice of reason? I stared at them both on the other side of the booth. Great. Now it was two against me. So much for mediating.

"And last I heard there was no father-finding in our

deal. Just your mother," Tre said.

"That was before. I didn't think the guy existed until now. It's kind of a bonus, actually. I wish you guys could be happy for me."

"I *am* happy for you," Aidan said. "But—"

"But what?" I asked.

Tre broke in. "You can't just walk into a man's office—an important man, with a lot at stake—and expect him to be thrilled to find out he has a long-lost daughter."

"We at least need Judge Judy and a DNA test for backup," Aidan said.

"It's not like I plan to come right out and say anything about the father part. I need to feel out the situation," I said. "But he seems like a nice guy. A guy with good morals. I think he would handle it gracefully."

Tre set down his cup. "You barely know him. You've seen what—a few TV ads? Listen to me, Willa. This is something I know about from my own experience: Kids who are abandoned by their dads are usually abandoned for a reason. *If* he's even your dad to begin with—and we really have no idea, do we?"

I must have looked hurt because he softened. "That sounds harsh. I want to protect you. Even Sly Fox isn't bulletproof, you know."

I gave him a twisted smile. "I'm not?"

"No. You're not. If this guy wasn't in your life then, he's probably not gonna want to be in your life now."

"Your dad took you in, right?" I pointed out. "You got

a second chance."

He shook his head. "Only because my mom strong-armed him. Threatened to go to the media. Yeah, we're cool now, but he wasn't popping Cristal when I came back into the picture, believe me."

"But I'm not asking him for money or rent. I just want to ask him some questions about his past. It's not like I want him to be part of my life or anything."

Tre leaned in, planting his palm on the table. "If their relationship was so innocent and he's such a good guy, then why did your mom have to move and change her name, huh? Why was Toni so afraid to talk to us? Don't you think it's a little suspicious?"

I showed him the poem. "Read this. She loved him. Once upon a time she really did, and chances are, he loved her, too. Maybe she needed to be independent and she didn't want them to stay together for the wrong reasons."

"This poem could be about anybody. And what if she dumped him?" Tre asked. "What if he's still pissed about that?"

"No," I said. "Something changed between them, and maybe it wasn't working out, but time has passed. People remember the good things, don't they? I mean, if you really loved someone in the first place?"

Tre and Aidan exchanged glances. "You're serious about this, then," Aidan said.

"When was the last time I *wasn't* serious?" They both

should have known that about me by now.

"Well, if you think it will help," Aidan said. "I'm just here to support you."

"Uh-uh. I can't let it happen," Tre said. "Someone's gotta make some sense here."

I drained my coffee, eyeing them up. "Look, if you don't want me to go see Granger, then can we at least check out this address she wrote down in the book? It could be someone else that knew her." I wasn't willing to admit what was becoming clearer to me by the second— that I *had* to solve the murder, and I was ready to try all of the angles until I did. "Can you please give me one more day?"

"One more day." Tre sighed. "But only because we've already wasted most of this one. You better not be setting us up for more trouble, though."

"I'm not," I said. "You'll see." I reached into my own pocket and uncoiled the chipped necklace. I replaced the pendant, and tied a knot uniting the broken ends of the cord. Then I pulled the whole thing over my head so that it was back where it belonged.

TEN

BENTON PLACE WAS just south of us by several blocks. It was a quiet, stately street, lined with beautiful, towering Victorian mansions, the kind that begged for singing nannies with umbrellas. Even so, number 14 stood out from the others with its alabaster front, its elaborate scrolling balconies, and slate-gray mansard roof. Outside, huge oak trees were shaking off excess snow onto the perfectly flat lawn. Big-money central.

"So we don't know who lives here, right?" Aidan asked, running to catch up with me as I stepped briskly down the walk. Since getting my hands on the book, I felt more eager and more determined than ever.

"Nope," I said. "But we'll find out."

The doorbell was of the old-school variety, a steady buzzing ring rather than a chime. A uniformed servant, a woman in her thirties, came to the door. "May I help you?"

An elderly lady with cropped silver hair and a sweet pink-lipsticked smile was quick behind her. "I got it, Stephanie. I could use the air, frankly," she said to us. "Oh, it's chilly out there." She pulled her lavender cardigan tighter around her small frame.

Sensing that she might be a chitchat type, I launched into it. "I know this is strange but I found your address in my mother's date book. I think she was planning to come here for some kind of meeting, maybe? This was fifteen years ago." I felt crazy even saying what I was saying but I had to try. "She died before she ever had the chance. I never knew her and I'm just trying to find out more about her. Do you remember her? Her name was Brianna Siebert. But she also went by Angela Chambers."

The woman frowned thoughtfully before turning away. "Danny?" she called over her shoulder. "Do we know anyone named Brianna or Angela? These young people want to know."

A man in a wheelchair rolled himself down the long, tiled hallway. He was middle-aged, with cleanly parted salt-and-pepper hair and a plaid button-down shirt whose edges pooled in his lap. It was clear he was paralyzed, and had been for some time, as his legs looked undeveloped, pin-like in his corduroys.

"Never heard of her. Or them." He smiled at us, too. "Hello there."

"Hi," I said. *What a friendly family*, I thought. But I

was disappointed all the same. Why was my mom so damn elusive? I'd thought for sure this would be a good lead.

"This is my son, Danny. He knows all the people I know. When did you say this happened?" the woman asked.

"Around 1997 or so. Did you live here then?"

"Yes, we did," the woman said. I saw them look at each other then. "We've been here since Danny was born."

"We have a picture of her, if that would help jog your memory," Tre added from behind me.

I'd almost forgotten. Tre clicked to the video of the rally before giving it to the woman. I didn't think it would really help, but it was worth a shot.

"Nothing." The woman shook her head, shrugging, and handed it to her son. I watched his face as he stared into the screen. How it morphed from a relaxed smile to a slow, dawning realization, something closer to fear, and then a dark furrow of anger.

"I think I do know this woman," he said. "Hang on." He wheeled himself briskly back in the direction he came from. A few moments later, he returned and handed me a white piece of paper. On it was a photocopied sketch. It was impossible not to see the resemblance in the hair, the eyes, the angles of her nose. My mom's face.

WANTED, it said at the top. SUSPECT IN HIT-AND-RUN ON JANUARY 3, 1997. So this was a police drawing.

"I don't understand," I said quietly.

"You don't?" The man's once-kind eyes were starting to go cold and hard.

"No. Maybe you can . . . explain?" The pause lingered as I looked from him to his mother.

"This is the woman who hit him. With her car," the older woman said. "Or so we think. We never did find her."

His jaw tensed in anger. "She's the reason I'm in this wheelchair."

They were saying my mom hit him? Could that be true? Was that why she'd moved and changed her name? To avoid getting caught? It made a certain kind of sense, and yet I couldn't believe that she could be so cold. What happened to the activist at the rally, the one who wanted to make people's lives better? It had to be wrong.

But what could explain the coincidence? I was still staring at the image and there was no mistaking it.

"Are you sure?" I asked stupidly.

"I saw her with my own eyes. It's an image you don't forget," he said. "A car coming straight for you. We locked eyes as it hit."

"But she was planning to come meet you, I think," I sputtered, scrambling for a reason. "So maybe she wanted to talk to you about it, set things straight. Maybe she wasn't trying to run away from this."

"So you say. All I know is I never heard from the woman. I was in a coma for two weeks. In the hospital for six months. A year of rehab. And as you can see, I still can't walk."

"Danny, don't get worked up. I'm sure there's an explanation," his mother said, putting a hand on his shoulder. "It might not even be the same person."

"What kind of explanation could there possibly be?" he spat, wriggling out from underneath her. And I agreed with him. "Besides, she's dead now so we'll never know."

I backed away from the front step, feeling dizzy. "I'm sorry," I said. "I'm sorry for coming here and bothering you."

"I'm sorry, too," his mother said.

"I'm not," Danny said to our backs. And even if he didn't say it, the tone of it was clear: *I'm glad she's dead*.

The words echoed and echoed as the house shrank behind us. But distance did nothing to minimize the shock.

"Damn," Aidan said when we reached the end of the street. "That was rough. Do you think it's true, Willa?"

I was still trying to process the information. This was even worse than imagining her being mixed up with Chet. She'd ruined someone's life. "I don't know," I said. "But I need to see Granger. Today. And please don't argue with me."

Granger was someone who may have known her. Maybe our only link left.

Aidan nodded.

"I don't want to repeat myself here—you know how I

feel," Tre said, putting a hand on my back. "So let that be on the record. I really hope you're not making a mistake, Willa."

"I might be," I said, stopping at a crosswalk. "But I don't have a choice anymore."

The local field offices for David Granger's campaign were listed right on his official website. I was surprised, in fact, that the information was so easy to access, but Tre reminded us that he wasn't likely to be hanging out at any of the offices.

"It's just for the volunteers, so they know where they can come in and give money and stuff." Apparently, Tre's mom had been pretty involved with the Obama campaign in Detroit.

"Then that's what we'll do," I said. "Pose as volunteers and find out where he is."

The Euclid Avenue office was the closest one so we started out there. It was a regular storefront, set between a dry cleaner and a pet store, and marked with a huge GRANGER FOR CONGRESS poster on the glass door.

Tre came in with me, but Aidan insisted on waiting outside. He said that he didn't believe in politics and that he would be our lookout in case any cops came along. Really, I think he wanted to check out the puppies tussling in straw in the window next door. I could give him a pass for that, since he was dog obsessed, something I learned the day we both volunteered at the animal shelter for our respective community service sentences.

The office was bustling, with dozens of volunteers huddled around tables, assembling mailings and cupping phones to their ears. Posters lined the walls, and strings of American flags waved from the ceiling. It was impressive, really, that so many people were here and cared about the cause. Or any causes for that matter.

I walked up to a tall, skinny kid with dark hair and a blue Granger T-shirt and requested to see the manager.

"You mean the volunteer coordinator?" he asked in a snotty voice. He couldn't have been more than twenty. A college student, probably. "The campaign manager is a little bit busy, I'd imagine."

"Fine." I rolled my eyes. How was I supposed to know all the lingo? "Yes, the volunteer coordinator."

"She's right over there. The woman holding the clipboard? Her name's Maria."

Tre and I followed his pointing finger over to an athletic-looking woman with cropped brown hair and thick-framed glasses, over which she glanced at us as we neared.

"We'd like to volunteer," I told her.

"Fantastic." She shook our hands and introduced herself. "I just need to you to fill out these forms."

She handed us our very own clipboards and pens, and Tre and I sat down in metal folding chairs. I wrote my name as Jennifer Price. Tre wrote his as Stephen Graham. Generic people. We put down fake addresses for other places, mine in Illinois, and Tre's in New Jersey, hoping they would think we were college students, too.

We gave Maria back the forms. "So when can you start?" she asked.

"We'd like to start today," I said quickly. "As soon as possible. But we don't have much time—probably only an hour."

She nodded. "We could use some help on the phone banks, and also door-to-door canvassing. An hour of that would be great if you could spare it."

"We can do the phones," I said, hoping to stay close to the information.

I could feel Tre's eyes burning into the side of my face but I didn't dare look.

"Here's the script and a list of numbers," Maria said. "Make a note beside each one, stating if they were home and if they committed to donate or vote. You can sit down over there at one of those tables and get started. If you need any help, I'll be wandering around."

"Um, I don't have a phone," I said, remembering that Aidan had our disposable in his bag, and that Tre probably didn't want to risk being tracked here on his.

"That's okay. We have extra over there." She pointed to a table where a number of landlines were arranged.

When she walked away, disappearing into a glass-walled office, Tre pinched my arm and I got the full burn of his straight-on gaze. "Are you cray? How are we going to find him if we're stuck here on the phones all day talking to cat ladies and shut-ins?"

"We have to have a cover. A believable one. She wasn't going to just tell us where he is," I said. "Besides, it won't be all day. I have a plan."

He gave me a slow headshake, which I knew by now could be roughly translated as "You're pushing it."

"I've got this," I said. "Just give me a little bit of time."

We sat down and I picked up one of the campaign's phones and started with the first name on the list.

"Is this Mrs. Callahan? I'm Jennifer, and I'm calling on behalf of the David Granger campaign. This runoff election is very important to St. Louis and the people of Missouri in general. We were wondering if we could count on your vote next month? We can? Great. And would you be interested in making a small, one-time donation of twenty dollars to help us get through the final push of our campaign? You would? Fantastic."

After a while, I started getting the hang of it. It was amazing, really, how easily some people were convinced to part with their money. (Especially when I thought of how hard I'd worked back in Paradise Valley to pick pockets.) Maybe they were all wealthy. Or maybe that was a testament to the power of David Granger. Everyone I talked to seemed to be a fan. One woman gushed to me about the new community center he'd helped establish in her neighborhood, how it had gotten the kids off the streets and reduced the crime rate, how she'd met Granger himself when he came to the ribbon-cutting and he was the sweetest man. He had that effect on people, apparently.

Tre was next to me, mumbling through his calls and eyeing me in between. He was clearly not enjoying this.

"C'mon, you've gotta get into the spirit," I said.

"No," he said. "I really don't. I just need to sit here and do this thing, until you get what it is you're looking for. Anything else goes beyond our agreement." He picked up his phone and dialed another number.

As I worked, I kept my eye on the office. Maria was sitting at a desk typing things into her computer and answering her own phone. Finally, she stood up to leave and I saw my opportunity.

When she was gone, I made my move. Her office was overloaded with stuff, stacks and stacks of papers and files—the natural habitat of a workaholic. I inched past the rolled-up poster tubes and the cardboard cartons of blue and red T-shirts. On the wall behind the desk was a whiteboard calendar scrawled with daily events. Today's date: *November 28*. At four P.M. there was a private event, a speech scheduled at the High School for Technological Arts.

Bingo.

"Can I help you?" Maria was back and standing in the doorway.

"I was looking for you, actually." I gulped down some air. *Don't blow it.* "I think we're done for the day so I wanted to thank you."

She frowned. "That was fast."

"I know," I said quickly. "We only had a short break today between classes."

She gave me another look but she seemed to be buying it. "You go to Wash U?"

I nodded, feeling my face warm. *Please don't ask me any more questions.* I didn't know how far I could take my fake story. And part of me was sad to lie. It felt good to contribute to something bigger than myself, a real cause. In another world, if I actually lived here, if I wasn't on the run from the police, I would've loved to volunteer on a regular basis. But in this world I had other things to accomplish.

"Did you see those kids on campus yesterday?"

"What kids?" I asked, the words garbling in my mouth. She was talking about us.

"The ones from—" Another volunteer, the first one we'd seen, was proudly handing her a stack of clipboards. She paused and in that moment I rehearsed a thousand denials. "Oh, thanks, Nate. Is this all of them?"

Then I saw that he was ready to start talking shop. "We really have to go," I said quickly, seizing on the distraction. "But thanks again!"

I moved away, but not as fast as I wanted to, not wanting to draw her suspicion. She tucked the clipboards under her arm. "Don't forget to take a T-shirt on your way out."

Even better.

I grabbed three shirts, including one for Aidan, and then nudged Tre. "You're off duty." Then I added under my breath, "And we need to jet."

I didn't explain, and I didn't have to. He nodded and we headed for the door.

Outside, we found Aidan, still ogling the puppies. A particularly fuzzy blond one was gnawing on a small bone and staring back at us with liquidy brown eyes.

"Have you been here the whole time?" I asked.

"He's perfect, isn't he?" he asked, and I could tell by his dreamy expression that he had been and he was smitten.

"He's pretty darn cute." *And so are you.* I handed him the shirt. "Sorry to interrupt, but we have to get going."

"Where to?" he asked us.

"The High School for Technological Arts. If we leave now, we can get there before Granger's speech starts."

No buses this time. The school was on the north side of town, and too far to walk. We hailed a cab, which let us out in front. The school was already packed, cars spilling out of its lots and lined up, end to end along its driveways. This was probably the biggest event they'd seen all year.

Aidan pointed to a few news vans with satellite dishes. "Willa, are you sure you want to do this?"

We were walking into the line of TV fire. I drew in a breath, feeling my heart pound out a quickened beat. I hadn't considered this possibility. But that was stupid of me—of course there would be news media at an event like this.

"They're not here for us. So we just have to be careful not to attract attention," I said. *You know, exactly what we didn't do on the last campus we visited.* I thought of Maria, and how it would have only taken a few more seconds to put it all together. How we were saved by the nerdy volunteer in the nick of time. Gaah. How much longer could I do this?

The snow had let up a while ago but the air was still damp. Our breath preceded us in clouds as we approached the front entrance of the imposing three-story brick building. It was nothing like Valley Prep with its elegant landscaping and fountains. No, despite the fancy-sounding name, this was an inner-city public school, with bars on the windows, metal detectors, and a distinctly get-your-butt-into-homeroom vibe.

At my insistence, all three of us had our T-shirts on so we could better blend into the crowd. We followed the swell of people in through the door and down a long hallway lined with trophies and student artwork. Men in suits were standing at either side, directing traffic. Security guards. The calendar said it was a private event, after all.

How were we going to get to Granger?

I stood on my tiptoes to get a better view of what was ahead. The crowd narrowed into single file as the people entered through the open auditorium doors. Inside, a huge banner with David Granger's name billowed across the stage, and a campaign sign was mounted on the podium. Hundreds of people were already seated and the room was filled with the ambient buzz of anticipation and chatter.

We pushed our way down to the front where the first several rows were blocked off with ribbons for VIPs. A very large black man wearing a gray suit and a headset was blocking the steps up to the stage.

"We'll meet you back here," Aidan said.

"No, we won't," Tre said definitively. "We're coming with. She needs us."

"Here goes nothing," I said under my breath. I turned to face the stage.

"Excuse me sir, we're late," I said, trying on my best girly charm. "Can you tell us the best way to get backstage? We're supposed to be back there helping out."

He gave us the once-over, with the small, slow-moving eye of a tortoise. "You working for the campaign?"

"That's right," I said.

He glanced at Tre and Aidan, then back at me, holding my gaze for what felt like an eternity. Yet again I played through the potential scenario—him pinning my arms behind my back, his fellow guards wrestling Aidan and Tre to the ground. The news camera operators rushing over to capture it all, barking out questions as we were dragged away. This guy boasting in a bar later that night about how he'd caught the Sly Fox.

He blinked again, his face unnervingly wall-like.

"Behind me," he said finally, moving his heft aside. We walked to the side of the stage, through a metal door marked EXIT.

It was just as bustling back there, with dozens of people running around, carrying more clipboards, wearing buttons. Small clusters of men and women in suits were conferring about issues and key words, polling results and TV spots.

"So where is he?" Aidan asked.

"The green room. Don't you know? There's always a green room for celebs and ballers," Tre said. "And they usually have the fancy stuff in there, like champagne and truffles."

I doubted the part about the truffles, but it was a nice image. He was pro social equality, but that didn't mean he had to live sparsely. I mean, wasn't that the point, that everyone should be able to enjoy the pleasures in life and not only the 1 percenters? I thought of the clothes in anonymous packages I'd sent to Mary, Alicia, and Sierra, underwritten by the money and stuff I stole from the Glitterati. The idea was to spread the wealth, and I still believed in that, even if my little plan seemed kind of silly now.

We wandered through the crowds, pushing past two women with coiffed hairdos and tastefully bright pant-suits. At least we fit in with our pro-Granger gear. No one seemed to bat an eye at us.

Finally, I spotted him. He was standing in a corner, holding a piece of paper and reading it over his bifocals. He had the same blondish hair and slightly pink complexion I'd seen on TV, only in person he seemed a bit older, his face more chiseled by time.

"This is it," I said, angling my chin in his direction. "Be right back."

"Are you sure you want us to leave you?" Tre asked.

"It's okay," I said.

"We'll wait here," Aidan said, folding his arms across his chest and leaning back against the cinder-block wall.

"Good luck," Tre said.

Emboldened by my two-guy support team, I walked toward Granger. Just like with Toni, I mentally practiced what I was going to say. I had to get the words exactly right. And there were a lot of them. But that visit seemed almost quaint by comparison. This was a million times scarier.

Before I could make it there, one of the pantsuited women got to him first. "We're going to need you in Dutchtown tomorrow," she was saying as she scanned her phone. "There's a barbershop meeting at four."

"I can't do it," I heard him say. "I have another appointment."

"David, we really need you there."

He turned to her and his tone was taut suddenly, almost vicious.

"And I said I *can't do it*, Libby. Tell them I'll come

another day. Your job is to protect my schedule, so do your job."

The woman, Libby, shook her head and walked away, simultaneously pecking something onto her screen. "Okay, D."

D. I guess that was what everyone called him. I now felt surer than ever. This was our guy. My guy. Or at least my mother's guy.

"Excuse me. Sir?"

"Yes?" He turned to me and gave me a dazzling smile. If there was a testy exchange with his aide it was already forgotten, bad vibes turned off in a flash. "Can I help you?"

His voice was clear, even as water. His skin seemed to crackle with electric energy, like one of those plasma globes. I felt myself inadvertently straightening my posture.

He held out a hand and I took it slowly. It was tight and broad, strong fingers that dwarfed my own. "David Granger, how do you do." It was uncanny, the way his warm gaze made me feel exposed and yet somehow comforted at the same time. Was that because we were related, possibly? Or just because he had some weird personal magnetism?

I searched his face for signs, for any features that looked like me. But his eyes were blue. Mine were hazel. Maybe the hair. It was hard to say. Either way he looked a lot older than he did on that video, but more polished, in much fancier clothes.

I took a deep breath. "I'm looking for information

about someone. She died a long time ago, but I think you might have known her. Her name was Brianna Siebert."

His expression softened at first in surprise, his eyes distant. Then his pupils glinted as he took in the sight of me. What did he see, exactly? Did he recognize her in me? Did he see himself at all?

"Who are you? Who sent you here?" His voice was hoarse.

How far to go? How much should I tell him? And how much time did I have? I reached for the necklace, running my thumb over its surface for support. It had become my talisman.

"I'm her daughter. . . ." I let it trail off there, allowing him to fill in the blank.

Confusion passed over his face, obscuring his features like a shadow. "But she only had one daughter. And she was much older than you," he murmured. Then, he looked up sharply but not unkindly. It was more searching. "Where'd you get that necklace? Who gave it to you?"

"She did," I stammered, though technically, it had been Leslie. "You might not have known about me." Again, I was hinting without saying it out loud.

But he seemed to get the picture because he pulled away, looked wary. "No. Now I know. You're that girl on TV."

I drew in a breath. I should have prepared for the possibility he'd recognize me, but I hadn't.

Not him. Not here. This was bad.

He glanced around to see if anyone was watching us. Then he leaned in close, bending down so that his blue eyes were lined up squarely against mine, so close I could make out the dilated blood vessels on either side of his irises. "I don't know who sent you, or what your agenda is. . . ."

"I'm not here for that. I don't want—"

I felt the bulk of him towering over me and suddenly I was afraid. That warm hand closed around my shoulder and I could feel those strong fingers pressing into the hollows around my bones.

And then, suddenly, the hand relaxed. The eyes, too. "Of course not. For a moment you had me confused. What a long day this has been. Anyway, thanks for coming and thank you for your concern, miss."

My concern? His voice was loud, his tone phony. He was speaking for the benefit of onlookers now.

His face had brightened again, but I knew it was over. Clearly, the brief moment of understanding we'd shared had drifted past and now he'd turned against me, shut me out with his little act. Who was he fooling?

This was all wrong. Not how it was supposed to go.

Time, the room, the words were slipping away from me. I was losing control. "She cut off ties with you when she was pregnant," I blurted. "She changed her name. She must have known something, something bad, and she didn't want you to know about it. There was an accident

157

and someone was hurt badly. Maybe she was trying to protect you from that, or from Chet—"

He spoke over me in a tone that was nearly theatrical. "Listen, I'm very busy and I need to get going. It's always great to meet young stakeholders. Keep spreading the word, okay? We need you out there. I'm sure you can find your own way out. Joe?" He waved to a guard standing nearby, a burly, bearded guy in a similar getup as the guy out front.

Maybe it was a misunderstanding. Maybe he hadn't heard me correctly. "I need to know what really happened to her," I said, my voice drifting up to a higher register.

Joe was closing in. The words were tumbling out of my mouth uncontrollably.

"Please. I traveled a long way to get here. I don't want anything else from you. Just some answers. If now's not a good time, we can meet somewhere else."

Granger was no longer looking at me. He was gesturing to the guard but talking through his impossibly white smile. He was impenetrable. "I wish you all the best, young lady."

"But wait!" I cried out. The guard's hand clamped around my upper arm, and his grip was tight. "I think she loved you. I found a poem—"

Granger's back was turned. He'd already moved away, down the hall. A shape in a suit. Gone.

Aidan and Tre saw what was happening and they were

following closely as Joe the guard dragged me away. "Let her go," Aidan called out. "She's just a kid."

"Orders are orders. I'll do my job, man, and you do yours, okay?" Joe said. He slammed on the push bar of the exit door and practically threw me out of there.

And then we were outside again, in the last vestiges of the afternoon light, blinking, stupid. I was off balance, stumbling to regain my footing.

The tears came then, all at once. "So much for meeting my father."

"He didn't admit it, did he?" Tre was the first by my side. "We don't know that was him."

As much as I wanted to, I couldn't agree. "That's the whole point. The way he was acting was like someone hiding something. It wasn't a straight denial. He knew more than he was letting on."

I replayed the scene in my mind. No, I was pretty sure he *was* my dad. Turns out he was just a jerk. A liar like everyone else. More than that. He was completely creepy, the way he turned on a dime.

"You were right, Aidan," I said through a choked sob. "Politicians are lying dirtbags."

"Don't cry, Willa." Aidan stepped in and put his arm around me. "Look, I wish I was wrong. I really do."

"The way he had me thrown out—that's not something an innocent guy does. He's afraid of something. I know it." Of course he *had* said he recognized me. If I hadn't been the Sly Fox, would he have done the same thing? Now I wondered. And for the millionth time I had to regret my mistakes, the chain of events that set this whole thing into motion. If I'd never stolen, I wouldn't be here at all.

"I don't want to defend the guy, but maybe it would help to put yourself in his shoes," Aidan said. "He's getting ready for his big election and some teenage girl pops up and hints around that she's his illegitimate daughter. The media goes crazy over stuff like that. That could kill the election. All I'm saying is maybe you don't have to take it personally."

I wiped away my tears with the back of my hand, though they were still flowing freely. How could this not be personal?

My voice was gravelly. "You'd think, if he was a decent person with good values like he pretends to be, that family ties would be more important than some stupid election."

"Hate to break it to you, Willz, but most people are not decent," Tre said.

"Except us." Aidan kissed the top of my head, his lips pressing into my hairline.

For some reason, I looked up at Tre. He caught my eye and then turned away. Was he embarrassed by our PDA?

Great. That was all I needed, on top of everything else: standard-issue high school awkwardness. Like we didn't have enough adult, real-world problems on our hands. I unhooked myself from Aidan's protective embrace and slipped a few paces ahead of them on the sidewalk.

"Where are you going?" Aidan called.

"Nowhere," I answered. "I just need to think."

I needed to be alone, really alone. The sky was darkening, the streetlights flicking on around us. The Christmas lights, too. They only depressed me, making me feel lonelier, and farther away from home.

I appreciated their help, but nobody could fix this for me. And knowing they were behind me, expecting me to keep it all together, counting on me to be optimistic and full of new plans, only made it worse. I was cold. I was tired. And for once I truly had no idea what to do next.

The only thing I knew now was that I had to figure this all out once and for all. I had to solve my mom's murder, no matter who was behind it.

ELEVEN

SO GOING TO see the man who was most likely my estranged father was a bad idea. Maybe the worst idea I'd had yet. And over the past few months, I felt pretty much like a bad-idea factory.

We were nowhere near close to solving this thing. We'd already been in St. Louis for three days. How much time did we even have left before the authorities closed in on us?

After a while, the walking quieted my brain, and the storm of emotion inside me subsided some. I just wished I had someone I could talk to, someone who knew about the past. Someone who had been there, someone I could trust.

Leslie was the obvious person. But she was off-limits—no more reachable to me than my real dead mother. I missed her so much it ached like a bruise on my ribs.

But at least she was probably safe, I reminded myself. At least Chet couldn't get to her now.

"What are you thinking about?" Tre asked as he caught up to me, his long strides easily narrowing the distance between us. I sensed he was handling me differently now, now that he saw how hurt I was over the stuff with Granger. They both were.

"I'm thinking we need somewhere to crash. Another public place we can sneak into."

"Why don't we get a room tonight?" he suggested. "I'll buy."

"Isn't that risky?"

"Not if I do it. Nobody's looking for me yet. I'll pay with cash. We can sneak you guys in."

Something told me I should take Tre up on his offer. The idea of sleeping on a real bed, of having a shower and watching bad TV, was too good to resist. Especially right now. Especially when it sounded so nice and legal-like.

"I vote yes on that," Aidan chimed in.

So, for the first time all day, the three of us were in agreement.

Tre got out his phone and keyed in his search. "There's a few spots on the waterfront."

Too exhausted to do much else, I let Tre lead the way. It felt good, actually, to give up some of the control. "Thank you," I said.

And I was grateful again, to have them both by my

side. I would have to make it up to them somehow, for going through all of this with me, but this IOU was bigger than anything in my book.

The hotel was a good sixteen blocks from where we were, and by the time we got there, my feet were covered in blisters after a long day of walking. Actually, it was more like an old-school 1950s motel that had been renovated into a boutique hotel. From the outside, it was all ground-hugging wings and balcony windows but the peppermint pink–striped awnings and the neon sign that said THE FAIRMOUNT in curlicue font was a giveaway that it had been fancified.

Tre went inside first, planning to check in while Aidan and I waited outside for a signal. It would be too strange if the three of us checked in together for a single room, and who knew what kind of security there was in the lobby?

"I'm sorry," Aidan said when we were alone. "About that guy Granger. Tre was right. We shouldn't have let you go in there."

"You both said it was a bad idea." I shrugged. "You were humoring me. I had to do it for myself. There's nothing to be sorry about."

"I always want to help you get what you want. You know that, right?"

I did, and it touched me. The fact that Aidan supported me no matter what had kept me going all these weeks.

He took my hand and squeezed it. "I guess we're not going to be able to make out in there, are we?"

"Probably not." I wasn't much in the mood, anyway.

"Waste of a good hotel room, if you ask me." He waved the hair out of his eyes, then paused. "Is something wrong? I mean, beyond the obvious?"

"No," I said quickly. "Why?"

"You seem distant. Mad at me or something."

"I'm not. It's just weird, you know? With Tre here. I don't want to be too couple-y."

Aidan frowned. "I don't know why that should have anything to do with anything. He's our friend. He understands."

"Guys!" Tre hissed, emerging on a second-floor balcony facing the street, waving. "I'm in. Jump up here."

"We'll talk about this later, okay?" he said.

So much for legal. Aidan and I ran toward the building. *Here we go again*, I thought. This was dangerously similar to the break-in we'd pulled back in Santa Barbara at Sam Beasley's house. Only this was a three-person maneuver. Aidan boosted me up, lifting me over his head, and Tre, hanging over the side of the railing, grabbed my arms, pulling me over in a swooping motion. I landed on the concrete deck. Then Aidan jumped up and took hold of the railing himself and, like some kind of ne'er-do-well gymnast, quickly cleared the barrier.

We went in through the sliding glass door. Easy. This

was our thing now, a fact that filled me with equal parts pride and shame.

Tre drew the beige drapes closed behind us, blocking out the night sky and the red and green shapes of light from the street, and turned on the push-button lamps by the bed. The décor was funky, with midcentury-modern furniture. It probably wasn't the biggest room in the whole place, but it was warm and dry, and, for that, it looked pretty great to me.

"One bed?" Aidan asked.

"Use your brain," Tre said. "I couldn't go asking for two twins now, could I? I can sleep on the floor. You two lovebirds can take the bed."

Ugh. More awkwardness. I looked from Tre to Aidan. "Why don't I sleep on the floor, since I brought you both here?"

"No offense to this guy, but I don't know if I want to get that close and personal with him," Tre said. "Seriously, it's fine."

I still felt weird. Tired as I was, I wasn't ready for sleep quite yet, anyway.

"Mind if I shower first?"

They both shrugged and told me to go ahead, so I did, spending an extra-long time scrubbing myself down with the thick and foamy soap, letting the hot water pool around my feet. I washed and conditioned my hair. There was no way to shave now, so that would have to pass for the time being. I dried myself off with the sweet-smelling towels, finger-combed a part, and changed into one of the extra outfits from Aidan's bag. There was no underestimating the value of cleanliness.

Once I was dressed again, I pulled out the files. Maybe another pass through the FBI documents with fresh eyes would yield some new leads, now that I was officially on the murder case.

I spread some of the pages on the bed, reread some of the parts I'd looked at before, like Chet's record:

FBI No. 356B290D
4/17/1994 Criminal trespass, private home
St. Louis, MO
Arrest Precinct: 2nd.
Arrest Number: 9823
Prosecution Charge(s): CTTL, CTTP, SOL
Disposition/Sentence: Found guilty, issued a
    citation.

1/3/1997 Suspected Robbery, First Federal Bank
St. Louis, MO
Arrest Precinct: 2nd
Arrest Number: 781
Prosecution Charges: None; not enough evidence

10/22/1997 Suspected Murder, Brianna Siebert
St. Louis, MO

Suspect was questioned in his home. No arrests made. Case still open.

It killed me. How could they have let him go free? What was I missing? I thumbed through the rest of the papers, most of which I'd skipped through before, not even knowing what I was looking for. I scanned through the dates again.

"January third," I said out loud. "The robbery was the same day as the hit-and-run."

"That can't be a coincidence," Aidan said. "Do you think it was part of the plan somehow?"

I shrugged and kept flipping. That would be odd, but who knew?

In the middle of the stack, I found a transcript of Chet's interrogation for the suspected robbery and pulled it out to examine it more closely. The first time I'd seen it on his rap sheet, the robbery seemed like an unrelated crime, but now I knew there was a good chance it was connected to the money Leslie had, which was definitely connected to the murder—somehow. I scanned down the page.

JANSON: What if I said we found your prints on the front door, the rope you used to tie up the clerks, and the safe?

TOMPKINS: What if I said you were lying?

JANSON: *So you're saying you were never at the bank? We have video footage of you there two weeks before the robbery and a few weeks before that. You weren't casing the joint?*

TOMPKINS: *We were doing our banking. You know, deposits and withdrawals.*

JANSON: *Who's "we," Mr. Tompkins?*

TOMPKINS: *A friend and myself.*

"This is interesting," I murmured, showing the page to Aidan. "He kind of slipped up here and said 'we.'"

"I would think most bank robbers have accomplices," Aidan said. "It's a pretty complicated feat to pull off. Does it say whether the other person was a man or woman?"

I shook my head, reading on. "It doesn't. And he was right, even though he was bluffing. The cop was lying. There were no prints. They never had enough evidence to charge him."

"So, hypothetically speaking, if he was the robber, who do you think this other person could be?" Tre said from across the room. He was sitting at the little desk, making doodles with the motel's complimentary pad and paper.

"Bailey? My mom? Granger? Toni? I don't know."

Everyone was suspect now. No one seemed innocent to me anymore. "All we know for sure is that my mom ended up with this money in her house somehow."

"So Chet was using her to hide it and he killed her when she started asking too many questions," Aidan said.

"Or she was his accomplice, they stole the money together, and they had some kind of blowup afterward," Tre said.

"Or she was keeping it for herself," I said, not wanting to admit it, but now that I'd heard about the hit-and-run, I was leaning in this direction. I could no longer think of my mom as someone innocently caught up in this situation. "Either way, Leslie took off with the money, and Chet couldn't find it until we were on the news, and that's when he came after us. I just don't know what the Granger connection is."

"Are we sure there is one?" Aidan said. "He could've been part of your mom's personal past. Maybe he had nothing to do with the robbery or murder. Maybe by breaking up with him she was trying to keep him out of all that."

"The dates don't add up," I said. "She definitely knew him around the time of that robbery. I was conceived around then, too. So if she was part of it back then, she was already exposing him to it. It was only after it all went down that she moved away and took on a new name."

"You still don't know he's your dad. Did you ask Granger specifically about Chet?"

I nodded. "He acted like he didn't know him, but he also denied everything else, so I don't know how good his word is."

"He's gotta know more than he's let on," Aidan said. "I wish there was a way to talk to him again."

"Even if there was, we don't have much time there," Tre pointed out. "The runoff election is in five days. Once that dude wins, and it sounds like he will, he's gonna be surrounded by even more guards and people all the time. Access will be limited."

"We could try to find some of the other witnesses. Or what about another source?" Aidan asked.

"Who?" I asked. "The police already interviewed those witnesses and came up with nothing. Who else is there?"

"Chet," Aidan said.

The very idea of coming face-to-face with him again was sickening, but I followed Aidan's line of thinking anyway. "And how would we find him?"

"I have his license plate number on my phone, remember?" Aidan said. I did: That day, which seemed like a million years ago, when we'd caught Chet running out of my house after he'd ransacked it, looking for the money. Aidan and I chased him through the back streets of Paradise Valley, to no avail. But I'd gotten the plate number, before Chet drove off, and typed it into Aidan's Droid.

"Naw, man. No way are we going to mess with that guy. And no way are we going to go looking for the murderer. That's not what we agreed on." Tre looked from Aidan to me and back again, registering the earnestness on our faces. "You people are losing your damn minds."

"I'm not saying we mess with him," Aidan said. "I'm just saying we do a little more research."

"Rule number one. You don't show up at a murderer's doorstep. You think that guy won't kill you if he has the chance again? Look, you guys, I've been really flexible here. I'm trying to be cool. But this goes beyond. When I talked to Cherise last night, she said this whole thing is like a snowball rolling down a mountaintop, and I agree with her."

Cherise said? When did he talk to her? I felt the sting of insecurity and something worse than that. Jealousy.

Well, that cleared up any suspicions I had—they were definitely a thing.

Aidan and I didn't say anything. Tre was right, even if we didn't want to admit it.

"It's been a long day. Let's just hang back and not make any decisions now, okay?" Tre got up and stalked across the room, turning on the TV.

The blare of a commercial filled the room in the spaces where our conversation had been.

Aidan gave me a conspiratorial look. "Says him. We'll talk about it again in the morning."

I nodded. I *was* tired. We all were. For now I would have to let it drop.

Tre changed the channel to MSNBC.

"No news, please," I croaked. I couldn't take any more interviews with Glitterati, teachers, cops, or any other reminders of the very thin ice on which we were presently skating.

"Fine," he said, cycling through the channels to a reality show about a movie star's teenaged kids. They were fighting over which kind of car to buy for the one girl's sixteenth birthday, a Maserati or a Ferrari. "How's this?"

We were all drawn in, silently, to the stupid drama as the girl whined about what her dad had promised her and how the dealership only had the car in black when she wanted red, and now she was going to have to wait because it wouldn't be ready in time for her birthday.

"Rich people problems," Tre said.

The girls were obnoxious and the show was obviously staged but for a moment I was happy to be sucked into their phony world. I envied them, actually. They were superficial, sure, but they had no reason not to be. Reality—true reality—was for other people.

The girl and her best friend were trading insults over whose dress was cheaper looking when there was a knock.

That jarred us out of our TV-induced glaze.

"Front desk," the voice behind the door said.

We looked at one another. They must have seen us sneaking in. Caught us on camera or something. Not knowing what to do, I dropped to the floor, rolled under the bed. Aidan jumped into the bathroom.

"Just a second," Tre called.

I saw Tre stand up and slowly make his way to the door. I clenched the cold metal frame of the bed, hoping against hope that there were no cops out there.

"Hi." It was a girl. Or a very young woman, in her early twenties at the most, with an auburn braid trailing over her shoulder, and a turquoise polo shirt with a name tag. A hotel employee? "Um, I know I said this was the best room I had for your budget, but I was looking over my register again."

What the—?

"I think, under the circumstances, that you might want some more space, in case any of your, um, associates show up," she said.

Associates? What was she talking about? Had she seen us on the security camera somehow?

"So I took the liberty of assigning you to a suite, on the third floor. Room 312. It will be much more comfortable. It sleeps three no problem."

She must have. She must have seen us. But she was giving us a *better* room?

"That sounds great," Tre said, his voice cracking the tiniest bit.

"I'll just leave the key for you. You can move there at your earliest convenience," she said.

"Thank you."

"And by the way," she said. "If you see the Sly Fox, tell her I said hi."

TWELVE

IN THE MORNING, Aidan tugged on my shirtsleeve, waking me. I'd zonked out in my clothes, and I was sprawled out on the bed on top of the covers.

In the swanky new room, there was a queen in our sleeping room and another pullout bed in the sitting area. Tre had slept there. Thanks to the kindness of our Sly Fox–fan desk manager we'd all had a comfy night.

I rubbed my face. "What time is it?" The drapes were drawn tight, sealing out the sky, and it was impossible to tell whether it was morning or night.

"Noon, actually."

What? How had we slept that long? But I knew how. It had been days since we'd had a good long sleep that wasn't interrupted by people coming and going, or the need to clear out before we got caught, or straight-up anxiety.

"That guy is still in la-la land." He pointed to the other room.

"How long have you been awake?" I asked. I knew that he'd laid down next to me.

"Since six." He grimaced. "For some reason I woke up at the crack. But I did get a little work done. C'mon, I want to show you something."

I followed Aidan out into the thickly carpeted hallway and down the mirrored elevator to the first floor. We stepped out into the lobby and eyed up the front desk. There was a guy there now but he didn't seem to notice us—he was busy on his computer, and, in any case, we were mostly concealed by a brass luggage cart holding a tower of Louis Vuitton bags. Aidan wagged a finger for me to follow him to an adjacent door marked STAFF ONLY. I withheld my questions for the time being as we walked down another hallway and then stopped in front of a door with a card slot.

He inserted a key card until it blinked, opening the door.

"Our friend left early this morning but she gave me the key," he explained.

It was an office room of some sort. "Are you sure this is okay?" I asked.

"Yeah, she said no one uses this room."

I wondered idly what else Aidan discussed with the young female clerk. Was he flirting with her? Had he told her more about me or our mission? Had he given himself away to her like he had with the dudes at Wash U? I quickly tried to tamp down my sudden flare-up of jealousy and distrust. He'd gotten us a computer and that meant more information. He was trying to help me.

Inside was a desk with two computers and a fax machine. Aidan sat down and started typing. I knew what he was doing: plugging in Chet's license plate number and running a search.

In the meantime, I made myself busy, Googling Granger. I couldn't get the image of his fake smile, his mesmerizing eyes, out of my head, and I wanted to know more about this guy and his history. Who was he really?

There was his page, of course, plus some official-looking bios on the Missouri House of Representatives and Senate pages and a Wikipedia entry.

David Granger
From Wikipedia, the free encyclopedia

David Daniel Granger (born 1960 in Maryville, Missouri) is the Missouri state senator and a member of the Democratic Party. He defeated Republican incumbent Fred Wilson in the 2008 state senate election. He previously served a term in the Missouri House of Representatives as the Minority Caucus Whip.

Personal life and education
David Granger is a lifelong resident of Missouri, born and raised in Old North St. Louis by a single mother. After graduating from Clayton High School, he attended Washington University and graduated summa cum laude with

a BA in political science in 1982. He gained early experience as a union organizer in the 1980s, working with neighborhood organizations in St. Louis before going on to law school. He received his law degree in 1998 from St. Louis University and is a partner at Lester, Granger, and Willis. He was married to Diana Robbins from 1999 to 2009 before her death from cancer. He has no children.

"Hmph," I said out loud. We'd see about that last part, maybe.

Political career

Though he was involved in social causes for all of his adult life, David Granger's official career in politics began in 1999, at age thirty-nine, when he was elected to the St. Louis Board of Aldermen. Shortly afterward, in 2000, he was elected to the Missouri House of Representatives and ran unopposed for reelection in 2004. In 2008, he was elected to the State Senate, where he served as chair of the Jobs, Economic Development, and Local Government committee and as vice chair of the Commerce, Consumer Protection, Energy, and the Environment Committee, where he wrote legislation to keep jobs in Missouri, protect citizens from environmental threats, and strengthen consumer and workers' rights.

More facts. But in the end, none of this was actually all that helpful. So he was a public figure—there was lots of documentation of what he'd done all these years, but there was no suggestion of any illegal activities or wrongdoings. There was also, I noticed, no mention of his activism before he went into politics, and no mention of the Equal Minority or casinos.

On the screen, at least, he seemed like a great guy. It's what everyone seemed to think about him, wasn't it? But maybe that in and of itself was suspicious.

Something else was bothering me. I needed to figure out the business of the hit-and-run and its connection to the robbery. I mapped the addresses of both locations, but they were on opposite sides of town.

"Got it," Aidan said, calling me out of my screen-inflicted daze. "The car. It was a rental. I found it registered under another name. S. Brightman."

S. Brightman. Who was that? "It has to be someone who works with Chet, right?"

"I have no idea. But there's an address here." He said no more, but I could read his meaning in the arch of his eyebrows: *only one way to find out.*

Back in the room, Tre was still asleep. "Come on. When he wakes up he's going to put you on the first bus back," Aidan goaded me, appealing to my Sly Fox side. "You're dying to know, aren't you?"

I hated to leave Tre like this, but Aidan was winning this debate. We already had an address. All we had to do was show up there and stake out the place. No one would even have to see us. And Awake Tre would not allow for our plan.

"Okay," I said, feeling a twinge of guilt for betraying Tre. The guy was too cautious, I told myself. We would never find out anything if we did things his way. Some liberties needed to be taken.

And Tre would certainly not approve of what we did next. Eighteen minutes later, we were standing across the street from the Four Seasons Hotel, watching the Jaguars and Mercedes pull in under the overhang. One by one, the vest-wearing valet attendants got into the cars and pulled around the block to an indoor parking garage. Then they came back and hung the keys on a board in the office.

"Just give me the word and I'll steal one of those keys," Aidan said.

I stared into the distance, squinting at a blue BMW as it pulled away from the curb. "No. Too risky. I'm going to walk up to that office and tell him I need to get into my car. I left something in there."

"But you won't have a ticket."

"I'll act entitled." I smiled. "I've seen enough Paradise Valley people do it."

Aidan looked away, and I could tell my joke stung him.

"I'm sorry. I didn't mean that. I didn't mean you."

"You didn't?" Anger flashed in his eyes—a tiny flame, and then it was gone. I was reminded that we were still on shaky ground.

"I was *kidding*."

"Whatever." He shook his head. "What do you want me to do?"

"Wait for me on the third level of the garage. I'll meet you inside and we'll get the car together." I couldn't drive—we'd established that long ago, so we needed him behind the wheel to pull off the actual getaway.

"Are you sure that will work?"

My heart quickened. We'd stolen cars before, a motorcycle, even. "I'm sure. It's easier this way. And we're not destroying property. They won't suspect anything for hours. We'll borrow the car and leave it where it can easily be found. You do want to find this guy, don't you?"

Aidan pressed his lips together in affirmation.

"All right, then. Do it."

I waited across the street as Aidan went into the lobby, acting like a guest of the hotel, taking his backpack with him. We'd been in the habit of taking it everywhere with us, ever since I lost my bag in California. I had my mom's date book in my jacket pocket—I was afraid to lose sight of it even for a minute. I even still had that stupid museum tag. I knew I could have thrown it out, but since I'd come this far with it, I wondered if maybe I should hold on to it a little while longer. I was well aware that I'd become a total flake, superstitious about everything.

In the meantime, I pulled on the fancy Barton Perreira sunglasses Aidan had stolen for me in California and smoothed my hair back before I approached the valet stand with all of the rich-bitch, Kellie-esque swagger I could muster. "I seem to have left my phone in my mom's car. Can you tell me where you parked it?"

The attendant, a bearded, potbellied man in a black uniform, looked up. "Which one was it, miss?"

"A gold Lexus? 2011?"

He nodded. "Do you have your ticket?"

"No," I said, trying not to panic, trying to sound official. "My mom lost it. But I'm in a bit of a hurry. She said you would be able to help me, that your job was taking care of the customers and that at the Four Seasons we could only expect the best treatment." I gave him a smile, playing it up.

The last line felt a little jerky but I was trying to cover my butt. It didn't even matter, though. The guy barely hesitated. He turned his back to me while he scanned over the keys on his pegboard.

As I stood there, I saw Aidan in my peripheral vision. He had a newspaper under his arm and a coffee (nice touches, I had to admit) as he headed out of the lobby and walked toward the garage.

"Here," the valet said, handing me a plastic fob. "You're on five C. Right over there through those doors."

Perfecto. Sometimes all you had to do was ask.

I found Aidan waiting and we rode up to the fifth level. The Lexus was easy to find. It was gorgeous, a four-door model, and the morning light streaming through the garage windows hit the contours of its chassis like honey pouring over a spoon. I handed him the key, and Aidan slid behind the wheel.

"It's a hybrid," he said, turning on the engine.

"Maybe that's good karma for us." If we were stealing, at least we could be mindful about our carbon impact.

"How'd it go?" he asked as I buckled in and admired the smooth and nice-smelling interior.

"I was kind of a brat, and it worked."

"So long as you're back to your non-brat self now," he said.

"I don't know. This car is pretty sweet. It could give a girl ideas."

He leaned over to kiss me and I kissed him back, feeling his stubble burn against my lips in the best possible way. This was the happiest we'd been in days.

The truth was, we both got that high when we stole something. It was almost like we brought out the need to steal in each other. A warning bell sounded in the back of my head. Was this really the best basis for a relationship? It didn't matter, I told myself. Not if we got along and cared about each other. Or it shouldn't.

I tried to focus on the car. It was a quality get, even for us. In the meantime, I'd have to add it to our IOU list.

He pulled out of the garage.

"Make a left here, and merge," I said, consulting the directions.

We hit the highway and went north for a few miles. It felt good to be moving fast in the car, the sky whirring past us out the windows. Aidan turned on the radio, and it reminded me of the days he and I spent on the road, fighting over what station to listen to in between breaking into houses, dodging cops, and eating convenience-store snacks. Everything was new then. It was the first time I'd been on a road trip without Leslie. At the time, I had been terrified for her life, but I'd had no idea what lay ahead, the search I'd be on now.

Well, the me of a couple weeks ago was a completely different person—that was for sure. I looked over at Aidan, whose eyes were trained on the road ahead of him. I wondered how he had changed.

"Get off on Broadway and continue on Bellefontaine Road," I instructed.

We pulled into a quiet-looking, middle-class neighborhood with small, boxy, one-story homes.

"Make a right on Criterion," I said.

The Lexus pivoted onto a side street where the houses were close together and the driveways were short. There were David Granger signs on some of the lawns, but that didn't mean much, because there were David Granger signs all over the whole city.

"This is it," I said. "Number 1305."

The house was as nondescript as the others around it, with gray vinyl siding and a fat, shapeless hedge standing guard out front.

"Park in the cul-de-sac." I pointed to the end of the block where we could stake out the house. "I want to see if anyone comes in or out."

So we waited. And waited. Aidan switched on the seat warmers, taking full advantage of the Lexus's luxury features. But we didn't dare turn on the radio, in case we'd miss hearing something important.

It didn't matter. Nothing was happening. No one was coming in or out. After a half hour or so, I started to wonder if this stakeout was really such a good idea. Maybe no one even lived here. Maybe it was a fake name and a fake address. S. Brightman? It sounded fake. What I thought was going to be a quick side mission was turning into an all-day event.

And Tre was undoubtedly awake by now, wondering where we were. When I thought of him, I felt my stomach turn with shame. We shouldn't have left him. What was I thinking?

"I don't know about this," I said out loud. "Not much to see."

"Be patient."

"That never was my strong suit," I said.

"No kidding. Let's give it another twenty minutes, okay?"

The next twenty minutes passed with geological speed, so slow that I half expected to be fossilized.

Just when I was going to suggest we head back, a red Pontiac came into view, rolling down the street. It pulled into the driveway and parked. We watched as a man got out of the car, slamming the door behind him, and jogged toward the front walkway.

"That's him," Aidan said.

But it wasn't Chet. It was Bailey. We hadn't seen him since Oregon, and he was better dressed now, in a sweater and jeans, but it was him all the same. "Does this mean he's S. Brightman?"

"Not necessarily," Aidan said. "He may be visiting whoever rented the Tahoe."

Bailey disappeared inside the house and we looked at each other. I was afraid to breathe too much. What was he doing in there?

In a few minutes, he came out, wearing a black jacket on top of his sweater. He locked the front door and got back into the car.

"Follow him," I said.

We got right back on the highway again, headed for the city. The Pontiac changed lanes a few times but Aidan maintained a respectably discreet distance without ever losing sight of it.

"Where's he going?"

"Looks like he's headed for the waterfront," Aidan said, braking slightly as a truck in front of him slowed down.

That's where our motel was. A chill ran through me. Was he coming for us, not knowing we were behind him? Did he know we were in town? It wouldn't be unheard of. They'd found us in Arizona, and Oregon, too. I could see the triangle of Bailey's elbow hanging out the window, flicking ash from a cigarette. The guy gave me the creeps. Or was he leading us into a trap?

"Don't slow down," I said.

"I have to. Unless you want us crashing into that truck. Please, Willa, don't tell me how to drive, okay? We've already established that this is my area of expertise and you suck at motor vehicle operation."

I couldn't exactly argue there. The Pontiac exited the highway, but instead of heading toward our motel, it turned to cross a bridge.

"East St. Louis," I read the sign. "Now we're heading into Illinois. What are we doing over here?"

It was just like in Tahoe, when we crossed the state line from California to Nevada without intending to. And here, too, there were casinos. Riverboat casinos. Were these the ones my mom was protesting? I could see their lit-up shapes on the water to my left. The sun was starting to set, tucking behind the buildings of the city, but these ships were blazing like fireworks.

"Maybe he's planning to play a few hands of blackjack," I said.

Bailey parked the Pontiac in a public lot. Lo and behold, we watched as he walked several blocks toward the entrance of a boat with the name *Lady Luck*, a wide, three-deck model of an old-fashioned steamer.

"Then we're going in, too." Aidan pulled up at the

valet station in front of the casino.

"Are you trying to be funny?" I asked.

"There's no point in parking as far away as he did when time is of the essence. Besides, it's free until four." He pointed at the sign.

"You do realize the irony of this, don't you? Valet to valet?"

"Just keep an eye on him," he said as he handed the (stolen) key to the attendant.

Bailey was already inside. At the door, a man in a suit was checking IDs from every visitor. All of them, I noticed, were dressed to the nines.

Aidan and I exchanged glances. We didn't have IDs. But I knew what we had to do. Same as earlier. Make up stuff. "Bring the bag," I said. "We should probably change into something nicer once we're in there."

"That's not going to help us get in, though."

"I'm working on that," I said.

"All right." He grinned, still enjoying the adventure. We walked up the pier leading up to the entrance.

I took a deep breath when it was our turn. Honesty, or semi-honesty, was the best policy here. "I'm sorry, sir," I said. "We're obviously underage."

He looked up at us, bushy brows lifted. He had salt-and-pepper hair, and a name tag pinned to his jacket that said SIMEON. "Looks like it."

"But our dad is in there." My eyes made a grim appeal. Sad, abandoned girl-face. It wasn't such a stretch, really.

All I had to do was think of my own family, or lack thereof. "It's been a long twenty-four hours. Please. We promised our mom we would bring him home."

Wow. Within the space of one afternoon I'd gone from rich, snotty girl to poor little abandoned child. Both acts were meant to get a reaction. Both made me feel completely terrible.

The guy frowned. I honestly couldn't tell whether my sob story was working or not. "He tell you he's in here?"

"He's at the craps table. That's where he always is. Can we just go and get him?"

He looked behind him and then back at both of us. "You have five minutes. If you're not back out here by then, I'm going to remove you myself."

I thanked him, trying to suppress my smile. Aidan and I stepped past him, hurrying on in. Our time was limited. We had to move quick. But first, we stopped in the respective restrooms. I changed into the red dress Aidan bought for me at the City Museum. He changed into a sweater-vest and button-down he'd acquired from the thrift store. When we emerged from the men's and ladies' we were like different people.

"You look hot," he said, blinking. "That dress is . . . perfect."

Perfect for me, or perfect for solving a crime? I didn't push him to make a distinction. "Thanks," I said, stuffing my old clothes back into the backpack. In an ideal world, I would have preferred to pair the dress with at least a kitten heel, but I only had a pair of flats and a pair of sneakers, so it was going to have to be the flats. At least this way, we would better blend into the surroundings.

In the lobby, we were greeted by a cacophony of jingling, jangling, beeping, metallic clacking, and the low-level din of chatter. It was like walking into the circuit board of the world's biggest computer. The red-and-orange-patterned carpet alone gave me a headache. And the lights—the flashing signs for slots and video poker machines, the spinning rainbow over the Wheel of Fortune machines, the spotlights at the top of each round pillar, the elaborate crystal chandeliers dripping glass beads from the vaulted ceilings overhead. All of these were dizzingly reflected and refracted off the mirrored surfaces on the walls and ceiling.

We scanned the aisles for Bailey, passing roulette and craps and rows and rows and rows of chirping machines, almost every single one occupied by a person pinching in coins and pressing a button or lever. No sign of him here.

As we passed the offtrack betting area, I couldn't help but think of Tre, who was involved in some kind of bookmaking, I suspected, for NFL games. How did people get into this kind of thing, the mindless sinking of money into long-shot hopes? You'd probably have to start off winning, enough that it would make you think you could keep winning. Of course, it wasn't so different from my robberies—once you got the taste of that buzz, you wanted to feel it again, to *prove* you could do it again.

I guess we all just wanted to be lucky.

Then I remembered the video I saw with my mom and Granger. They wanted to protect people from the evils of gambling, because it was addictive and it only made the rich richer. But the riverboat people had won after all because here we were.

"There he is!" Aidan said, pointing.

The shiny black of Bailey's jacket was visible ahead. He was headed into a smaller room off the main area. It looked like a private suite. But inside there wasn't much gambling going on. People were dressed up in suits and cocktail dresses, holding drinks and chatting. A party of some kind, I assumed. The room overlooked the water, which glittered with the reflection of the boat lights.

We couldn't go any farther, not without being seen, so we ducked behind some slot machines to watch Bailey as he approached another man in a charcoal-gray suit with a red tie. A man with blondish hair.

Could it be?

It was.

"Granger," Aidan said out loud.

I remembered his conversation with his aide the other day. So this was his personal private meeting or appointment or whatever. He knew Bailey. Which meant he probably knew Chet, too. I shouldn't have been surprised but the revelation still rang through me, as loudly as the machines blurting around us.

Granger lied to me. He was in on this somehow.

And what was he doing in a casino? Hadn't he been protesting these very same riverboats in that old video?

Our view was framed between the metal cases of the slots. Bailey's back was still toward us but we could see him leaning in close, whispering something into Granger's ear.

Granger's eyes widened as he listened. Then he whispered something back to Bailey. It took a pickpocket's eye to spot it, but I watched their hands as Bailey passed Granger a folded slip of paper. Granger took it from him without reading it, folded it into smaller quadrants, and put it into his back pocket. Bailey's other hand slid into his pocket, and it looked like he was fiddling with his phone.

"We need that paper, whatever it is," I said to Aidan.

I was going to have to go in and get it myself. The reefing technique seemed like my best bet—inching up the lining of his pocket from the outside until I could grab the note. But I still needed a distraction. He would remember me from the other day, but he probably wouldn't remember Aidan out of context.

"I need you to walk right up to him and bump his shoulder," I said.

"Won't he recognize me?" he asked.

"Not right away. He'll be confused in the moment,

and that will give me enough time," I said. "But we'll need to move quick."

I waited until Bailey walked away, passing back into the larger casino room. We ducked down as he neared us. Then, when Granger's back was turned, I saw our chance.

"Ready?"

Aidan nodded. I went first, positioning myself at a bar ledge nearby. I picked up someone's old drink, and pretended to be busy with it while I watched our mark. My heart thundered while I waited for Aidan to close in.

I watched with admiration as he marched straight through the door, heading right for Granger like he owned the place. But he'd added his own spin—a drunken spin. He was killing it. I crept up behind Granger just as Aidan plowed into him. The movement jarred Granger's body.

"Watch it, buddy," he said.

By then I already had the lining reefed, the corner of the paper in grabbable reach.

"I'm thso thsorry," Aidan said, slurring like he'd had five martinis. "I didn't thsee you there, thsir."

I pinched the paper, closed it inside my fist. Within seconds, I was back out the door, hiding behind another row of machines, feeling its sharp edges press into my flesh while I watched for Aidan. He was done now, too. He walked away, hands raised in apologetic retreat, while Granger scowled at him. He even faked losing his balance a little along the way.

"Amazeballs," I whispered to him when he was back beside me.

"Why thank you," Aidan said. "So what's it say?"

"I haven't looked yet." I wouldn't dare until we were alone and away from here. I'd stolen a lot of stuff, but this might be my most valuable take ever, at least to me personally.

"So where's that dad of yours?" asked a voice behind us. The guard from the entrance. His face, doubtful before, was fully suspicious now. It took me a moment to remember our lie, to realize he wasn't talking about Granger.

"We haven't found him yet," I stammered.

"Ah, but I see you've had time to change your clothes. Nice sob story." He pulled us both to our feet by our elbows. "Well, your five minutes of scamming are up."

There was no need to struggle now. We'd gotten the paper. Best to act natural, go with it without making a scene. He didn't need to drag us.

"Okay," I said. "We'll go."

So we went with him, the three of us walking back out into the lobby, the guard lecturing us about how he could lose his job and how underage gambling was a serious problem and blah blah blah.

The timing was all wrong, though. As we passed the men's room, Bailey came out, stuffing his phone back into his pants pocket. We were, undeniably, face-to-face with him. It took a second, but his eyes widened in surprise as he lunged in our direction.

"You two," he growled.

"Are these your kids?" the guard asked, forgetting that he'd already written us off. "They really shouldn't be here, sir."

Bailey shoved past him with a violence that quickly solved the dad question for even the most casual onlooker. He lunged at us. I didn't need to have a flashback to our confrontation in the Painted Hills to know we were in deep. My muscles tensed automatically, firing up to launch.

"Run!" I yelled.

THIRTEEN

THE ARCH WAS just up ahead. By the time we crossed into Jefferson National Expansion Memorial Park back in St. Louis, we'd been running for a good twenty minutes. It was eerily silent behind us. Bailey was nowhere to be found. Even so, we were still looking behind us now and again to make sure.

"I think he's gone," I said to Aidan.

He exhaled through his nose. "Yeah. That was tight there for a minute."

As we got closer, I could see that the Gateway Arch was more metallic than it had seemed from a distance, the carbon steel surface contrasting the now early evening sky. The park's trees, skeletal in winter, were dwarfed by the enormous structure. I'd been looking at it for days, and we were finally here. It was massive. It was stunning. But this was not how I wanted to see the famous landmark.

And then in the distance, I saw a familiar figure. Was that Tre? Sitting on a bench outside the Arch? *How did he get here?* It was like he knew we'd be coming.

And then I had to smile. My legs were sore. I was cold. My dress was a less-than-optimal running outfit. I wanted nothing more than to sit down. But now I knew we had something to run toward. Safety. Maybe I had been right about the Arch all along—it was here to protect us.

"Let's get Tre and get out of here," I said to Aidan. We just needed to get back to the motel and figure out our next steps, the three of us. I imagined the walk back, how we would fill him in on everything we'd learned. How he would probably try to convince us to get the next bus home. How Aidan and I would argue that we were really onto something. For the first time, I believed we could actually solve this thing. I felt it in my bones— a vibration, almost.

Or maybe that was the car engine gunning behind us. I turned to see the red Pontiac careening up the park's driveway.

I screamed, clutching Aidan's arm. He grabbed me back and yelled, too.

Turns out, Bailey was very much not lost.

The car gained speed, and soon it was next to Aidan, swerving dangerously close. We jerked to the left, tried to move out of the way.

Then the car spun around and screeched to a halt in

front of us, completely blocking the path.

There was nowhere to go but up and over. Aidan and I scrambled over the side of the car, feeling its cold metal burn our fingertips, and pushed off across the top, catching air and landing in a run.

The car door slammed shut. Bailey was running, too, and yelling. "Get back here! You almost blew it for me, you brats."

We stepped up our efforts, pounding harder against the pavement. All I could think of was getting to Tre. Tre would know what to do.

Two bundled-up joggers came by, moving in parallel along the path. Then a man pushing an extra-wide stroller with twins. We pivoted left then right, then hopped over a post-and-chain barrier as we reached the inner perimeter of the Arch.

By now, people were stopping and staring. Two kids being chased by an adult. It had to look bad. Anyone who was watching could've put two and two together— no, I couldn't think of that.

Tre moved toward us in quick strides. My fear churned with the bubbly mix of happiness and relief.

"He's after us, Tre," I panted, afraid to slow down. I should've told him to stay out of it. I should've just let him be. This was our mess, after all. But I knew we needed his help, now more than ever.

He looked back over his shoulder. "I see him. Come on. We'll make ourselves disappear."

"How'd you know we'd be here?" Aidan asked.

He raised both eyebrows in disbelief. "I didn't. I woke up alone and figured I would at least see the city before heading back home."

"I can explain . . ." I said between raspy breaths.

Now we were all running. "I know you can," Tre said. "But not now, Willa. We need to disappear."

Crowds were useful. Ask any pickpocket, and they'd tell you how easy it is to pick victims when there's a bunch of people standing around. Yet Tre was right— there was shelter here, too. This was different from before, when we'd been in an abandoned state park, after-hours in a desolate area. Even if Bailey found us, he wouldn't shoot at us in here, would he? In public? Risking the lives of innocent bystanders? No, I had to bet that he wouldn't. He was evil but probably not that insane.

Tre hurried us into the underground entrance to the Visitor Center, where there were metal detectors. So Tre knew exactly what he was doing.

Inside was total noisy chaos as the teachers tried to herd groups of school kids around and settle them down. Clueless tourists walked in aimless packs, blocking the path. Animatronic Native Americans moved robotically in front of a two-dimensional desert, while real human guides in National Park Service gear were leading tours. This was as good a place as any to get lost.

I looked back and saw Bailey slip through the

underground entrance. He would be held up at the metal detector. They'd never let him in if he was packing. We were safe in here.

"C'mon," Aidan said. "Stop looking for him."

Tre pushed us ahead of the crowd to the front of the tram line. There were two more trams left before the monument closed for the day, I heard someone say. Surely, there would be a good mess of people up there to hide in, at least for a little while.

"Excuse me, emergency, coming through," Tre called out as he scooted us through to the narrow doors of the tram. It wasn't a lie. It *was* an emergency, though they probably thought we were typical obnoxious kids. We followed him into one of the cars and sat down on the mod white plastic seats.

"Ladies and gentlemen, please stand clear. Tram doors are now closing," a woman's voice announced from unseen speakers.

And then we were going up. I gulped. I'd always been afraid of heights. And this was just the tallest monument in the United States.

I. Can't. Even.

The white double doors slid shut, and the tram lifted with a disconcerting creak as we mounted the curve of the Arch. Panic set in. This thing was not only super high up—it was also *old*. It had to have been built in the 1960s. You rarely saw cars from the 1960s on the road anymore, so how was I supposed to trust that this thing wasn't going to snap on its chains? I chewed the inside of my cheek and tried not to think about it.

Through the windows we could see the hollow, skinny body of the building with its cables and girders and bolts and the endless staircase folding in on itself. The tram picked up speed, sounding almost like an airplane. Then it slowed down again as we approached the top.

The Arch swayed in the wind. I could actually feel us tipping ever so slightly. I grabbed Aidan's hand and crunched it hard.

Assuming we survived this rickety death trap, what would we do when we got to the top? And where was Bailey? Would he be waiting for us outside? Maybe this plan wasn't such a good one after all. I tried to close my eyes, but that was scarier because there were no boundaries—I felt like I was plummeting into nothingness.

The tram began to settle and the creepily calm woman's voice chimed in again through the loudspeaker. "Welcome to the top of the Gateway Arch. Please be careful as you exit."

Thank God. The doors opened, and we, along with the rest of the passengers, stepped out into a narrow, low-ceilinged walkway. The lack of space above us was disorienting, like a fun house, and Tre had to bend at the waist so as not to hit his head. On either side of the room were views through recessed areas. In the darkness, you could still see the Mississippi, with its casino riverboats that looked like little lit-up toys from this distance, the

Old Courthouse with its dignified blue roof cap, and the cars passing on the highway as though they were tiny golden beads sliding on a string. Once again, I had to give St. Louis props. This was a really cool city. I mean, we were standing on the top of a freaking arch.

I had to remind myself.

The building swayed again and nausea swelled into my throat, obliterating all other thoughts. Rationally, I knew we weren't going to fall. But I wasn't necessarily feeling so rational.

We started to make our way through, Tre moving ahead of us past the people gathered in packs at the horizontal windows. Three little freckled kids running their fingers on the smeary glass. A couple of South American guys with backpacks and baseball caps. A young woman carrying a baby in a front sling. The last one gave me pause. Had my mom ever been here? Had she brought me? Something else I'd never know, another bit of information lost forever. But if we could just get away from Bailey, we could finally figure out what the hell happened to her.

"Excuse me," Tre said as he nearly bumped into a senior citizen in white sneakers and a blue-flowered shirt, a large camera bag slung across her chest.

"Watch yourself," she said, none too pleased.

"Maybe *you* should watch *your*self," Aidan said.

"Don't mind him," Tre said, glaring at Aidan. "We're sorry, ma'am."

"Where are your parents? They should teach you some manners," she huffed, taking her husband by the arm as they moved on.

"What's your problem, man?" Tre asked Aidan.

"Nothing. I just don't like old ladies telling me what to do."

"Show some respect," Tre said.

They launched into a spat as they walked, sniping and gesticulating at each other like two ruffled birds.

A young girl, maybe eight years old, stepped in front of me, holding a phone. "Can you take our picture?"

I looked around, and Tre and Aidan were well ahead of me, lost in their disagreement.

That's when I caught sight of Bailey, pushing through the crowd. Our eyes locked. His narrowed. He was close, maybe thirty feet away.

So they hadn't stopped him at all. But he couldn't have been on the same car as us. We would have seen him. He must have been on the last one of the day. The bastard. How had he made it?

We were screwed again. Tre's escape route was now a dead end. Literally.

"I'm sorry," I said to the girl through clenched teeth. "I can't right now."

I leapt forward, desperately pushing myself into the thicket of bodies.

"The exit tram will be leaving in one minute," the woman's voice announced.

We had to make it across the Arch to the other side in order to get out of here, to get back down. Aidan's and Tre's heads were barely visible over the crowd. They didn't even know Bailey had gotten up here. If I got left behind, Bailey would grab me, probably take me back to his house, or his headquarters, or whatever it was. Question me about the money, maybe torture me until I gave him some answers.

And then what? Kill me?

"Aidan!" I yelled, panicked, as they receded farther. "Tre!"

I imagined bullets in our heads, our bodies dumped somewhere like a junkyard or the bottom of a lake. The queasiness I'd been feeling gathered into something stronger, a violent urge to throw up. I tried to breathe in through my nose. We'd come close to death before, I reminded myself. And we'd won.

I twisted onward, bumping into chests and backs and not caring. Where were they? It was too slow, to get through all the knots of people rushing for the tram. I was losing valuable time.

The air came through my lungs in limited gasps. I had to find them. We needed to get out of here.

Finally, Tre's blue jacket came into view, a little patch of it.

I reached out for his sleeve, grasping it with the very tips of my fingers, and he turned around, startled.

I didn't bother to whisper. "He's HERE."

"Oh crap," Aidan said. "Oh sweet crap."

"C'mon," Tre said, pulling me in front of him, guiding me with his hands on my back.

We were almost to the tram when a man in a park ranger uniform held out his arms.

"We're full. You'll have to wait for the next one."

We watched in horror as the doors slid shut in front of us, coldly and with finality. As if they couldn't care less that our lives were hanging in the balance.

I let myself look back again. There he was with his big, dumb, unshaven face, bullying his way closer. Now he was smiling—he knew we were in reach. If only we had really ruined things for him back at the casino; if only that guard had realized what was going on.

We couldn't wait for the next tram, not unless we wanted to face off with Bailey, so we pivoted away, looking for another exit, or somewhere to at least hide and wait him out.

In the corner was a smudgy door marked EMERGENCY with a red-and-white sign. Without hesitation, Aidan slammed his shoulder into it, and the alarm sounded as it opened, a bleating low-pitched honk.

Stairs. We ran down them, zigzagging, trying to ignore the sound of the alarm, the flashing strobe of the lights. Aidan and Tre jumped the bottom few of every flight and I tried to do the same.

Suddenly, I remembered the overhead voice in the tram telling us that there were in fact a thousand steps here. Now that we were going down them, I believed it.

They wound around and around in a never-ending spiral. No wonder they weren't open to tourists. You'd have to be insane to choose this route over the tram. Either insane or running for your life.

After a while, my brain dulled to blankness. Every bit of mental energy was spent on trying to descend as quickly as possible, trying to follow Aidan's and Tre's rhythm, trying not to break my neck.

Step step step step jump turn step step step step jump turn.

All the while the alarm blared around us.

By the time we got to the bottom, we were thoroughly dizzy, weaving a little as we went through another door back out into the darkness. No stopping now. We had to get as far away from the Arch as possible. Away from Bailey.

The three of us ran furiously, ran maniacally, for blocks. I kept hearing the alarm in my head, like a deafening, overplayed song. The streetlights were on but everything was closing down, all the stores locked up.

We needed a destination. Another place to hide. Back in the Painted Hills we'd hid in a cave. We needed the city equivalent of that. And soon. I was losing steam.

I stopped in front of a bus stop and bent over, breathing hard. "You guys, I can't—"

"You have to," Aidan said, pulling me along. "You have to force yourself. I'm not letting you stop."

"There," Tre gasped, pointing. Up ahead was a

stadium. EDWARD JONES DOME, it said. "We just need to make it there."

I forced myself. When we got to the sidewalk in front, Tre stopped a couple of scalpers.

"What are we doing?" Aidan asked. "You're not serious, are you?"

Tre reached into his wallet and handed one of the men a wad of twenties for three tickets.

"Deadly, son. This buys us some time. And shelter."

"I had no idea you were a Rams fan," Aidan joked as we went through the turnstiles and were swallowed up in hollowed space of the concourse.

"I'm not," Tre said. "But they're playing the Bears and I hate the Bears."

He still wasn't really looking at me, and I sensed, even through his joke, that he was angry. "Tre, let me explain what happened today."

"I told you. I don't need to know. Let's just go, okay?"

I followed, still dizzy, still traumatized. Now sweaty, I was shivering cold. As I reached my hands into my pocket I felt the note. After all of that, I'd almost forgotten about it.

"Wait, you guys." I stopped and took the paper out. It was a lined page with handwriting.

Crow and broadbill spied
the lark. The nest has fallen.
But nestling fledges.

Incomprehensible. It reminded me of the pages I'd seen in my mom's book. Why were they exchanging poetry? Neither one seemed the type.

"What does the note say?" Aidan asked.

"I don't know," I said. "It's a poem of some sort."

Aidan grabbed it out of my hand. "Well, it's a haiku. Five syllables, then seven syllables, then five syllables. Yeah, this must be some kind of a code."

After all that? All the risks that we took? This is what they exchanged? Some random note in a language we couldn't decipher. What was I supposed to do with this?

I was heavy with disappointment and something worse. Because it was clear now. Granger knowing those guys meant he was a criminal, too. I raced through the other possibilities I'd been trying out in my head before, but they no longer worked. There was no theory to explain this. There was only one truth and it rose up on my tongue, stark and undeniable as blood, but I couldn't say it out loud.

"We'll figure it out," Aidan said, trying to comfort me. "Every code can be cracked."

"Well, we do know one thing," I said. "If they're exchanging notes in this code, then the connection between those guys and Granger probably goes way back."

Back to when my mom was still alive. Was she the one who made up the code? She was a poet, after all.

Tre nodded and pointed to a clothing shop. "Look, we

can figure out the code later. I'm gonna go in there and get us some new gear, so we can blend into the crowd. You guys wanna wait it out here?"

"We'll stand by this hot-dog guy," Aidan said. "Then we can find our seats."

"Just don't bounce again, okay?" Tre said, and I heard the bite in his tone.

"We won't," I promised.

Aidan and I stood and watched what we could see of the game from where we were. The second quarter was coming to a close, and the Rams were up by seven. With three seconds left, the Bears had the ball, but they weren't able to do anything with it. Now it was halftime. People were getting up out of their seats and coming up to the hot-dog stand. Others went to get in line for the bathroom.

A golf cart came down the concourse, with a security guy behind the wheel. He was talking into a radio and peering around, like he was looking for something. Just what we needed.

"Crap," Aidan said as he nudged us closer toward the entrance of the stands, so we'd be out of security sight lines.

We heard the footsteps slapping behind us. Was he off the cart now? I turned, shaken, only to see a fuzzy goatlike creature in a blue football jersey and white pants. He was running headfirst, or should I say, horns-first, and right in our direction.

"It's Rampage," Aidan called over his shoulder as the blue thing was upon us. He knew I was a sports idiot. "The mascot."

Before we knew what we were doing, Rampage was circling around us. He'd grabbed Aidan's hat and was tossing it back and forth, inviting a game of Monkey in the Middle. Aidan's face was now exposed. We froze, stunned and terrified.

Rampage threw Aidan's hat to another man in the stands. And now it was gone forever.

"Willa, look around," Aidan said through gritted teeth. I looked.

Everyone was staring at us. Well, we were in the middle of the freaking stadium, being harassed by a man in a big furry suit. But that wasn't even the worst of it, apparently.

The worst was what Aidan pointed out next. "We're on the FanCam."

FOURTEEN

SUSPENDED OVER THE goalposts, our faces were magnified two hundred times in full high-definition LED color—on not one, but two JumboTrons. I gasped. Everyone and their mother could see us.

We moved as fast as we could, running back to the concourse as the crowd simultaneously cheered and booed. I could've sworn I heard some teenage boys chanting "Sly Fox," but maybe that was in my imagination.

Tre was there already, holding a plastic bag full of jerseys and hats, his face scrawled with disgust. "A couple people blinked. Wanna go back and make sure all forty thousand of them peeped the view?"

No time to dignify this question. We ducked out through the west side exit, skittering across the street. The headlights of passing cars swept by us as we ran by block after block of parking garages, convenience stores, high-rises, pizza joints.

"Where are we going?" I asked Tre as I tried to keep up with his naturally longer stride.

"As far away from here as possible," he snapped.

We were sucking air, dodging parking meters, and charging forward, the rhythm of our feet on the ground the only sound in our ears. Yesterday's blisters rang out painfully with my every step. Running again. How many times would we run away? When could we stop running?

A few days ago this city had seemed so foreign. Now we passed by a familiar park, post office, and a sprawling churchlike building with a red roof. There was the library again. St. Louis was no longer anonymous, and neither were we. I didn't want to think it, but maybe that was a sign.

Tre stopped in front of Union Station. We followed him through an arched doorway, across an indoor plaza, and into an enormous hall. I looked up at the elaborately painted ceiling, covered with gold vines, then down at the clusters of art deco streetlights lining the center of the old waiting area.

"What are we doing in here?" Aidan asked.

"Getting you jokers off the street," Tre said.

From his body language and the hissing of his voice, I could tell he was furious. This was bad, I knew it was without him saying anything. We were really dead now. If they'd only had glimpses before, the cops and the whole world now knew exactly where we were. And it was only a matter of time until Tre let us have it.

I counted silently: *Three . . . two . . . one . . .*

"I can't believe you two," Tre said as we followed him down a staircase to the lower level. Suddenly, we were in a mall, with the usual array of stores and fast-food restaurants. "I really can't believe it. The JumboTron? How stupid can you be?"

"It wasn't our fault," I said, scrambling to explain. "The Ram—"

He pointed a long finger at me. "I could have been on there. You could've gotten me a ticket straight back to boot camp."

"But you weren't. And we had no choice," I tried again. We were all in danger, weren't we? "We didn't mean to—"

He was undeterred, talked right over me. "After everything I've done for you both. I just saved your asses from that dude. I came all the way out here, risked everything to give you an assist. And this is how you repay me, ditching me at the hotel to do God-knows-what stupid stuff, and then getting caught on TV?"

"If I remember correctly, you came here to save Willa. It had nothing to do with me," Aidan said. "So maybe leave me out of this."

"That's right," Tre said, his eyes venomous. "You're beyond my help. And this thing is your fault, like every-thing else."

I looked from one to the other, not knowing who to

side with. I was too risky for Tre, and maybe not risky enough for Aidan. Either way, I was caught between them.

"How can you say that?" Aidan asked. "We were there and you weren't."

"Because I know you, Murphy. You're careless. You enjoy getting yourself into bad situations. Because little rich boys like you never have to pay the price, do you?"

"You don't know anything about that." Aidan was getting ruffled now, I could see. His lips were pinched together and he shifted his weight from side to side.

I couldn't be sure, but I sensed that Tre was referring to what went down at Valley Prep.

"That woman was crazy," I jumped in, trying to defend Aidan. "She was out to get him."

"Oh, come on," Tre said. "You don't think he led her on, just a little bit? Mr. Playah over here? Everyone at school knows the guy thinks with his gonads."

I looked at Aidan. Now he was angry. Could this possibly be true? "Shut up, Tre," he mumbled.

"You didn't, did you?" I asked.

Aidan wasn't looking at me at all. He was picking at his cuticles, looking nervous.

I felt heat rise on my cheeks. He could at least answer the question, couldn't he? I'd been trying to give him the benefit of the doubt all this time.

Even if he was flirting with her to begin with, it wouldn't justify her actions, her attempt to blackmail him. She was still in the wrong.

But what if Tre was right? It would be one more thing Aidan conveniently left out of the story. One more reason to give me pause about whatever it was that he and I were doing together.

"It's not true, right?" I tried again. All he had to do was say no. I was more than willing to believe him. I looked at Aidan, tried to home in on what he was thinking. When we'd first left Paradise Valley, the three of us were on the same page: With Tre's help, Aidan and I were supposed to go find my missing mom. Of course everything had twisted and turned since then. Now, I no longer knew where I stood or who I could believe in.

And Aidan, meanwhile, wasn't denying anything. He just heaved his shoulders. "This is all old news. It happened a while ago."

Was that a tacit admission? "It was only a few months ago," I said. "Not that old."

He turned to me. "I'm with you now. So what does it matter?"

"It matters," I said, "because I've been trusting you. And I need to know if you're the kind of person who takes responsibility for their actions. Or if, like Tre said, you stumble into these situations, worm your way out, and blame someone else."

Something broke inside him then. He no longer seemed like he cared what I thought. "You know what?

Screw you both. I don't need this crap," he said, his face scrunched up in disgust. "It's like I'm on trial or something. I shouldn't have to explain myself to my friends."

"Answer the question," I said quietly, staring him in the eye. "Can you at least do that?" How could he be so cavalier right now? Didn't he understand that our whole relationship, whatever it was, was riding on this?

His mouth went bitter and mean. "Why? Tre will answer it for me, obviously. I'm sure between the two of you, you can figure this out. I'm gone."

He charged out through the center aisle of the mall, knocking into a little kiosk with sunglasses, shaking its flimsy structure so that mirrored pairs of them went flying, rattling across the tiled floor. Aidan's lone frame stalking away was reflected in every one.

"Hey, wait a minute," the salesman said, but Aidan didn't turn back or even flinch.

We watched as he passed under the ramp of the escalator and then disappeared through a set of double doors. We watched as he became smaller and unreachable, narrowing to a dot in the distance.

"Wow," I said out loud. How could Aidan walk away, just like that? Then I remembered how dismissive he'd been about his parents. A few slipups and he was done. This was Aidan. This was who he really was, temper and all. I wasn't sure I could be with someone who gave up on the people he loved so easily.

But I also felt the panic I'd felt when I'd lost him

back in Tahoe, when he'd stormed off a bus and I was convinced I'd never see him again.

"He'll be back," Tre said after a while. "He's probably blowing off steam."

I nodded, hoping like anything that Tre was right.

Not knowing what to do with ourselves, Tre and I walked around the mall. Never in my life had a shopping trip been less fun. There wasn't much in the way of fashion—the Glitterati wouldn't be caught dead here, I thought—but there was a Foot Locker, and some cute gift-type stores, and a lot of sports memorabilia that we had no use for. By now, we'd already put on our Rams gear, just as a safety measure, and I'd taken off the ridiculously impractical dress. Our matching outfits were ridiculous in their own way.

Tre led us toward a bagel place. "I don't know about you, but fights make me hungry."

I nodded my assent. Food was a good thing. A distraction. He bought us sandwiches and sodas and we sat down at a little table to eat them.

"I'm sorry I yelled at him," Tre said.

"Are you sorry to me or to him?"

He thought this over, chewing. "More to you right now. I still think he's been acting stupid."

I didn't know what to say about that. I was afraid of Aidan's carelessness myself, worried about what he could be doing at this very moment. I was mad about the Sheila thing, too, and I was afraid that if I opened my mouth about that a whole torrent of feelings would come out.

"So how long have you two known each other, anyway?" I asked. I'd always wondered—it seemed like when I came to VP, they were already pals, but Tre started there the same time I did.

"We met over the summer. I moved in at my dad's, and he started taking me to the golf club. He plays with Murphy's dad all the time. I have no clue how to play, so one day Murph and I hung out by the pool and started talking. I guess you could say he was my first friend in town. I think my pops was hoping the whole golf thing would rub off on me, that Murphy would be some kind of good influence, but Murphy hated that place. All he wanted to talk about were ways we could mess with them. You know, pranks and stuff."

"I think he mostly just hates his dad," I said, tearing off a piece of my bagel.

"I can see that. The guy's your typical CEO cornball. He puts a lot of pressure on him. Wants him to be the next one in line for the dynasty, or whatever."

"I haven't met him," I said. "But that sounds about right."

He dug his straw into his waxed cup. "That's the way rich people are, man. They like to control their kids. But it never works out."

"What about you? Your parents, I mean?"

219

"My dad's okay. A little out of touch sometimes. A little obsessed with his work. He doesn't want me to embarrass him, is all. So I have to toe the line if I want to stay in Paradise Valley. Right now he thinks I'm in Colonial Williamsburg. I told him we weren't allowed to use our phones, for the full old-timey experience."

"And he bought it?"

He shrugged. "More like he didn't bother to *not* buy it. He's a busy guy. But my mom . . . she's great. She wanted more for me than she could provide, you know? I mean, I didn't even know who my dad was until I came to live with him. She wasn't just going after his money. She wanted to do it on her own."

I thought of Leslie, and then my real mom, and a lump lodged in my throat, along with a surge of loneliness. They wanted more for me, too. I put down my bagel and tried to regroup.

Tre must have noticed because he looked at me with concern. "Did I say something wrong?"

"No, not at all," I said. "Remember when you said I wasn't bulletproof? You were more right than you know."

"Nobody is. Hey, I cry." He looked up at me with a funny little smile. "Well, not a lot. Like, once a year."

"Once, huh?" I teased.

"Look, you don't have to be bulletproof. You're plenty tough. It's gonna be okay, Willa. I promise you it will."

But I wasn't sure he or anyone else could make that

kind of promise. "I'm sorry for being a bad friend," I said. "And for ditching you earlier. I guess I kind of took you for granted. I want you to know how much it means to me that you're here."

"I'm over that now," he said sheepishly. "It was stupid."

"No, I mean it. We need a chance for a do-over. A time when we can just hang out without all this other stuff going on."

"I'd like that," he said, dimples emerging.

I crumpled up my napkin and got up to throw out my food, then placed the tray back in its slot on top of the trash can. There were so, so many things I wished I could do over.

We walked a bit more and then, at Tre's suggestion, got some ice cream. "We deserve it," Tre said, spooning up butter pecan. "Listen, you don't have to decide now. But I want you to think about turning yourself in tomorrow."

"You've been saying it ever since you got here," I reminded him. "I know. You want me to do the right thing, pay my dues." He thought I should pay for my crimes as he had with his.

"You keep saying that, but it's not about me. Believe me, I don't want you to go to juvie. I don't even like to think about you being away that long, in that place. . . ." He looked away as the words trailed off. "Just, I've been mulling it over and it's gotta be the best option. The safest. Think about it, okay?"

I agreed to at least think about it. "I don't think I've ever had ice cream in winter," I said, smoothing down the top of my cone, feeling the cold sensation numb my lips.

"Are you kidding? That's the best time."

"Speaking of, what time is it?" I asked.

"Eight forty-five," he said.

An hour had passed and there was no sign of Aidan anywhere. And that's when I realized that he'd walked off with his bag, with all the FBI files, our changes of clothes, and our temporary phone inside it. Great. I'd relied on him to take care of all of our stuff. Well, it served me right for not doing things myself. At least I still had my mom's date book.

Tre checked his phone. Nothing. We were both getting annoyed. Where the hell was he? This wasn't the time for dramatics, for storming away in a huff. We had serious problems on our hands that were way bigger than this fight.

"What do you think?"

"I think he's trying to prove a point," I said.

The mall would be closing in another hour, so we decided to stay on for the night. That way, when Aidan came back, we'd be right where he left us.

As usual, Tre knew what to do. We hid in the Santa's workshop display, me crouched in between some elves with hammers and toys, and Tre curled up under a blanket of fake snow. We waited for the guards to do their rounds.

When we heard the footsteps receding, and the overhead lights in the mall dimmed, we freed ourselves and found a couple of benches to settle down on in the shadowy center of the floor, overlooking some topiary arrangements in the shape of candy canes.

This had to be least comfortable of all of the temporary sleeping arrangements we'd come up with and the silence in the mall was stranger, more disturbing, than anyplace else we'd squatted at night. In the library and museum, at least, it had seemed peaceful. Here it was just lonely. I tossed and turned on the narrow slats, trying to drift off, but unconsciousness wouldn't come. All I could think about was what would happen to us tomorrow, when we would reunite with Aidan, and what we—or I—would do next.

In the morning, we woke to sunlight streaming through the mall skylights. I was up first. I shook Tre. He rolled over, his mouth parting, eyes rolling beneath their lids.

"Tre. Come on." I touched him again.

He sat up, startled. "Yo."

"We should get up," I said.

He rubbed at his eyes with the heels of his hands. "Right."

We waited for the mall to open and we did a lap around, and when there was still no sign of Aidan, doubt began to creep in. Maybe he wasn't coming back at all.

"I hope the guy wasn't just wandering around waiting to get picked up by the cops," Tre said.

"Who knows?" I said. "He could have turned himself in by now."

"Do you think he would've done that?"

"I honestly don't know," I said, though I was reluctant to admit it to Tre. "As much as I want to think otherwise, there's a lot I don't know about him."

If Aidan went to the police, he could give me up, too. I still didn't think he would do that, but who knew? I was going to have to make a decision on my own, anyway. I felt it looming over everything, along with Tre's words from the night before.

"Maybe something else happened to him," Tre said.

"Like what?" I asked, afraid of the answer.

He didn't say anything, and for a split second, I felt guilty for thinking the worst of Aidan, for assuming everything was his fault, and I could tell Tre was feeling the same way, too.

With an ache, I realized how much I missed Aidan. He'd been with me for weeks, and other than that short time in Tahoe when we'd been separated for a few hours, we'd pretty much been together 24/7 all that time. Now I wondered if I'd see him again. Had he really left for good?

I was still angry, don't get me wrong. Still bothered by his behavior. But I was also pretty sure I loved him. And he cared about me, didn't he?

How had this happened to us? I replayed all of my memories, looking for answers, everything from our first kiss outside of my house to the days snuggling on the long bus rides and our nights in the library, the museum. It had all seemed so right at the time, but now I didn't know. Maybe I had been fooling myself. I had to have been. There was Sheila to think about. His deceptions. His inability to play by the rules when I needed him to.

"Should we go out and look, walk the streets?" Tre asked.

"No," I said. "If we stay here, he knows where to find us."

Probably, he was fine. And if we didn't hear from him in a couple of hours, we'd have to go on without him. We'd just have to assume he had turned himself in.

So we sat back down on our benches, watched the other shoppers passing us. The stores weren't open yet, but people were already wandering around—tourists, mostly, and a few elderly mall walkers in coordinated sweat suits and Nikes. Instrumental music played overhead, cheery brassy versions of Top 40 hits. The smell of cinnamon buns started to waft through the air.

At 9:45, Tre's phone rang.

I grabbed it instinctively and answered. It had to be Aidan. I knew it was. He'd be wanting to know where he could meet us. He'd have changed his mind, and he was ready to come back to our mission. He needed us more than we needed him, obviously. And I'd have to decide whether I was ready to forgive him.

But the voice that came out of the other end wasn't Aidan's. I didn't know who it was because it was distorted through one of those voice changers, deep and burbling like the person was talking through water, or on the wrong speed of a recording. "We have your friend. Listen very carefully," it said.

My heart stopped, or at least it felt that way as the words echoed through my brain. They were talking about Aidan. They'd found him. He *was* in danger after all.

"We want the money. All five million. And we need it within twenty-four hours. We'll call you back and tell you where to meet us. Make sure you follow our instructions very carefully. No cops. No telling anyone. Get us the money and your friend will live."

I gasped. The unspoken suggestion left at the end of that sentence chilled me to the deepest cells of my being.

I clicked the phone off and slid it back to Tre, wordlessly.

"What was it?" he asked.

I stared at him, wide-eyed. "Aidan. He's been kidnapped."

"Who called you? Was it Bailey? Chet?"

"Impossible to tell," I said, stunned, staring out into the bright, busy space of the mall.

"Well, what did they say exactly?" He pulled on my shirtsleeve, impatient for the whole story.

"They want the money. Leslie's money. All five million. And they want it within twenty-four hours, or else. . . ."

"Or else what?"

I winced, feeling like a guillotine was hanging over all of us. I could barely bring myself to say it—the words came out in the hoarsest whisper. "Or else they'll kill him."

FIFTEEN

I CHOKED DOWN the bile that had risen in my throat. They were going to kill Aidan, yet the world around me was oblivious. It all felt very wrong, these mundane details, life going on as usual when we were in the middle of a crisis.

The sunglasses guy was back on duty. Across the way, a woman was pulling up the security gate on a Claire's Accessories. To my left, a fountain burbled lazily, water recycling itself over a scattering of pennies. If only I could dive in and steal a lucky one. But I needed much more than that right now. It occurred to me that in all my stealing, I'd never actually come away with lasting good fortune—just some fleeting breaks, and I was sure I had finally used those up.

Think. I had to think. Aidan was out there, he was in trouble, and we had to do something.

But what? I knew these guys, and I knew they didn't

play around. Tre and I didn't have guns or a crew to help us. We'd scraped together some clever ideas in the past—some plans, sure—but no amount of planning could get us out of this situation.

The choice was simple. There was none. I had to go to the authorities. I had to call Corbin. Yes, he was FBI, but he'd helped us in Oregon. Of course we'd ditched him, and he'd probably be angry about that. But maybe he would be willing to help us again, if I offered to turn us in. Promised him for real this time. We could make a deal. Surely, he would care that Aidan's life was at stake. He would want to save him.

Tre didn't resist. He was relieved, I think, that I was finally ready to turn myself in. "It's the right thing," he said.

"But this is it, Tre. If I do this, it's over."

He simply nodded. So be it, his expression said. We were living on borrowed time, anyway. And at least we'd be safe.

Hands shaking, I took Tre's phone and dialed the number.

Corbin answered on the third ring, his voice gruff. I could hear typing in the background.

"It's Willa," I said, and my own voice sounded small and metallic. "We're in St. Louis."

"I know," he said, salty as ever. "Give me some credit, will you?"

The words came tumbling out then, all at once. "They

have Aidan. They kidnapped him. Chet and Bailey and whoever they work with. They called, demanding a ransom—five million dollars. I need your help. I'm ready to cooperate. And I have a deal for you."

There was a pause. A sigh. Then, "I'm listening."

"They want me to hand over the money. I mean, it has to be me, since it's Leslie's money they're after. If you can help us figure that out—how to get it to them, real or fake—we can rescue Aidan. And then I promise I'll turn myself over to you and forget about my mom's murder and all of the rest of it." My voice broke some. "Please, Corbin. Can you come out here?"

"It's nice of you to offer to give yourself up, Willa, but it's a little too late. I'm off the case."

My heart sank. "But why? They're still looking for us."

"We've been down this road before, haven't we? With your promises." Now he sounded like a stern teacher. "And how am I supposed to know you're not playing me again?"

"This is different. I swear . . . I'm not making it up. I wouldn't lie to you, not about Aidan."

"What you did in Oregon, that was unforgiveable." His voice sharpened, intensified in volume, almost as if he was holding the receiver directly in front of his mouth like a microphone. "I helped you, I helped Leslie, and what do you do to repay me? The two of you take off, like Thelma and Louise. Like it's some kind of game you're playing, without regard for your own safety or others'. Do you have any understanding of what I put on the line for you? An eighteen-year career, Willa."

"Listen, Corbin," I said, feeling humbled by his chastising tone. "I never meant to hurt you or your career. I appreciate all that you did for us. I do. But I had to know more about my real mother. I was afraid I'd never have the chance again."

I could explain but I couldn't bring myself to apologize. Maybe I was stubborn or just plain stupid, but somehow, even after everything, all of my mistakes, I still stood by that decision.

I looked at Tre and he was watching me, brow furrowed.

"And what have you learned? You've been there less than a week. It's a cold case. Did you really think you'd uncover what the FBI and local authorities couldn't?"

"I've learned a lot of things—"

He talked right over me. "I don't know what you expect to find but the facts are there for anyone to see them. She was in a mess of trouble, that woman. Whatever happened to her, she brought it on herself."

My voice dropped to a whisper. "So you're saying she deserved to be murdered?"

"No," he said. "I'm not saying she *deserved* it. But it's like I said to you before. It's about choices, Willa. And choices have consequences. The same is true for you. If you think I'm going to drop everything and come out there to save you when you've shown yourself to be a thief and a liar, then you're wrong."

"You also said that it's not always black and white," I reminded him. "Remember that?"

He huffed impatiently, clearly not interested in the full blow-by-blow of our conversation. "Forget what I said. Now listen: The local cops are still investigating our little explosion in Three Rivers. Just so you know, just so we're absolutely clear: If they come to me, if it's a choice between my job and protecting you again, I'm going to choose me."

"I know," I said, the guilt about our actions swirling into the larger surge of guilt I felt about everything that was happening now. I was responsible. I knew it was my choices that had landed us here. Did that mean I couldn't try to make to things right, though? "But what about Aidan?"

He was out there. His life was at risk. I would never forgive myself if anything happened to him.

"What about him? I don't owe you anything at this point. Do you hear me? I'm not responsible for either of you. I was looking out for your sister. That was all."

Leslie. "How is she?" I asked quickly, realizing that he was my only link to her at this point. "Have you been in touch with her?"

"She's doing just fine," he said, his tone softening. I was pretty sure he had deeper feelings for Leslie—I'd seen something pass between them in Oregon—but I wasn't about to point that out to him. Especially not now.

"So you talked to her?"

"Yesterday, actually." He paused, then added almost reluctantly, "She's all set up. She misses you, of course."

And I miss her, I thought, the feeling echoing in the deepest part of me. It was too much—losing Leslie, and now losing the mother I'd never even met yet. And Aidan . . .

"Look, I feel for you, Willa. You're in a tough spot there."

"But you won't help me," I finished for him.

"Not after everything, no."

Feeling desperate, I tried another tack. "What if I told you there was more to this case? What if I told you I had reason to believe that a senatorial candidate was involved, a man named David Granger?"

"I would tell you that you're out of your mind. You need to stop playing Nancy Drew, okay?" He choked out a bitter laugh. "Forget it. Why am I even trying to offer you advice? Not like you listen to me, anyway."

"I might have new information, though."

"And I might be distantly related to the Queen of England. Like I said: Not interested. Not my responsibility. Not my case. Call the local police. They'll help you."

He hung up the phone and I held it to my ear for a moment, listening to the blank sound between the click and the dial tone, a silence that seemed to stretch on into infinity.

"No go?" Tre said.

I handed the phone back to him, feeling dizzy. "No go. I guess I burned that bridge back in Oregon. He said we're on our own. He thinks my mom probably got what was coming to her and that we should call the local authorities."

He shook his head. "Sounds like a smacked ass."

"He pretty much is," I said, shutting my eyes, feeling everything close in on me. But could I blame Corbin for it? Not really. "What are we going to do, Tre?"

"I don't know."

"I got Aidan into this. If it wasn't for me, he'd be home right now, hanging out at the animal shelter, or driving around Paradise Valley or geeking out over some computer thing. Instead, he's . . ."

The image of Aidan, tied up somewhere, gagged, tortured, was too dark for me to even conjure.

Without Corbin, we were screwed. I didn't have the slightest clue how to fix this. I was exhausted. I was scared. Most of all, I was tired of feeling like all these things were so much bigger than me. I wanted to give up.

I looked down at the tiled floor. "I don't know. Maybe we should take Corbin's advice and just go to the local police."

Tre had been ready to turn us in for days. I figured he

would jump at the chance. So it surprised me when he shook his head vehemently. "Nah."

"What do you mean?"

"If Granger's really behind all of this, then who knows what kind of connections he has? He could have the local police tied into his scheme and that could backfire quick. Cops can't always be trusted." He caught a corner of his lip between his teeth as he thought it through. "I want to take care of this ourselves."

"Really," I said, disbelieving.

"It's my fault. I drove the guy away. I was too hard on him. I shouldn't have hinted at that stuff about the teacher. I was just trying to—I don't know. I was just trying to get it all out in the open, I guess. I wanted you to know the truth." He looked up at me from under his long lashes, almost shyly. "Anyway, I'm not going to let you shoulder all the blame for this. I'm going to take care of it."

"How?" I asked.

"I can get the money. I'll call home. I can get my dad to liquidate some assets, tap into my trust fund—*something.* I know he has it."

"You'd do that? For him?" A few hours ago, he seemed like he hated Aidan.

"We have our differences, me and Murphy. But I made a mistake," he said. "And we can't give up now. The guy's life is on the line."

As if I could forget. "Getting the money, that makes you more of an accomplice. That ties you to me and

Aidan. Are you sure you want to get deeper into this?"

"Am I? Not really." He gave a little shrug. "You know, at first I thought I could come out here and save you but this situation is deeper than I realized."

"Yeah," I said, allowing a smile to tease at the corners of my mouth. "And there's also the little problem that I didn't exactly want to be saved."

"There's that."

"Back in California, you told me you had boundaries that you weren't willing to cross," I reminded him.

"I know," he said. "I still think that. But this is life or death. I can't sit back and pretend like I'm not part of it."

"You know, I think you're getting warm and fuzzy in your old age, Tre."

"I like to think of it as changing my priorities. Not going soft."

"Either way. You're pretty much the best." I gazed at him gratefully.

"So I hear. C'mon. Let's get out of this dang mall."

We walked out past the stores with their arrangements of goods and promises of convenience and better times, and into a restaurant called Duff's, offering an all-you-can-eat breakfast buffet. We went in and got a table, though I wasn't feeling especially hungry. If nothing else, it was a place to sit and think things through.

We sat down at a table for two close to the back of the room. The waitress brought us some coffee, set down some cream and sugar, and told us to help ourselves to the food. I let Tre go first. The room was only half full, a couple with two little kids occupying a corner table, a few businessman types scattered around drinking coffee and reading newspapers.

I pulled out my mom's date book again. In all of the action of the past few days, I hadn't had time to go back to it again, to really take another look. And something was bothering me—it was that weird code.

SPARROW
DOVE
CROW
BLUEBONNET
BROADBILL

And then there was the paper we'd stolen from Granger. I drew that out of my pocket, too, and unfolded it:

Crow and broadbill spied
the lark. The nest has fallen.
But nestling fledges.

I knew the two were related. It was obvious. But I couldn't decipher them.

Tre sat down with his plate overloaded with eggs and sausages and fruit and muffins. "Your turn."

"Hmm," I said, distracted by what I was seeing on

the paper. I paged through the book again and saw the tattered edges where the missing pages had once been.

He forked some yellow clouds into his mouth. "So we agree I should call my dad," he said.

"No," I said, holding up a hand. "Not yet. We need to go see Toni again." If she knew more than she was letting on, then we needed to know what that "more" was.

It was a weekday morning, so we could only assume Toni was at work with the rest of the world. I looked up her company, Belles Nuits, and found a downtown address. Tre and I walked there and found a brick building taking up most of a block.

We asked for Toni at the front desk—no point in breaking in or doing anything disreputable. She would either see us and cooperate, or she wouldn't.

The older blond receptionist looked at us over red-framed bifocals, then got on the phone and called Toni's office. "There are some kids here to see you."

Toni herself came out a moment later, carrying a sheaf of paper and frowning. "I should have known I'd see you again."

"We just have a few questions," I asked.

She looked around behind us, checking, perhaps, for the presence of policemen or unsavory characters, and then put the paper on the receptionist's desk before ushering us back to a small conference room. We all took seats at a round table.

"Shoot," she said, still looking uncomfortable. "I don't have much time."

We didn't, either. About an hour and a half had elapsed since we got the call, which gave us precisely twenty-two and a half hours to come up with the money or another solution. Part of me wondered what the hell we were doing here, but another part of me knew that the only way we could help Aidan is if we understood what was really going on.

"I want to know about the book," I said. "My mom's book."

"The one you stole from my house?"

"That one," I said, allowing a smile. "There are some missing pages—pages that look like they were ripped out. I think they could be important in telling us the story of what happened to her, why she was murdered."

"Are you sure you really want to be involved with this?"

"How could I not be?"

She rubbed her temples worriedly. "I got the book when they cleaned out her locker at work—our boss asked me if I wanted something to remember her by, so I took it. I always loved her poems and I thought that's all it was, a poetry journal. Until I realized that some of those pages might be code. I could never figure out what it said but I knew they could explain something about what happened. I was afraid, so I hid the book away all these years." As she spoke, the doubt fell away and

239

I became certain: She wasn't guilty of anything except being my mom's friend.

"And then when we came to your house, you ripped out the code pages."

"I wanted to protect all of us, okay? I figured the past was past."

"And now?"

She shook her head. "Look, I'll tell you everything I know—you can decide to do with it what you will."

I nodded.

"Angie—that's what I always called her. She was a sweet girl. We met at the restaurant. She'd just moved to the area. She was older than me, but we were fast friends. You know how that is, when you connect with someone, and it feels like you've known them all your life?" She looked up. I did know how that was. That's how Cherise and I had been, back when I started at Valley Prep.

"We both daydreamed about what we were going to do with our lives. She talked about her writing, how when she saved up enough money she was going back to school. My passion was cooking. I always wanted to start a catering company." Her dreamy gaze broke off as her eyes trailed downward. "Well, here I am. It happened for me."

"But she never had the chance to pursue her passion," I said.

"No."

"So what do you think happened?"

"I knew she had some secrets. There was a dark feeling to her, a shadow that kind of stuck to her. I knew she'd had a baby real young—too young."

"Leslie," I said softly.

"Angie's parents threw her out because of that. By the time I knew Angie, Leslie was a teenager. Angie was always worrying about her grades and whether she was getting mixed up with boys. She said school had to come first, that a degree in boys wouldn't get you anywhere."

I had to laugh. "That's what Leslie always says to me. Now I know where she got it."

She looked at me. "And you. You were just a baby. I watched you a couple of times when she was out. She worried about you, too. She really wanted to do the best for both of her girls. I got the feeling that's why she'd moved. She was trying to get a fresh start for you all."

My throat tightened. "So did you know what she was running from?"

She closed her eyes, as if conjuring some image on the backs of them. "One night, this man came into the restaurant. She took one look at him and her face turned real white. I asked her what was wrong. She said, 'It's some guy I used to know. I can't face him now.' So I told her I would cover her table."

"Did you get any information about this guy?" Tre asked. "Did you get a good look at him?

"I did. I mean, after she had such a strong reaction,

I remembered his face. It was only years later, when he was on TV all the time, that I realized who he was."

"David Granger," I murmured, locking eyes with Tre.

She nodded. "I assumed something personal, maybe something romantic was going on, but I was too afraid to ask her—I guess I was watching my own back in those days, trying to stay out of trouble. I'd had my own issues as a teenager—some struggles with the wrong type of people. So I drew a line in the sand. It seemed that whatever she'd been involved in was bad, that maybe she'd made some mistakes that weren't just relationship mistakes."

I had to ask—the question rang through all the other noise in my head, sharp and clear as a whistle. "Is he my father?"

"I honestly don't know the answer to that." She twisted her wedding band.

"So then?" I asked.

"So then the next thing, maybe a couple of months later, she was gone." She paused, letting the last word rise up and hover over us.

"Do you—" Tre started.

"Do I think he had something to do with it?" She nodded. "He's done a lot for the state of Missouri, but there's always been something off about the guy. Like he's too good to be true. Typical megalomaniac cult-leader type. And knowing that your mom was that afraid of him, well . . ."

So she thought he was guilty, too. "But you never said anything to anyone?"

"Not until yesterday. I emailed his office after I saw you all, letting him know I was onto him. I said the truth would come out, that his whole campaign would be over, and that her family deserved to have closure." She clasped her hands together. "That was probably a crazy thing to do. But after all this time, after I let him get away with it before, I needed to speak my mind before he gets elected again. He has to come clean—and in a public way."

Fat chance of that. I sighed. "We already met him and he denied everything," I said. "But you really think he was the one?"

"I'm not saying he murdered her outright. But in my gut? Yes. I think he at least knows what happened."

We let that sink in.

"Did she ever mention anything about a hit-and-run?" I asked. "Or a robbery?"

Toni shook her head. "No. That's all I know. I promise."

I believed her.

"I just wish Angie—Brianna—had lived. She would have had a better life. My business really took off after I left the pub." She waved a hand around the room as if to show us all that it had bought her. "Maybe her life would have, too. And I wish I hadn't been so afraid of getting involved. I wish I'd spent more time listening to her, asking her questions, demanding answers.

Maybe she would still be alive."

Sensing that we were coming to an end, I stood up. "Well, thanks for your time and for sharing this information with us. It's really helpful. But do you mind if I ask what happened, why you talked to us today and not the other day?"

She gave us a tight smile. "Seeing you at the house was very startling. I wasn't prepared for it. But I guess I have these regrets about your mom. Not doing anything or talking to the police back then has haunted me. And all these years, I wondered what happened to you and your sister. So I'm just glad to see you're okay." She reached inside her purse and produced some folded sheets of paper. "Here. Take them. Do what you have to do. I know it's not my place, but I'm a mom, too. Whatever happens, I hope you'll try to stay out of trouble."

We would try, I told her as I accepted the missing pages. But what I didn't say was that trouble was something we were still very much in.

SIXTEEN

ANOTHER HOUR HAD elapsed and we were still in limbo. I felt the clock ticking. Back on the street again, I thought of Cherise. Talking to Toni reminded me of her, and more than ever I needed her advice. Even hearing the sound of her voice would comfort me. But there wasn't time to call Cherise now. We had to look at the new material Toni gave us. We slipped deep into a bookstore, way back in the travel aisle, where I eyed up the blue-and-white covers of guides to places around the world, wishing I could be in any of them right now, anywhere but here.

The new pages matched the book in size and shape, their ripped edges ragged and yellowing. On them were more haiku.

Sparrow in morning
Bluebonnet + dove migrate
Drop feathers; eggs in thicket.

Crow wings west alone,
Waits for thaw. Bluebonnet stores
The eggs in winter.

I opened the book. I had to figure out this code of hers. Again I thought of Cherise—we'd taken English class together and she was good with language. Maybe she could make sense of this jibber-jabber.

SPARROW
DOVE
CROW
BLUEBONNET
BROADBILL

I read and reread the words. As far as a code went, it was a strange one. There were no numbers, no calculations to make. But the same bird names kept reappearing. Was the list a key of some kind?

There was the bird doodle, and the reference to birds in her poem, too. What was up with all of these damn birds? Chet had a bird tattoo, I suddenly remembered. And there was the frieze at the museum, and the motto that connected up with my mom's sign. Welfare for All. That had sparrows on it, too. My hand went to the pendant at my throat.

"What do you know about sparrows?" I asked Tre.

"Nothing much. In Sunday school they always said

the sparrow stands for the common man. It's in the Bible."

"Could 'Sparrow' be the name of their group?" I asked out loud. "I mean, it's a perfect symbol for the things they stand for."

"But it says 'sparrow in morning,'" Tre said. "That makes me think it's not people but a thing. Maybe Sparrow is the name of their plan, like Operation Sparrow?"

An interesting idea. It sounded like something out of the military. But I could go with it. I started to read the rest of the poems out loud, over and over, including the one I nabbed from Granger.

Crow and broadbill spied
the lark. The nest has fallen.
But nestling fledges.

"The nest has fallen," Tre repeated back to me. "Whose nest? The lark's?"

That gave me a chill as I remembered the explosion. *Leslie*. Was she the Lark? Was Bailey reporting back to Granger to tell him what happened in Oregon?

But nestling fledges.

That was me.

"He's warning him that I'm around," I concluded. "Because they still think I'm *Leslie's* daughter."

"So Granger doesn't know, either, then?"

"I don't know." I looked at the words in the date book

again. "Bluebonnet must be Brianna."

Tre picked up where I left off. "Dove is David Granger and Crow is Chet. Broadbill is . . ."

"Bailey," I finished.

Now we could fill in the rest. "Sparrow in morning. They robbed the bank in the morning." This fit with the newspaper reports we'd seen.

"Brianna and David migrate . . ." Tre said. "So if we go by these poems, they were definitely all in it together. But then somewhere along the line, your mom must have changed her mind."

"Where were they going, though? Migrate to where? And to do what?"

He flipped the page in the book and then held the whole thing up to the light. "There's an imprint of numbers here. Like someone wrote them on a different page in the book and they transferred."

He held them up to the light and took out his phone to take a photo.

"What are you doing?"

"Reading them. I learned this trick on TV. The photo captures the shadows around the imprints."

"Whatever it takes," I said.

He murmured as he looked at the screen and traced his finger over the numbers. "38 dot 5498. And 90 dot 2926."

"More code?" I asked. "Or a combination of some kind? For a safe or something?"

He shrugged. "Or an account where they planned to store the money?"

Ugh. These numbers could be anything. "Now what?"

"Now . . . we have to match them up to something. Unless you think they're meaningless."

I didn't. Nothing was meaningless at this point. "Google it," I said. "You never know."

Tre typed the numbers into his phone. Within a few seconds a slow smile spread across his face. "Well, look at that," he said, looking up from his screen. "They're map coordinates. According to the trusty internet, it's the location of Cliff Cave Park. Just south of the city."

"We need to go there," I said, understanding all at once. "There's something hidden in the park."

Cliff Cave Park was a good twenty miles away. We agreed that we didn't have much time, and we couldn't risk a cab, and there was no public transportation to the park. In this extreme situation, stealing another car was our best bet.

"You sure this isn't another boundary we're stepping over?" I asked Tre, not wanting to push him beyond his comfort zone.

"Forget the boundaries thing, okay, Willa?" he said, eyeing up a junker with mismatched door panels on the side of the street with five tickets in the windshield. At least some of it looked like a Subaru, circa 1990. "Besides, I think we'd be doing this guy a *favor* if we take this piece of garbage off his hands."

The street was relatively quiet—it was now well beyond lunch hour. But still, it wasn't a place I would *choose* to steal a car. If I had my druthers, I probably wouldn't choose to be trying to solve my mom's murder or rescue my boyfriend from kidnappers, either.

Choice, then, was kind of a moot point.

We had no tools at our disposal, not even a wire hanger to pick the lock. So Tre went low tech: He quickly pulled down his jacket sleeve and wrapped it in his fist. With a punch, he shattered the glass.

"Wow, it worked," he said as he reached through and opened the door.

"You didn't think it would?" I was surprised he was surprised.

"Let's just put it this way: Back in the day, my buddy did the breaking in. I was mostly the driver. And I never saw anyone try it this way. Get in."

Huh. You lived and you learned and you could still be caught off guard by the people who pretended to be experts. All this time I thought he had firsthand experience. He bent down, cursing under his breath, quickly removed the ignition cover, and reconfigured the wires. I'd say it was two minutes, tops, until the car started.

"Next you're going to say you can't believe you wired the car," I said. "Don't even front."

"No, no. This *is* my specialty."

On the way down, I talked out loud as Tre drove,

trying to be heard over the air noisily and freezingly rushing in through the hole in the window. I wanted to get us up to speed and sort through our unanswered questions.

"So Bailey and Chet came after me and Leslie, following us to Oregon, and then reported back to Granger." And then there was the worst part of it, the fact that my probable dad was the killer. "If Granger was the head guy and called the shots, then he was the one who murdered my mom and had them try to kill Leslie."

"And they think Leslie died in the explosion," Tre said. "Which solved that problem. Except it didn't."

"But why would Granger do it?" Well, it was becoming obvious, at least partially. I answered my own question. "He's been trying to cover it all up for the sake of his career. Because if anyone knew he was ever involved in robbing a bank, let alone killing someone, the election would go right down the tubes. He'd be ruined."

"It makes sense," Tre said.

"It makes perfect sense." The question was what we'd do with this new information. And what we'd find in this park. I had no idea what we were looking for, but I knew there was something important there.

I watched cars zoom past us out the window as I went back to the poems, mentally reviewing them. *Feathers.* What could feathers be? Money, like feathering the nest? Did they hide the money here and move it? Or had they planned to?

"This is the exit, right?" Tre said, pointing to the sign for Exit 2/Telegraph Road. About a mile later, we were at a green-and-white marker announcing the entrance.

The park ran along the Mississippi River and there were recreational trails, for biking and running and that kind of thing. Like everywhere else, the paths were covered in snow. Only here it was pristine and untrampled, because how many people went hiking in the winter? Only crazy people like us.

Doubts flickered. So we were here. How were we supposed to find anything in a five-hundred-plus-acre span of woods?

I pointed to the woods on either side of the parking lot. "Should we just start to walk and map ourselves as we go?" We didn't have much time.

Tre shook his head, registering the unlikelihood of us finding anything. "Let's do this for an hour, and if we don't find anything, we turn ourselves in. Deal?"

"Deal," I said, a little relieved to know we had a plan B.

He set his phone to satellite map so we could read the coordinates. We set out into the forest, our feet crunching on the snow and the dead leaves below it. In the distance, I could hear river water churning. The Mississippi was always close by, it seemed. I thought of Leslie, and how much she would enjoy hiking here. I hoped she was okay.

I hoped *Aidan* was okay. Oh God. Every minute that

passed was another minute he was in danger. *Please let him be safe. Please, please, please.*

I watched a hawk circle beyond the reaches of trees, its wings dipping through the air. Feathers. They were what allowed birds to move from one place to another.

I knew then.

We were looking for a car.

"Go to the right now," Tre said. "Stay straight."

The woods seemed to slant at an incline and there were sinkholes here and there where water had naturally eaten away at the stony terrain. I walked quickly, pulled along by my sudden conviction.

We found the car about ten minutes later, buried under snow and sheltered by a large rock formation. I wouldn't have seen it if the tailpipe hadn't been peeking out, if I hadn't known that we were looking for something in this exact spot. But there it was. And it was no coincidence.

We ran toward the rock, almost tripping over the debris on the ground.

The car was pretty well preserved for being half buried for fifteen years. There was no license plate.

"Take a picture," I said to Tre.

"You think this is it?"

I nodded, sure as I could be about anything.

I ran my hand along the frozen metal of the car door and noted the bashed-in armature at the front. This car had definitely hit something. A sickening sense of foreboding came over me. I withdrew my hand, quick as if I'd touched a flame.

My mom had driven this car. Danny said he'd seen her behind the wheel.

That last poem: Chet was going to wait. My mom was going to hold the money, or deposit it somewhere. I wiped snow with the inside of my arm to access the passenger side. I could see that the glove compartment was left ajar. That wasn't an accident, either.

She was supposed to leave the money here. So why did she take it?

"The hit-and-run," I said, sliding the last pieces together like a puzzle. "That ruined the plan. That was why she changed her mind. They robbed the bank, and my mom nearly killed someone during the getaway. It was too risky. So after they'd hidden the car like they were supposed to, she decided she wanted out."

My heart sank with the certain weight of it. I'd thought she was like me, doing the wrong thing for the right reasons, but that was giving her too much credit. She was all wrong. If this was who she was, I didn't want to be anything like her.

"She took it?"

I nodded. "After the accident, she came back here and took all the money, all five million dollars, for herself— that's why Granger killed her. And that's why they were after Leslie." "Well, she was trying to meet the victim, wasn't she? At the end? Maybe it's not as bad as you think," Tre said, trying to be comforting.

It was bad, though. I didn't want to pretend anymore. "For all we know she was going to bribe him. Or do something to silence him. . . ." I shook my head. "It doesn't matter—she never got there. But she did this. I know she did."

He didn't say anything, just finished taking photos with his phone, photos of the car and the details of its location.

We considered cutting out a piece of the remaining upholstery for any possible DNA, but Tre said we shouldn't tamper with the evidence. "The cops will want it intact."

Besides, we were running out of time. We finally had the information we needed and we had to use it. Quickly.

"Twice in one day? I must be dreaming."

I ignored him. "Listen, we don't have much time but we've pieced the story together now, and if you'll just hear me out, you'll see that it makes sense."

I could practically hear him frowning through the receiver. "Go on," he allowed.

"Granger and Chet and my mom—maybe Bailey, too—were involved in something we think was called Welfare for All. Ever heard of it?"

"Enlighten me."

"It was a local political activist group back in the

nineties. Granger was the front man."

"So they were a bunch of Ralph Nader–type hippies."

"Not quite. They robbed the bank. First Federal? It's in your file on Chet."

"Which you stole from me," he said pointedly.

I ignored this and kept going. "The cops were right back then, that Chet was involved, but they didn't have enough evidence. Granger's group was going to use that money for future plans—I don't know what they were but it had something to do with their cause."

"Which was?"

I couldn't answer that. It was a big hole, I had to admit. But it didn't mean we were wrong. We just didn't have the whole story yet.

"So you don't even know?"

"All I know is that they were all trying to change things—they didn't like the direction the city government was taking with gambling—and the robbery was going to help somehow." As I said it out loud, I wondered if the whole thing was a front for Granger's own slimy scheme. Maybe he was just going to take the money for himself. He was convincing enough to get people to do something like that. I'd seen it firsthand. "But something went wrong. My mom was driving a getaway car and hit someone. Then she left the group, not wanting to be found out, and took the money. That's why she moved away and changed her name. She stopped seeing Granger, too."

"So what's this have to do with him?"

"See, they were together. He's probably my father."

"David Granger. Is your father." He sounded skeptical.

"I think so. If you look at the dates, she was pregnant with me when she got out. Maybe she was worried about me and Leslie, that something would happen to us if the truth ever emerged. But either way, she didn't want to get caught. Only Granger wasn't letting her go. He stalked her. My mom's friend remembers seeing him one night at the restaurant where they worked and my mom was avoiding him."

"So you think he came back and killed her for revenge?"

"That, and the money."

Corbin was silent on his end.

"I have her date book, her writings, and there are references to Operation Sparrow, which is the robbery, plus a love poem about Granger. I have a note to Granger that ties him into this. We're standing right here with the car, the hit-and-run vehicle—it's in pretty good condition. If you can figure out the model, maybe you can run some kind of registration or car rental records. I know it will be connected back to one of them."

"But do we have anything actually tying Granger to the scene of either crime? Physical evidence?"

"DNA was never run on the case. I'm willing to bet if you dusted the car you could get DNA for both of them."

"Assuming that DNA is still viable. What about the

murder? We'd need evidence for that, too."

"I don't know about that part," I admitted. I couldn't solve the case single-handedly. I was just an amateur, after all. "There's gotta be something that could match up. Look, it's worth a shot, isn't it? Granger and Chet and Bailey have been hiding these secrets all these years. And now they've got Aidan. They want their money so they can hush everything up. But we can't get him back alone. You have to help us. What do you say?"

Corbin was silent.

I tried to sweeten the deal. "I'll do a DNA test, too. If we can prove that I'm Granger's daughter, that will be more evidence for my theory."

"I don't know. I'm not exactly in the business of bringing down corrupt pols, Willa."

"This murder has bugged you all these years. Now's your chance to solve it. I'm giving you everything. Do it for Leslie. She would want you to finally put these cases to rest."

A hard exhalation.

"All I need is for you to get the money, and come out here. You can do that, right?"

"All right," he said finally. "I'll be there. Give me two hours. Lucky for you I happen to be in Kansas City today. I'll meet you at the Hyatt Regency hotel and send one of my guys to the car. You should leave immediately. I don't want to risk anyone seeing you there."

"Thanks, Corbin," I said, feeling relief pour through me. I knew playing the Leslie card would work.

"And, Willa? Don't let me down again."

How could I? All I wanted was for Aidan to be safe. For this nightmare to be over.

"I won't," I promised. And this time I really meant it.

The last time I saw Corbin, he was in plain clothes. Now he was wearing more official gear—a black suit, crisp white shirt, black tie, and a navy-blue windbreaker with FBI lettered in yellow over the chest and back. It was as if he wanted to remind us that there was no playing around, no bending or breaking the rules. His face showed a day's worth of stubble but his dark hair was neatly parted to one side and combed back.

"Come on," he said, angling for me across the lobby and grasping my elbow. He never was one for big greetings.

"Is this fully necessary?" I asked, meaning the leading-me-by-the-arm business.

"You're lucky I'm here and don't forget it."

Somehow, I had a feeling that he wasn't about to let me.

"This is Tre," I said, trying to be polite as we moved awkwardly, the three of us in a triangle, toward the elevators.

"Yes, I know all about him."

"He's not involved. He's just here for support," I said quickly, hoping Corbin didn't have the wrong idea about him.

"I know that, too."

Tre didn't say anything. He followed us silently. I hoped he wasn't panicking. Most likely, Corbin had no interest in ratting him out, but Tre didn't know that. We got on the elevator and went up to the sixth floor, where Corbin had hired out a suite for us. Our war room.

Corbin pulled out two chairs at the round table in the living area. "Have a seat. We may be here for a while."

"What's the plan?" I asked.

"The plan is we wait for your friends to call back."

"I wouldn't say they're my friends," I said.

"Whatever," Corbin said. "I'm having Tre's phone tapped in the meantime so my guys can listen in and record it."

"My phone? Tapped?" Tre looked nervous.

"You want to catch them, right? How else are they going to get in touch with us? When we hear from them, we'll make a meeting place, fit you with a wire, and have you go in with the money." He patted a computer bag that looked, to my eye, to be filled with stacks of bills.

The old Sly Fox urge pulled at me for a second, seeing all that money in a hefty pile. It was so big, so . . . grabbable. I swallowed and looked away.

Corbin continued. "I'll be in an unmarked raid van, listening in. We'll have a SWAT team for backup. Then, we go in and nail the sons of bitches. How does that sound?"

"You're bringing in the HRT?" Tre asked.

"This kid is good," Corbin said to me, and I could tell

Tre was pleased. "Actually, it's a typical SWAT unit."

Tre nodded. "Will you have snipers?"

"Probably not."

"You might need them."

Corbin actually smiled. "I'll take that under advisement. Do you guys want anything? A soda?"

"I'll have one," I said.

Corbin grabbed two Cokes for us from the minibar and slid over a pad of the hotel stationery and a pen.

"So they said no FBI, no police, no media," I said. "No marked bills, no consecutive bills. I want to make sure we're doing this right."

Corbin nodded. "We've got all that. Willa, we wouldn't send you into this if we didn't take all the precautions we could."

"What do you think they're doing with him?" I asked.

"They've probably got him restrained somewhere," Corbin said. "I don't think they'd hurt him, maybe just enough to scare him. They're not stupid, these guys. They're just after the cash they think you took from Leslie."

I wasn't so sure. "I wish they'd call already." I got up and started to pace the room. The waiting was driving me crazy.

Corbin put down his drink. "And you're sure you want to go through with this? If this guy Granger is your dad, you could be sending him to jail for life."

I didn't need to search my soul for answers. I had no

feelings for Granger. If he was my real dad, he'd never been part of my life, not like Leslie had. Not like my real mom would have been. He was a murderer. Toni was right. He was too good to be true, and he'd fooled everyone all this time. He'd killed my mom, and I would never be able to forgive him for that. It was that simple. He was getting what was coming to him.

What I did feel bad about were the people lined up at those rallies and speeches. The people who believed in him and had no idea how evil he was. They deserved someone better. Someone who wasn't going to lie to them just to hang on to his power.

No, I couldn't feel guilty about turning Granger in. Not now. This was his fault, the results of his choices, as Corbin would say. And my mom was guilty, too. Only she wasn't here to deal with her own consequences.

"I've thought about it, and I say go ahead," I told Corbin.

"Just want to make sure you're not going to get cold feet at the last minute. Blood is thicker than water, and all that."

"I'm not," I said firmly. Was blood really thicker than water? Sure, I had this biological family, but I also had my adopted family, and that included Aidan and Tre and Cherise, the people I'd chosen to surround myself with. And I felt just as loyal to them, if not more so. They'd stood by me, and I'd fight for them—to the death if necessary.

262

Tre's phone rang, and he placed it on the table in front of us.

"Okay to answer it?" I asked.

"Go ahead," Corbin said.

I picked up the phone and I could hear the voice pouring out, deep and burbling as though it were coming from the bottom of the sea. Spooky. "Is this Willa Fox?" Was it Bailey, Chet, or Granger himself? I had no way of knowing.

"Yes, speaking," I said, feeling my heart accelerate.

"We want you, and only you. Meet us at 1305 Criterion. I believe you know where that is. Seven P.M. this evening."

I did. That was where we'd just been the day before, when we traced the car registration. I picked up the pen and the pad of paper and wrote down the address.

"Seven P.M.," I said. "I'll be there."

"No cops. No FBI. No media, or we'll kill you and your friend. Understand?"

My stomach lurched. This was potentially the most serious lie I had ever told. Was I making a terrible mistake? But Aidan was out there. He was depending on me. "I understand."

"Make this easy, do what we say, and no one gets hurt." The phone went dead and I gripped the piece of plastic in my hand, because at least it was something I could hold on to.

SEVENTEEN

WE CALLED A cab from the hotel to take me to Criterion Avenue. Tre and Corbin were going to follow closely in the raid van. Corbin tried to fight Tre on it, saying it was too dangerous for him to come along, but he wouldn't budge. There was no way he was gonna wait back in the hotel for us, he said, keeping his eyes on me the whole time. Corbin finally relented. I guess Tre was in too deep now.

Corbin went to pick up the van from the parking lot, leaving Tre and me in the lobby to wait for my cab.

"You really want to do this?" Tre asked me.

I nodded, feeling the dime-sized microphone I'd stuck under my bra strap. It connected to a transmitter inside my waistband. The device was small, imperceptible from the outside, but just knowing it was there made it a princess and pea situation.

"Look, if you need me in there with you, just say . . ."

He looked around and his eyes fell on a police car across the street. "Just say 'bulletproof,' okay? That will be our code."

I smiled. "It's going to be okay," I said with whatever false bravado I had left. "Look, this will all be over before we know it and I bet you'll be back in Paradise Valley with Cherise by tomorrow night."

"Cherise?" he asked, puzzlement glancing across his brow. "What about her?"

"I thought you two had something going on. . . ."

"No," he said. "I guess we flirted a little bit for a while back there, but she told me she wasn't interested in your leftovers."

I frowned. "What does that mean?"

"Just, she thought I had a thing for you."

Now I did a double take.

Wait. What?

His face held no signs of a joke. What did she mean by that? Tre? And me? He wasn't agreeing or denying. He was simply offering it as a statement of truth.

And now I was embarrassed, too. What had they said about me? How could I not know any of this? Most important, how did I feel about it?

But there wasn't time to process the information because the cab was pulling up in front of the hotel. I hugged Tre.

"Good luck," he said, pulling away so I could look into his eyes. "Be careful, all right?"

"I will. Over before we know it."

"I hope so." He ran his thumb along my jawline. Gently. I felt myself dissolve under his touch, and I realized I'd never been so close to Tre. Or at least not like this. "I'll be right behind you."

Before I could think or say anything else, it was over and we'd broken apart.

I got into the backseat of the cab, the vinyl seat squeaking on its springs beneath my weight. I dropped the computer bag of money down next to me.

"Where to?" the driver asked, meeting my eyes in the rearview mirror.

"1305 Criterion Avenue," I said. "But my friends will be following us, so hang on."

When the van pulled around to the front of the hotel, I watched Tre get into it and I felt a vague tug inside me that wasn't just worry. Like I was forgetting something. Or maybe just remembering.

The cab pulled away from the curb, with the van behind it. I bit my lip and turned to face forward as the cab drove on.

There was no time for feelings now. I had a job to do.

We followed the same sequence of streets we'd taken the other day—the highway, then the neighborhood with its orderly rows of homes. As we approached the address, I could feel nervousness prickling in my veins. I turned around to look behind us. The raid van—disguised as a painter's truck, complete with a ladder on top—was there, pulling into a neighboring driveway. Four cars were arranged in what Corbin said was a stakeout box. They would never leave me alone, I knew that. This was the FBI. They had protocols to follow.

I zipped up my FBI-supplied bulletproof jacket—a cheesy black bomber that I'd never otherwise be caught dead in—and paid the driver with cash Tre gave me. Then I got out of the car, carrying the bag of money. It was heavy, the handle biting into the flesh of my upper arm as I started down the paver-stone walk. Good thing I didn't have to go far.

All I had to do was meet them at the door, hand over the money, like Corbin told me to, and wait for them to bring out Aidan. I was not supposed to make any sudden movements or use my hands below the belt—this last, I assumed, was so they wouldn't think I was pulling a gun. I had the FBI phone Corbin had given me in my pocket—if I had to, if something went wrong with the wire, I could always pick that up and call for help. I was not, under any circumstances, to go inside the house.

Up close, I could see it was an ordinary suburban split-level, not unlike places where I'd stayed with Leslie before we moved to Paradise Valley, before we'd started living large on the five mil. For a moment, I was overtaken with the strongest urge to go back in time to when we were living in Washington or Colorado again, to that simple era in my life where I was still a kid. When I'd had no idea what had happened before I was born and hadn't given a thought to consequences at all, let alone the consequences I would inherit. Or all the ones I'd bring on myself.

But I couldn't. *Aidan's in there. He's depending on me.*

If I needed courage to do this thing, I was going to have to take it from that thought. I felt ridiculous, though, as I approached the door. *Um, hello? I'm here with your five-million-dollar ransom.*

No. I had to be businesslike. Confident.

Let's just make this quick. In and out.

I'd hand over the money and they'd hand over Aidan. When Corbin and his guys heard me say "Thank you," they'd come through the back door and surprise the bad guys. Meanwhile, I was supposed to tackle Aidan and pull him to the ground, roll out of the way. I had to stay on top because I had the bulletproof jacket on, and Aidan would have no such protection if gunfire was exchanged.

Gunfire. I couldn't even think of that. *It's the worst-case scenario*, Corbin had said. *We won't let it come to that, but just in case.*

Hand shaking, I reached up to press the illuminated doorbell button.

I heard footsteps inside and then the door opened. Behind it was Bailey, his dark eyes glinting like bits of mica. Chet appeared next to him. He was as I remembered him: a big dude—maybe two hundred fifty pounds—with curly, auburn hair sprinkled with gray, and heavy-lidded hazel eyes.

"So you finally decided to do the right thing, huh?" Chet asked.

"Yes," I said, biting my tongue, trying to swallow my hatred of these people. Right thing? Whatever. Like he knew what that meant. And where was Granger? I looked around, but there was no sign of him. Was he out campaigning while these two handled his business? Pathetic.

"I'll take that."

He grabbed the bag and yanked both me and it closer. Before I knew what was happening, Bailey had a hand clamped over my mouth. He dragged me over the threshold.

Oh God. I wasn't supposed to be inside. Already I'd messed up. Could Corbin hear what was happening? Then Bailey lifted up my arms while Chet patted me down roughly.

I panicked. *Please don't let them find the microphone or the transmitter.* It was small, the size of the most recent generation iPod, and clipped to my underwear, but still.

His hands slapped their way around my torso and down my legs and up again. I squeezed my eyes shut, willing this to be over. Not to mention trying to block out just how disgusting it was to have this pig touching me.

The bulletproof jacket was already crumpled on the

floor. He found the phone first and handed it to Bailey. Then he lifted up my shirt and pulled out the transmitter, wound it back to the front of my body, and violently ripped off the microphone sensor.

He found it. Oh crap, he found it. Chet threw the device at the wall until it cracked, the plastic chipping off in several pieces. "Get the kid and get rid of that phone."

My connections to Corbin, to safety, were now gone. It had all happened so fast. My only hope was that maybe they'd heard something over the wire before it was destroyed.

Bailey thundered down a set of stairs that must have led to the basement. Chet's fist closed around my bicep. I forgot how to breathe. With the pressure of his fingers, I imagined my blood slowing down, stopping. Bailey dragged Aidan up the steps to where we stood. He looked dirty, disheveled. His arms were hoisted behind his back. His mouth was covered up by tape. But he was alive. He was okay. For that I was immensely relieved. Our eyes met and I could see the alarm sparking in them.

"Take the money, let Aidan go. Let me go, and we can forget all of this happened."

Chet reached out and slapped me. Blackness filled my vision, but not before I caught the violence in his face. The pure hatred. A chill curled up the length of my spine to the back of my skull.

The raw, burning sensation on my cheek came next, the pain so intense I could barely feel anything else. I crumpled, and my head hit the floor.

And then, blackness.

EIGHTEEN

IT WAS LIKE my eyes wouldn't open, it was so dark. I wasn't blindfolded, though. I felt the other restraints—my arms wound behind me. A piece of tape covering my mouth, so tight it was cutting off the circulation in my face. It took a minute before I completely understood that the reason I couldn't see, the reason for this suffocating darkness, was that I was actually staring at the inside of a car trunk.

A body shifted next to me, and I knew that it was Aidan's.

"We're screwed," I said, beneath my gag.

I couldn't exactly make out what Aidan was saying, as his words were equally muffled, but I think it was something to the effect of "Nice to see you, too."

Things were looking bleak. I was pretty sure they wanted us dead. It was only a matter of time, really, and what method they chose. As the car swerved, the force of motion threw Aidan and me together and flung us apart again.

I had no idea where we were going or what came after that. Where were Corbin and Tre in all of this? Clearly, Bailey and Chet were trying to throw them off. We were on our own.

But that didn't mean I was just going to sit here and wait for them to call all the shots.

No, my sister hadn't raised me to give up. Ever.

First things first. I had to get the gag off, so Aidan and I could communicate. I tried using my shoulder with what little give the rope had, rubbing it against the smooth tape's surface, hoping to roll or lift up a corner, but that didn't seem to be working.

The only choice was to work from the inside. I started poking the tape with my tongue, trying to dampen the surface. It had a foul metal taste, but when the adhesive started to dissolve, I knew I had to keep going. After a few moments, the edges of the tape give way, the material softened, and I was able to draw it between my teeth in small amounts at a time, chewing up the artificial fibers and then spitting out the destroyed bits on the floor of the car.

"Aidan! I got it off. Lick the tape."

I couldn't see him in the dark of the trunk, but I imagined his brow furrowing over the silver rectangle where his mouth would be.

"It's gross but just do it!"

I heard him steadily working away for a few more moments until he had the tape off.

"We're really in deep," he whispered, and I was never happier to hear his voice, despite what he was saying. "What happened to you?"

"I was wearing a wire. They found it. Corbin's out there somewhere."

"But what you're saying is he won't be able to find us."

"He might . . . ," I said, but I knew the truth. The car had stopped its frantic swerving. It was likely that Chet and Bailey had slipped Corbin's people. Sweat beaded on my neck and temples. How were we going to get out of here? "And you?"

"They found me on the street, dragged me into their car. Bailey must have been behind us the whole time, waiting. They took me here. Searched my wallet and everything. Then I guess they found out who my dad was, because they called him, trying to get more money. That was Bailey's idea."

The darkness of the trunk was impossible to penetrate; there was no adjusting to it. I could only feel his breath next to me and fill in the image of him with my memory. "They called your dad? Did you get to talk to him?"

"I was in the basement the whole time, but I could hear them on the phone. It sounded like he was ready to sell me out."

"What do you mean?"

"They were bargaining. He wanted a lower price. For

his *son*. Nice, right?" His voice faltered. It was the first time I could remember him crying in front of me. That was something the Aidan I'd known in Paradise Valley would never allow. I worried, suddenly, that there was no going back. That whatever he'd been through was big enough to change him forever.

And what kind of person did that to his son? "How could he be so cold?"

"I guess he decided I wasn't worth that much to him after all. But if they have their way, they'll get more out of this than they ever dreamed. Millions on top of millions. They hit the jackpot when they kidnapped me."

"We can't let that happen." I explained to him everything we'd learned while he was gone.

"So they'll kill both of us if they want to. No one would stop them. Granger wants us dead."

We were in the same boat, really. Both of us had fathers who didn't seem to care whether we lived or died. But that only made me angrier. Were we supposed to just accept this as fact? Because I wasn't going to.

"Corbin and Tre are out there," I hissed. "They'll find us. They will—"

But the truth of it was we were cut off from them. My voice trailed off.

"Face it. We don't have much time, Willa."

What he meant was the air in the trunk was limited— I felt it dwindling as we filled the space with exhalations of carbon dioxide. The longer we were in here the harder it was going to be. I'd learned about suffocation in health class. We'd start feeling dizzy, then lose the ability to concentrate. Our hearts would beat faster as we gasped for air. Our extremities would turn blue, and then our vision would close in on us.

But I could still think. I had to snap into gear. "Look, we can't just sit here feeling sorry for ourselves. We need a plan. How can we get out of here? How can we untie ourselves?"

"I've tried, Willa. Believe me." His voice was quiet, defeated.

I struggled against the ropes, trying to find an out. They were too tight. We'd have to wait.

The car swerved again and I rolled on top of Aidan, which was strangely comforting. I couldn't hug him, but I could feel the familiar topography of his muscles and bones under mine.

"I want you to know that I'm sorry," I said. "We shouldn't have let you walk off like that."

"Willa, if we get out of this alive, that'll be the least of our concerns."

What could we do? Charge them when they took us out of the trunk? Try to grab their guns? That wouldn't work. As long as our hands were tied, we didn't have many options.

Another turn and we were thrown apart. The car pushed along a heavily rutted road, and every bump vibrated beneath us. Where were we going? Around a mountain? Around something. Back and forth, the car twisted, and with each curve, I felt the hotness of our breath filling the trunk, the frustrating distance between me and Aidan, the futility of our situation.

Dizzy. I was getting dizzy. My lungs drew up as much air as they could, but I could tell that between the two of us, we'd already hit the peak level of oxygen. Maybe that's what they wanted. To kill us like this, a slow death in the dark. I closed my eyes and tried to think of other things, because the more I thought about breathing the harder it became. At this point, even speaking would be using up too much precious breath.

Finally, the car pulled over and came to a stop. The engine turned off.

We waited, clenched tightly, to see what would happen next.

The trunk's lock released with a clink and then a tiny white crack appeared. A few seconds later, the crack widened, blinding us with the brightness of the sun.

"Time to get out," Bailey said. In the flood of light he was a black silhouette, but his hands were rough as ever, pulling me to my feet.

"These two little punks got the gags off," Chet said, grabbing me once I was upright.

Bailey dragged Aidan out of the car and held on to him by his hair. Aidan winced in pain. "Well, it don't matter out here, do it?" Bailey said. "No one around to hear them scream."

That's when I saw where we were. Some kind of abandoned electrical plant along the river. At least I assumed the massive, angry body of water to our right was the Mississippi. On the other side, an ancient-looking structure towered over us, its railings, ductwork, and ladders rusted, the windows broken out, brick smokestacks crumbling from age. Whatever walls were left were covered in layers of blue and silver and red graffiti. Bailey wasn't kidding. It was deadly quiet out here—no-man's-land. If there was a sound, you couldn't hear it over the vicious rush of the man-made falls. I looked and looked but there was no sign of Corbin's van or the other FBI vehicles.

I had no plan. For the first time since I'd become Sly Fox, I felt completely, utterly defeated. Terrified beyond my most harrowing nightmares. Because this was real. And death felt certain.

"What are we doing here?" I tried to shout over the water. But I knew. It wasn't a place you brought your buddies for a picnic.

"You'll find out on a need-to-know basis," Chet yelled back.

They dragged us to the edge of the concrete, overlooking the falls. Chet slammed me down hard enough that my ribs banged against the railing and I cried out. Bailey did the same with Aidan.

I heard a length of chain unfurling behind us, then felt it winding, tightening around both of our waists, pinning us against the cold, rusted metal bar, so that we dangled face-first over the crashing water. The lock clicked shut.

I struggled, flailed, but there was no give, only metal cutting into me. "Just hang tight," Chet said as he retaped our mouths and stepped away. "Your daddy should be here soon."

Stunned, I stared into the river's violent oblivion. We'd be powerless to swim against it, the strong pull of gravity sucking us in, churning us downstream. It would be days, weeks even, before our corpses floated to the surface.

Blood rushed to my head and my heart raged. So Granger was coming here after all. And they knew he was my dad even though Bailey lied about it before.

I didn't know which was worse—the crushing pain in my abdomen, the freezing wind and fantasies of drowning, or being forced to wait for Granger to show up. Why not just throw us in? This was torture.

I thought about Aidan, how sorry I was to have dragged him into my crazy life. How I'd never meant for him to risk his future for me. How love could be so damn twisted that it could end like this.

And my mom. I wondered how I could possibly love her, when she was the one who brought the situation on all of us. And yet, I knew I still did, in the softest parts of my heart. Mostly, I thought of Leslie, who was out there, safe, and who'd be horrified to know that despite her attempts to protect me all those years I was still going to die at the hands of these scumbags.

The screech of a car behind us broke through my thoughts. A door slamming. Close enough to hear over the water. Footsteps crunching on the gravel.

I tried to turn but couldn't. That tiny, hopeful voice in my head piped up. Maybe it was Corbin. He'd somehow found us and he was here to rescue us. . . .

"You made it," Bailey said.

"I'm not here to play games with you two degenerates." A man's voice. Familiar, Granger. Again I twisted my head—but there was no moving.

What I heard next came in fragments, the words only semidecipherable over the cascades.

"You told me she was Leslie's daughter . . . until I get an email from Brianna's old friend. . . ."

Was he serious? He didn't know? I highly doubted it. He was a criminal and a world-class liar. The great mastermind behind Operation Sparrow.

What a joke. I thought of their rallies, the state motto that inspired their name. It was all BS. They'd stolen a serious concept of human goodness, an idea that was inscribed on buildings, for God's sake, and appropriated it for their own selfish gain.

Then it hit me. The frieze at the City Museum. The City Museum admission tag—it was still in my jacket pocket. I reached up reflexively but my wrist was bound.

Bailey's voice: "Take a step back now, Senator. Don't

280

do anything you'll regret."

"You think I'm gonna let you shoot me? . . . After all I've worked for?"

Fighting was good. That meant they weren't paying attention to us. More time to figure this out. I wiggled my hand, trying to create enough slack in the rope. I had to get into my hip pocket. It was just a little too high, a little too far.

"Don't need to shoot . . . ," Bailey said. "I've got a better weapon."

The words became fragments again. . . . I was too busy trying . . . stretching . . .

Granger: "Did you know your friend paid me a visit yesterday?"

"What were you doing?" Chet asked.

"Ask him," Granger said.

Salty blood filled my mouth. I hadn't realized I'd been biting the inside of my cheek. But finally my fingertips dipped into the fabric, brushed against smooth metal. If I could only get close enough to pinch the tag. . . . I reached again, willing my body longer. But I had to be careful. If I dropped it . . .

There.

I clutched the tag and maneuvered my hand out of the pocket.

I tuned in again to the shouting voices. "You both knew. When were you gonna tell me?" Granger asked. "You knew it would change things."

"Like you care about her. You and your phony high principles," Chet was saying. "Don't act like you didn't want me to kill her. You let me do it, comrade."

So it was Chet after all. But Granger knew.

I needed a C shape with little tabs on both sides. The metal gave easily as I folded it—more pliable than a soda can. Now I just needed to wedge it into the lock. I felt around, shaking the chain a bit to find the lock, and the tiny space where the shackle met the latch. It was exactly like I'd done back at Valley Prep when I broke into Drew Miller's locker. It wasn't a complex move, not for an experienced thief. But with the restraints and my awkward position, the degree of difficulty was a thousand times greater.

"We're not comrades," Granger's voice echoed, even louder now. "I could destroy you. . . . You're not . . . bulletproof."

Wait. What? That was our code word.

How did he know?

It couldn't be a coincidence. The way he'd paused, amplified that word—he wanted me to hear.

The explanation was obvious. Granger must have talked to Tre. Granger must have been in communication with the FBI. He was on our side. Somehow, and I didn't understand how, he was on our side.

C'mon. C'mon.

The shim was in. It took a few jabs, until the latch finally released.

The loop of the lock swung open. I flung the whole thing off, and the links of the chain tumbled away as I stood up.

I'd done it. Aidan and I were free. He looked at me in disbelief as he pulled himself up, too. Feet on safe, solid ground.

Run! The command sounded in my head.

Our hands were tied, our mouths still covered, but we could run. We could hide somewhere, maybe inside. . . . The FBI would be here soon. . . .

Before my brain could signal my legs to move, hands grabbed my waist, sucking the air out of my lungs. I screamed under the tape. This time Bailey didn't hang me over the rail. He was lifting me over it, ready to throw me into the water. My feet kicked helplessly at the air.

So close, and yet so far.

"You're not as sly as you think," he grunted.

The wind whipped and the water roared. I closed my eyes, clenched every muscle, and waited to plummet the hundreds of feet below.

This was it. This was how it was all going to end.

"Oof!" Bailey flinched, his rough hands loosening. "Son of a bitch!" He dropped me and I fell onto the rail. Crushing pain shot through my belly.

I recovered to see Aidan's foot jammed into Bailey's gut a second time, and Bailey stumbled.

Bailey lumbered back toward Aidan like a bear. He grabbed Aidan and choked him in a headlock.

"Let him go!" I tried to shout through the gag.

"What was that?" Bailey gave me the sickest sort of smile, and I knew for sure then that he'd kill either of us without a second thought. He would enjoy it, too. All along I'd thought Chet was the scarier one, but now I wondered if I'd underestimated Bailey.

Well, screw him.

Pain or no pain, I had to try. I flung myself at his feet, twisting and jabbing the pointed metal edge of the tag into Bailey's ankle.

He cursed loudly and, in the moment of shock, Aidan squirmed out of his grasp. Bailey went for him again. Now they were pressed together against the railing. Without the use of hands, all Aidan had was the force of his chest to keep Bailey at bay—that was the only thing standing between him and drowning.

I watched, horrified, as Bailey grabbed him by the throat.

"Stop! Don't kill Moneybags," Chet called out. "I'll take care of this guy."

I looked up to see Chet pointing a .38 at Granger with one hand, dragging him across the pavement toward us with the other. Both of Granger's hands were in the air.

"Keep back!" Bailey fired his gun in Chet's direction, but the bullet ricocheted off the metal façade of the electric plant. Then the psychopath pointed the barrel at Aidan's face.

At least three cars ground through the gravel at that

moment, brakes squealing. Doors opened and slammed shut.

"Freeze. FBI." Corbin trained his gun on Bailey. "I said *freeze*."

Nobody froze, though. Granger made a grab for Chet's gun. They both held on tight, dodging forward and back until the weapon spun out of anyone's grasp, falling to the ground and kicking up dust.

Granger slammed his fist into Chet's jaw. Chet came back swinging wildly but Granger ducked his punch.

Behind them, against the rail, Aidan was choking in Bailey's grip, his face going red. I felt helpless. I couldn't watch Aidan suffer. I couldn't just stand here.

"Willa, don't—" Corbin yelled and then Bailey pointed the gun at me as I came closer. "Drop your weapon! Immediately!"

"Come on. You think anyone's gonna miss this trash?" At that, Aidan kneed him in the groin, and Bailey crumpled, his back on the rail.

Corbin wasted no time. He threw himself on top of Bailey, trying to pin down his arms and grab the gun. An errant shot went off, and Corbin dropped to the ground.

Aidan tried to shield me, so I couldn't see much of what happened next.

The power of the explosion must have shook Bailey off balance. He was too far over the edge. He slipped, headfirst, his scream reeling out of him as he tumbled through the air.

The sound of the splash was drowned out by the river.

And then came the gunshots behind us. Deafening. The next thing I knew, Granger was on the ground and Chet was standing in front of Aidan, both hands squeezed over the trigger.

Even though my arms were still tied I knew what I had to do.

I launched myself in their direction, knocking Aidan to the ground. He yelped in surprise at first, and then probably pain. The impact, with no hands to stop me, was harsh, and I felt the gravel rake against my cheek as soon as I hit.

There might have been more shots, or more shouting—I was deaf and blind, everything blanked out.

When the world came back, it was completely still. My ears were ringing. I heard breathing first, then smaller sounds filling in the gaps—feet scraping the pavement, a bird calling out overhead.

Corbin was doubled over, clutching at his leg. He called for medical assistance while the SWAT team, three guys in black-and-yellow uniforms, did a sweep of the area, making sure there were no other surprises.

But it was over. Chet was sprawled on the ground, bleeding. The SWAT guys quickly went to work, handcuffing him and reading him his rights.

I slid off Aidan, allowing him to sit up.

"We're okay," he said, pressing his forehead to mine. "Oh my God, we're okay."

NINETEEN

THE NEXT MORNING, Aidan, Tre, and I were escorted into a back entrance of the FBI field office in central St. Louis. The media was camped out in front for blocks, but for once they weren't here for me. They were trying to get a glimpse of Granger, now in custody. A press conference was scheduled for later in the afternoon.

A lanky, bald officer with milky-blue eyes and a pencil line of a mouth led us to the elevator and up to the third floor. We walked down a narrow fluorescent-lit hallway to a conference room. Aidan and Tre and I were seated opposite Corbin at a small table. Corbin had been treated for his gunshot wound, held overnight, and released just that morning. The bullet only grazed his lower calf, thankfully, and it was all bandaged up now, though he still winced in pain when he showed us the dressing.

Chet was in the ICU, fighting for his life with internal

bleeding. The FBI was waiting by his bedside for him to come to and answer some questions. Bailey's body hadn't been recovered yet, but a team was out dredging the river.

Agents had already found recordings of phone conversations with Granger during a search of Bailey's house and phone—he was apparently hoping to blackmail Granger *and* Chet. Turns out that's what he'd been doing at the casino, gathering evidence against Granger. Other agents had hauled my mom's hit-and-run/getaway vehicle from the park—if they could positively ID it with a DNA swab, they'd have almost everything they needed to convict all four of them, even though only two were still alive.

"We have some business matters to discuss," Corbin told us. "The case came with some financial rewards. The local government's offering five thousand dollars to anyone who solves the murder—a typical reward for a cold case. And Brianna's parents—your grandparents—put up another fifty thousand before they died."

He removed an envelope from his pocket and slid it across the table to me. "Do with that what you will."

He also handed me a plastic bag. "Here are your mom's remaining belongings—mostly clothes, things we won't be using in the trial. With Granger's confession, we have more than enough evidence. I thought you might want them."

I grasped the bag. "Thanks. Yeah, I do."

I could look through her stuff later. But for now I

opened the envelope and took a peek at the check. Fifty-five thousand dollars was a lot of money.

Corbin tapped his fingers on the wooden surface in front of him. "If you want my advice, I think you should start a bank account, invest it, so that when you get out of juvie, you have a nest egg."

It was sound fatherly advice, but typical Corbin to always act like he knew what was best.

"No," I said, realizing that I knew exactly what to do with it. I looked at Aidan and Tre. "I have some debts."

I had that list of IOUs. There were people we owed, people in California whose homes we'd borrowed, and whose stuff we'd taken. There was a wrecked stolen car, another borrowed car, and the motorcycle. Clothes. Fancy sunglasses. There were the nights at the library, the City Museum. Bikes. The Lexus. I owed them, too.

"Okay. But that's probably ten thousand maximum," Aidan pointed out. "You didn't steal any fur coats or ruby rings. Most of the other stuff was in perfect condition when you left it."

"We could split the rest," I offered. "Three ways."

"No," Aidan said. "Tre and I don't need it."

It didn't feel right, somehow, walking away with cash. This had never been about money for me. Money had only been a corrupting influence for everyone involved in this case. "Can we donate it then?"

"You can do whatever you want. It's yours." Corbin

looked at me like I was crazy. "But like I said, I think you might need it later."

How could I explain that I wasn't thinking about later? That now was the only moment I could be in. As soon as I went to juvie, life as I knew it was over. "I want to donate it," I said firmly.

"I guess idealism runs in the genes in this family," Corbin said, shaking his head.

I met Aidan's eyes. "What about the animal shelter in Paradise Valley?" It was where our whole adventure had started, and it seemed a fitting cause. Orphaned animals that had no one else to help them. We couldn't give them homes but at least we could try to improve their lives.

"I'd vote for that," Aidan said.

Just then, the uniformed officer who'd brought us into the building appeared in the frame of the glass door and knocked. "Agent Corbin, can I come in?"

Corbin nodded, and the officer stepped into the room. "We have a request for Ms. Fox. Senator Granger wants to talk to her."

"What does he want?" Corbin said.

"He just said he wants to see her. He didn't say specifically. I can wait outside the door."

"You okay with that, Willa?" Corbin asked, looking protective.

I was. Granger was probably going to be locked up for a while, at least until the murder, hit-and-run, and robbery trials, and we were leaving. This was my last chance to talk to him. I wasn't sure if I was going to like what he had to say, or if he had any answers at all, but there was only one way to find out.

I left the three of them behind, and the officer led me down the hallway to what looked like an interrogation room.

I took a chair across from Granger, who looked exhausted and unshaven. On the table in front of him was a Styrofoam cup of coffee, which he grasped with his handcuffed hands. He'd probably been in here for close to twelve hours now, answering questions. The investigation and the events leading up to it had clearly taken its toll on him. He looked smaller to me now, broken down. The officer shut the door but as he promised, he was waiting on the other side of the glass, watching, in case anything went wrong.

"Hi," Granger said.

"Hi." I felt tension build in my throat, tightening around my vocal cords as we sat in an awkward silence. Maybe this wasn't such a good idea after all. Was he going to scold me? Blame me for wrecking his campaign, nosing around in his business? I mean, he'd be right to. It *was* my fault, even if I didn't feel sorry.

"Look, we don't have much time to talk. But there are things you need to know," he said, leveling his eyes with mine. "About me and your mother."

So he was finally going to open up. I watched him, waiting.

He cleared his throat. "After the *incident*—"

"The hit-and-run?" I offered. If he was going to come clean, I wanted him to speak as plainly as possible. No politician mumbo jumbo.

"Right. After that, she didn't want to support our plan anymore. She wanted us to turn ourselves in. I said no—I thought what we were doing was more important. He was one guy, but we could help thousands. Millions, even."

"Just what was the plan, exactly?" I asked.

"We wanted to take the gambling money from the bank where the riverboat kept its account, and return it to the people of St. Louis, to the homeless shelters and soup kitchens. Sparrow was just the beginning—we had other actions planned, too." Up until now he'd spoken slowly, haltingly, but now it was like he was caught up all over again in the excitement of his ideas. "I knew I had a lot to give the world—I just needed a voice. The actions would do that. The stuff that Occupy has been doing? We were doing that fifteen years ago."

I had a lot to give the world. Even if he thought he was trying to do this great, noble deed, it was all about his ego. Toni had said it best: megalomaniac. "But where did all of this start?"

He rubbed the skin of his forehead. "I was working as an organizer, and I met Bailey and Chet at the Sheet Metal Workers Union. That was when I realized how easy it was to get people to listen, if you made your message clear enough. They seemed to really get it. I asked them to work for me."

"And my mom?"

"She was a bookkeeper at the union office. We got . . . involved. She was so smart, so full of life. With her by my side, believing in me, and these other guys hanging on to my every word, I felt invincible. When the riverboat thing began, I started to go to rallies and speak out about the casinos. It was the perfect cause for our mission. Your mom always came to support me. But it wasn't enough to just talk. We needed to do something big, something that would shake things up."

"So you planned the robbery."

"I did, and it went off without a hitch," he reminded me. "Until we hit that guy. Brianna wanted to get out, set the record straight. She thought it wasn't worth it. I had no idea she was also pregnant at the time. I was too young and too dumb to realize it then."

He shook his head and regret furrowed his face, deepening the lines across his forehead. I still didn't understand exactly what kind of person this man—my father—was, but the pain tracing his eyes and lips was real. I knew because I was young now, and I was living with my own mistakes. That was what it looked like when you wished you could go back and make different choices.

"We had our meeting time arranged—the money was supposed to be in the car. And it wasn't."

293

"She disappeared then," I said.

"She stayed in the city and changed her name—I guess she thought if she could hide in plain sight she wouldn't have to move the whole family around. And she'd taken the money with her. I thought maybe this was her revenge. She was angry at me for letting her go, not doing the right thing, so she was taking it out on all of us. Chet said he was going to go after it, get it back, that we couldn't let her derail the plan—he called her a crazy bitch, I remember that."

I just stared at him.

"Oh God, this feels like I'm in a confessional or something. You don't know how hard this is to talk about." He tapped the cup and sighed. "Chet was sure but I kind of never believed she would do that. She just wasn't the type. She had the purest heart."

"I guess you never know about people," I said. I didn't want to believe my mom would take all the money for herself, either, but what were the other possibilities?

He continued on, his tone high and defensive like he was making a case to a jury. "I felt so betrayed. I loved her. And worse than that, the plan would never work if our group was falling apart. And if I got into trouble, if it got traced back to me, I wouldn't be able to help anyone. My whole mission would be over before it began. So I made an even bigger mistake. I let Chet do what he needed to do, to get the money back. I figured if I couldn't have her, I could still have our plan, still change the world, which was almost as good."

"So you let him kill her," I said. "So you could be some sort of superhero."

"No!" he yelled, and the force of it startled me.

"What, then?"

"I didn't know it was going to end up like that." He paused, shuddering, and closed his eyes slowly. "Not like that. . . ."

Anger flared in my chest. He could apologize, do the sad act all he wanted to, but it didn't mean anything to me. He'd killed my mother, maybe not with his own hands, but he'd stood by while it happened. And for that I could never, ever forgive him.

"I'm so sorry, Willa. I never wanted it that way. It was like . . . a big ball of yarn, unraveling. The more I lied, the more I had to lie to cover my tracks. I guess I started to believe my own lies after a while."

And what lies they were. I shook my head.

There was a sharp intake of breath before he continued. "You might as well know. *I* was driving the car, Willa. It was me who hit that kid."

So the hit-and-run was his fault, too. I felt a tiny sense of relief that it wasn't my mom, but it didn't change the fact that an innocent person was hurt and never got justice.

"You," I said, letting the idea settle between us.

He nodded.

"And you kept that little secret, too." He couldn't

stop here. As angry as I was, as hard as all of this was to listen to, I had to hear him say it.

"Years passed."

"You went legit," I said.

"Well, I built my career. I swore off that other stuff. I figured I could give back, but do it the right way this time. Then one day, I was sitting in a hotel room after a campaign event, and I get this call from Chet. I haven't talked to the guy in fifteen years. We'd gone our separate ways. He says he saw Leslie on the TV, that her daughter had gotten into trouble in Arizona for stealing."

I nodded. That was me. Sly Fox. That part I knew. They were worried the cops knew of her whereabouts and it would only be a matter of time until Leslie's real identity, her scam, was uncovered. The money would be traced back to them.

"Chet said he and Bailey wanted to go out there and get the money back. I was in the middle of this campaign; my hands were tied. I told him we should finally put all of this behind us. I told them they could keep the damn money. By then I realized that's what they were in it for all along."

"You were more interested in erasing your own tracks," I said. "Looking out for yourself."

"That's right," he snapped, looking mad for the first time since I'd sat down. "Look, you don't know me. You think the worst. I'm not proud of my past, believe me. But I've always had a cause, at least. Unlike those guys.

You have no idea the good I've been able to do for the people here. Is it wrong that I tried to keep at it? That I didn't let some bad judgment I'd made when I was in my twenties ruin everything I'd worked for?"

"That bad judgment included the murder of my mother," I broke in.

"And that's haunted me every day of my life. You have no idea!" He hit the table and looked away then. "I'm trying to explain it to you, okay? I'm trying to be honest here. You could at least listen."

He had me there. I twisted up my mouth and stacked my arms across my chest. "I'm listening. Go on."

"So, you know what happens next. I did it again. I made the same mistake twice. Trusting these thugs, looking the other way."

"But thankfully, they came back empty-handed. They never found the money. He never solved your problem or found Leslie."

"That's right. She was killed in the explosion in the trailer park. Another senseless loss." He looked sickened.

I didn't correct him. The fact that Leslie was alive was a secret to everyone except me and Corbin and Aidan and Tre. He didn't need to know it. Sure, he was coming clean to me now, but I still didn't trust the guy. How could I? He was a proven liar.

"We thought it was over, that the money must have gone up in flames with her in that trailer."

"Until I showed up in St. Louis."

"Exactly. After I saw you, I called Chet and told him about it. He was convinced it was a setup and Leslie was still alive. I told him he was crazy. He assured me you were Leslie's daughter, that you were probably only coming after me with your story because you were on the run from the police and you thought you could get some kind of handout or legal protection from me. He said Leslie had lied to you, probably because she was ashamed of having a daughter so young. So she said you were Brianna's daughter."

"But he still thought I had the money?"

"I was there at the casino, you know."

"I didn't. I didn't know lots of things, clearly. And no, I don't know what he thought. That's when it gets hazy. They went rogue. They were trying to blackmail me. Bailey was going to double-cross us both. All I know is that by that time, Chet wanted to get the money and kill you. He figured I wouldn't say anything because he'd be doing what I wanted in the first place, which was to erase the history."

"Unless you realized the truth about me." I couldn't say the exact words out loud.

"Right."

"But he knew?"

"I think he suspected. I think he was watching your mom for a while before he made his move. He must have seen you as a baby, all those years ago. Maybe he didn't know for sure until he actually met you."

I remembered, again, the moment when Bailey and Chet were chasing us through the Painted Hills, threatening to kill us. When Chet glared at me with disgust and said, "You're just like her." At the time, I'd thought he meant Leslie. But he meant Brianna.

"If I'd known, everything would be different, Willa." So he was going there. "I'm still adjusting to this idea that I'm someone's father. I mean, I would've been in your life all this time, helping raise you. I wouldn't have let you go. I certainly wouldn't have let any of this happen."

It was hard to hear, this admission. Because what did it matter? What had happened was done. I'd never had a father. I pictured briefly, what it would have been like to grow up with a famous politician for a dad, a real mother, a real sister. All of the luxuries I could have had. All of the holidays and celebrations. A steady home.

But I'd had a great childhood with Leslie. I had my adopted family of friends in Paradise Valley. I wouldn't trade that for anything. In the end, cause or no cause, my real mom and Granger were thieves—and liars, too.

He was still lying, for all I knew. It was easy for him to say all this stuff now, wasn't it?

Still. I could see the pleading in his eyes, the tight clasp of his hands, held together almost in prayer. I could see some of the conviction I'd seen in his commercials and when he spoke at the rally. He seemed to believe what he was saying. Maybe he wasn't a bad man. Maybe he was a good man who'd made bad decisions. I, out of everyone, could understand that, couldn't I?

And yet, he'd lied. About lots of things. He was a criminal. He was also my dad.

It was very confusing.

"So what were you doing in a casino, anyway, after all of that?"

"They're my biggest donors," he said.

"Hypocritical much?"

"Sometimes you make compromises."

"I don't," I said flatly.

"No. Maybe you don't." He shook his head. "Look, I don't know what's going to happen to me. My political career is probably over. I'll most likely have to serve some time. And I know there's no way to make up for all the lost years we've missed. But I'd like it if we can leave the lines of communication open in the future."

"I can't promise anything," I said. "I'm headed to juvie myself." And beyond that, my future was blank.

"You don't have to promise me now." His voice was quiet and small and I remembered that for all of his power and scheming he was human, like the rest of us. "Just think about it, okay? That's all I ask."

"Yeah. Okay," I said, getting up from my seat. Was I supposed to shake his handcuffed hand? Hug him? It was too weird. Instead, I gave him a smile. He smiled back, for the first time.

"Good-bye, Willa. Good luck," he said.

"Thank you," I said, feeling tension in my throat again. No, it was more like a fluttery feeling. Anxiety, maybe, of losing something I never knew I had. "Take care of yourself."

The officer opened the door and led me back out into the hall, and I left Granger behind.

Back in the conference room, Corbin had a small box in front of him.

"One more thing we need to take care of, as per our deal," he said.

He opened the box and pulled out some purple latex gloves, which he slid on his hands. Then he produced a cotton swab with a plastic cap. He popped off the cap and said, "Open up."

I opened my mouth and he rubbed the swab on the inside of my cheek, then covered it again with the cap, detaching the handle from the cotton and covering up the plastic with a plug.

"We'll send it off to the lab this afternoon," he said.

I watched as he took the vial, no bigger than a large pill, and put it in an envelope. There it was. The scientific proof. The answers to all of my questions. Some lady in a white coat would make a determination within hours. But it didn't matter at this point. I knew in my heart of hearts what the truth was.

TWENTY

AT TWO P.M., Corbin went to make some calls and Tre stepped out to go get some cash. That left me and Aidan in the conference room. It was the first time we'd been alone together since the trunk. His hair was still long and shaggy, but he'd gotten a shave and his face looked soft and pink. He was wearing some fresh clothes, too, a clean white T-shirt and jeans supplied by the FBI.

"So how are you doing?" he asked. "It's been a lot at once."

"I'm okay," I said, sitting across from him. "You?"

He shrugged. "Happy to be alive. I should thank you for that."

"No." I shook my head. "Don't ever thank me. You wouldn't have been in that situation at all if it wasn't for me. At least it's over, you know? We can go back. We can give up." I savored the relief. Not worrying about where our next bed and meal was coming from, not worrying about who would recognize us and turn us in. We could at least predict where we'd be for a while, and after a lifetime of moving around the country, and the past several weeks of living on the road, that was something I looked forward to.

"Yeah, well, I don't want to go back, Willa." He was shaking his head, but unapologetically.

For him it wasn't just juvie, I remembered. It was real jail time and I certainly understood why he was anxious about it.

"It might not have to be that bad. I'm sure your parents could hire someone, a fancy lawyer. You could fight the charges."

He leaned forward in his seat. "That would mean being part of my family. I told you, I'm done with them."

"They do love you, Aidan."

"How can you say that? You didn't hear my dad on the phone. My life was on the line and he was worried about minimizing his losses."

How *could* I say that? They had to love him, didn't they?

But I didn't know, not really. There were so many variations on families, I was learning. And parents operated in strange and unpredictable ways. Says the girl who didn't know who her real mom was until she was fifteen. I really didn't know the first thing about parents, when it came down to it.

"I just can't go back to living there like nothing

happened. I can't let them control my life anymore."

"So then what?" I was afraid of his answer. He was slipping away, the distance between us widening—physically it was only a table's surface, but emotionally it felt like a much greater expanse. After all that happened we should have been closer, but now I was less sure than ever.

"So then I stay on the road." He ran a hand through his hair. "I've thought this through. You can stay with me. It will be like it was before. Only this time, we'll be smarter. We'll plan it out. No one will find us. I have a way to get new Social Security numbers. We can move somewhere far away, start over. I can develop some software and we can make a fortune, like my dad."

I realized then that, for all his school visits, he'd never planned to go to college in the first place. He didn't need to. He was probably as smart as his father, if not smarter, and he'd go farther than him, I had no doubt about it.

For a moment, the idea was tempting. We'd had fun together these last few weeks. Driving on the open road. Our night at Sam Beasley's. Playing in the City Museum. Even running from the police had somehow turned into a fond memory. It had always seemed like it was me and Aidan against the world. We were free, we'd broken all the rules, and we'd had each other. And this plan of his, it didn't sound half bad, except for the Social Security fraud. I'd already been down that road with Leslie.

But so much had changed, also. I was run-down. I felt

304

like I'd given up too much already.

"I don't know if I want to live that life anymore," I said. "I'm only fifteen years old. There's a lot of time ahead of me, Aidan. I still want to finish school and go to college and get a job, live in a house. I don't want to be someone else again."

He gave me a cocked smile. "But you're Sly Fox, and I'm your partner. We have more adventures to live out, Willa. This is only the beginning."

I let his words hang in the air. Was it really the beginning? To me it felt like the end. Sly Fox—whoever that girl had been—was gone. I didn't want to break the rules anymore, even if it was to do right.

I looked at Aidan's eyes, the green eyes that had captivated me for weeks now.

I cared about him. I was still attracted to him. The idea of losing him, of us being separated by jail and juvie, terrified me. Other people our age were in long-distance relationships at college, but this was completely different.

Maybe I could try to help him, I thought. Maybe if we both gave ourselves in, we could work together to turn things around, build a better relationship with his family. I imagined us writing emails, keeping in touch. It would only be a matter of months.

I could be a good influence, a calming one. Supportive.

But I also knew Aidan would never agree to that.

He could never give in. That wasn't his style, to surrender. He was more suited to life on the road. He was truly rootless—in many ways, he was more of an orphan than I was. I wanted family; I wanted to be cared for. I couldn't live the way he did.

And, as deep as my feelings went, I knew I could never really do anything to make him a different person. Love wasn't always enough. It wasn't with my mom and Granger, that was for sure. Their love had ended in tragedy. I couldn't stand to see anything like that happen to me and Aidan. I loved him too much. I'd almost lost him already.

"What do you say? Come with me?" he asked, and he looked so hopeful it almost broke my heart right then and there.

"I can't," I said finally.

"Why not?"

"Because it's not a good idea." We'd tried so many bad ideas out by now, and I couldn't knowingly fling myself into another one. "I don't think we're the best influence on each other, you know?"

"How can you say that? Me and you?"

"It's not you. It's me." His eyes flashed and I cringed at my own cliché. "What I mean is, this is about me. I feel like I need to start taking responsibility for what I've done. I need to try to take care of myself, because there's no one else out there who can do that for me."

He cupped a hand over mine. "But we love each

other, don't we? Shouldn't that be enough?"

It wasn't. "I care about you, Aidan. I really do. You are the first person who ever made me feel this way. You changed my life, and you're amazing."

He nodded slowly, drawing his hand away from mine. "I guess I didn't change your life for the better, though. Otherwise you'd want to be with me."

"That's not true." The tears came then, clouding my vision. It was hard to separate out what was him and what was this impossible set of circumstances. "I just— I just can't see it working. Not this way. If things were different . . ."

He closed his eyes. "I get it. You don't have to explain any more."

"I'm sorry." And I was. I couldn't stand knowing I was causing him pain. I sucked in a breath, as I returned my hand to my lap. "But you have to promise me you'll be careful out there. I don't want anything to happen to you."

"Okay." He looked away. That was what killed me, when he shut me out of his vision, like he was already trying to forget, block me out.

The door opened. Behind it was Tre carrying three coffees. He set them down on the table. I watched him do this act slowly, with care, his long fingers grasping each cup as he lifted them out of the cardboard carrier. His timing should have been awkward, but actually I think both Aidan and I were grateful that he showed up when he did. There was no sense in prolonging the conversation any further.

"You wanted milk, no sugar, right, Willa?"

"Right," I said, feeling dizzy.

What had just happened? I brought up my palms to my eyes, tried to press back the tears. I was a mess. An embarrassing, horrible mess. This was the worst moment I could imagine.

"I'm sorry," Tre said. "Was I interrupting something?"

"No," Aidan said. "I think we're finished."

"You want me to leave you two alone?"

Finally, Aidan met my eyes. There was, at least, some agreement between us. "Nah, man. Have a seat."

Tre sat down and the three of us sipped at our coffees, together for the last time.

TWENTY-ONE

AIDAN MUST HAVE slipped out in the middle of the night. We'd all been sitting around in the conference room, dozing off in uncomfortable arrangements of chairs, because according to Corbin it was easier for us all to stay here under supervision. Personally, I would have preferred the hotel room. When I woke up, at the crack of dawn, there was a handwritten note from Aidan on a napkin on the table.

> *Gone back on the road. Good luck at home. Tell Tre thank you for his help. I'll miss you, Colorado. We might not work together as a flavor anymore but you taught me how to be free. You were right, though. This is probably for the best.*
> *Love, always,*
> *Aidan*

I'd known it was coming, but even so, my eyes filled with tears. He was really gone. This was it. Would I ever hear from him again?

I wondered how he'd pulled it off. If he'd used Sly Fox techniques or his own. Probably his own.

I looked out the window into the city, the streetlights flicking off, and the bruising morning sky settling over everything. The world seemed huge, suddenly, now that Aidan was out there. Away from me.

Tre, who was too tall for chairs, rolled over on the floor, and opened his eyes. "What time is it?" he moaned.

"Six A.M.," I said. "Aidan's gone."

"He did it, huh?" Tre said, smiling. "He actually snuck out of the FBI offices. That's one for the books."

I smiled, too, vicariously enjoying the badassness of it all. Somehow Aidan had become the slickest of the three of us. How had *that* happened?

He put a hand on my shoulder. "You all right?"

"I guess so. Yeah." I mustered a smile. As devastating as it was to lose Aidan, it also felt right, letting him go. "It's going to be hard without him around."

"You've been through a lot together."

I nodded. "Individually, too."

"But this whole thing, it was worth it?" He rooted around in his pocket for his phone.

"It was."

"You have no regrets?"

"No, not really. There was so much I didn't know when I started out, and it seemed like the more I found out, the less I understood, not just about my mom and who she was, but about myself. But I guess this whole journey has helped me understand. I mean, we always carry our families inside us, whether we realize it or not, and we have to learn to live with that, even when we don't always agree with them." I looked up at Tre. "I didn't even know what I thought was right or wrong when this whole thing began. I just did what I thought I had to do, trying to fix the problem I inherited. But now I see that you don't have to play the cards you're dealt. Bottom line, you have to be able to live with yourself in the end and be good to the people you care about."

"So you're done with being Sly Fox?"

"Well, it's come to an end. We've achieved what we wanted. I have to turn myself in now. I can't speak for Aidan or why he's made the choices he made—I don't have the right to do that anymore. But I think he's going with his heart and that means being on his own, for now. I'm really going to miss him."

"I'm sure he'll miss you, too."

I frowned, registering that he was still holding his phone. "Is this some kind of interview?"

"Actually, yeah," Tre said. "Don't kill me, but I got all that on video."

"For what?"

"For the fans." He gave me a crooked smile as he pressed a few buttons. "I'm posting it to Facebook."

I looked at him to see if he was kidding, but he was

completely serious. It wasn't that I'd forgotten about the Facebook page, but in the midst of everything, it wasn't exactly my top priority.

"Hey, they've stuck by you through all of this, and they've supported your decision to stay on the run. So we need to give them an update. And I knew it would be better to get it in your own words, when you weren't self-conscious about being on camera."

He had a point. "Can I see it at least?"

He handed me the phone, and I watched it play back, cringing only slightly at the sight of myself on video.

Tre was right, and if I owed an explanation to my online fans, then I definitely owed one to my real-life friends.

I dialed Cherise's number. She answered on the third ring, even though it was eleven A.M. on a school day. "Hello?" she half whispered, and for some reason I pictured her with her backpack on, springy hair held back in a headband. "Tre?"

"It's Willa. Where are you?" I asked.

"Willz! Precalc. Where are *you*?"

"At FBI headquarters in St. Louis. Everything's okay."

"Okay okay?"

"Okay okay. We did what we needed to do. And now I'm in custody. Tre's on his way home. Aidan left."

I could hear her pause hanging. "And how is that?"

"It's all right. It's over, I guess." My voice constricted over the words. "We talked it through and we're both doing what we need to do."

"I'm sorry, Willz. Really, I am."

"He won't be coming back to Paradise Valley, I don't think. He's a good guy. We just want different things. Can you do me a favor, though, and make sure that people know that? That no matter what's going around the grapevine, he's not what they think? Not some player or derelict?" It seemed important to me, suddenly, that his reputation was protected, even if he himself had allowed it to be tainted.

"Sure," she said. "I can do that."

"And we made a video for the fan page. It explains everything."

"That's great. We desperately needed an update on there. When will I see you?"

"Soon, I hope," I said. "Very soon."

"Okay. So long as you're all right and everything, I should probably go. I'm kind of under the table right now and I don't want to get busted with this phone."

I laughed, picturing the sight. Also remembering how Cherise was a stickler for rules. She was always going to be a much better person than I was in that way. In most ways, probably.

"Get out from under the table. I'll call you when I can," I said. "Miss you lots."

"Miss you, too. Be safe, Willz."

I sighed as I clicked off the phone. "This is all harder than I thought it would be."

"That's 'cause people care about you, Willa." Tre's brown eyes burned into mine. His lips parted slightly, and I found myself transfixed by them, for a moment.

Corbin limped back in the room. The bullet hadn't gone in deep but he was bandaged and still in pain. "Where's Mr. Murphy?"

"He's gone," I said. "He must have left in the middle of the night."

His face reddened and he slapped a hand to his forehead. "That kid . . . he'll have me in a grave by forty-five. So he just disappeared? No word?"

"He didn't tell us where he was going, I swear," I said. That was purposeful, I was sure. He wouldn't have wanted us to put ourselves on the line for him. Our time of crossing boundaries was done.

"Goddamn."

"Are you going to send someone after him?" I asked.

"I have to. Even though it's a colossal waste of our time and resources. And you?" Corbin asked Tre.

"I'm on my way out, sir. Catching a 10:15 back to Phoenix."

"I don't have to worry about you skipping the bus or going somewhere you shouldn't, do I?"

"No, sir. I'd like to stay a free man."

"Stick with this kid, Willa," Corbin said. "You could learn something from him. You and Murphy both."

"I already have," I said, smiling at Tre.

"I can call you a cab to the station," Corbin offered.

"That would be great," Tre said.

When Corbin was gone, I turned to Tre. "Okay—you can't leave without telling me how you and Cherise got past that checkpoint."

He grinned. "Oh that. It was really just a good story I gave them."

"What'd you say?"

"I said there was an emergency backup at the bakery plant and we had to deliver the goods ASAP. At first he was looking at me like, 'What's this black kid doing driving a truck?' but Cherise and I told him it was our dad's truck and we had to get to L.A. by sundown or there would be a shortage."

"The cops weren't suspicious?"

"I can be pretty convincing," he said. "Also, we gave them a case of crumb cakes."

"Everyone's a sucker for Betelman's." I shook my head. "So there was no gun?"

"Are you crazy? That was some rumor that got on to the internet. You know how they do."

"Well, I'm relieved." If Aidan was more of a badass than I thought, then Tre was less of one.

We stood up to face each other. "So you'll take the money and deposit it, send the checks for me?" I'd signed the checks over to him.

"Will do." He gave me a hug and I felt my whole body enveloped by his. It was warm there, and I knew I was taken care of. "You're going to be okay?"

"Sure," I said, trying to fake it. "No safer place than jail, right?"

He raised an eyebrow as we broke apart. "I can think of a few. I'll visit you, okay? Call me when you can."

"I will," I said, feeling something catch in my throat. Something unfinished between us, something familiar. But there wasn't time to sort it all out for myself, let alone try to articulate it to him. "Thank you—for everything. I couldn't have done this without you."

"Yeah, yeah, yeah," he said with a wink.

We hugged again and then he kissed me softly on the cheek. "Be good, Sly Fox."

Then Tre left and I watched him from the window, swinging off his backpack to get into the cab. As it pulled away from the curb, I swallowed hard. First Aidan. Now Tre was gone, too.

I looked out at the blocky, mirrored, and shadowed shapes of the city, this city I had come to know so well over the past few days, and felt a surge of affection for it. It had soul and history. People chose to work and love and have children and build their lives in St. Louis, and their energy hummed in the streets.

I understood, finally, why my parents had been fighting for this place, even if their plan had been the wrong one, and why Granger had stayed on all these years to try to represent its people. As someone who was shuffled around from home to home, in town to town, I almost envied them—they had a home of their own.

A few minutes later, Corbin came back into the room. "Your friend leave?"

I nodded. "So I guess someone will be escorting me back to Arizona?"

"Well, I've been thinking about that. You don't really need to go back there, do you?"

"You tell me." I frowned. What was he getting at? "Are there any other options?"

"I have one. Why don't you join Leslie in Mexico? Neither of you needs to be in hiding anymore, but you could at least get a fresh start out there. I can arrange it so you have amnesty for helping us solve the crime. Consider it my last gift to you. Well, to Leslie, really."

"You'd do that?"

"Look, family's all we have, right?" His eyes were kind, if a little sad. "You belong together. And I think your mom would have wanted it this way. All along, I wondered how she could have been mixed up with these people, and something Granger said last night cleared it up for me. He said she'd always been poor, and her parents had pretty much abandoned her when she had Leslie as a teenager. I think being part of something bigger like that group gave her hope. The point is, I think you need to be part of something, too, Willa. We all do. I don't know . . . maybe that's why I was stuck on this case, on finding Leslie all those years. And heck, maybe that's why you guys had so many fans, you know?"

I stared hard into his face and I could see that it was

finally relaxed. He had all of his answers, after all of these years. This was his way of telling me he was grateful for helping him put the case to rest.

"Let me make a few calls, and then we can have you sign some documents and get this together. Stay put, now."

I sat at the table, feeling newly excited and relieved. No juvie? That was awesome. I would see Leslie again. We'd be together. And Mexico . . . Where would we live? Where would I go to school? I let the daydream unfurl in my head. It would be a new life, and this time we were both choosing it.

Alone in the room again, I started looking through the contents of my mother's bag. There was a soft fuchsia turtleneck sweater, a pair of gray corduroys. I'd seen photos of her and lists of her other belongings. But touching these items, fabrics she'd worn against her skin, was different. I unfolded a pair of jeans, ran my hands over the denim. As I grazed the back pocket, I felt the shape of a folded piece of paper tucked deep within its crevice.

I reached into it and pulled the paper out. An envelope. No address, but a name. The Franklin family. No return address, either.

Franklin Family. My heart started to race. I slid my finger under the flap, which was already open, and removed the letter inside.

I've been trying to avoid this situation for too long.
I want you to know how sorry I am about what's

happened. Not a day has gone by when I haven't
wished we could go back and change it. While I
can't make it right, and I can't change any of it,
I can help you with your care costs. There's more
where this came from, but for now, please accept
this check.

Folded inside the letter was a yellowed, brittle check, written to the Franklin family for the sum of a million dollars. I stared at the typeface so long that it blurred into indecipherable scratchings, barely believing what was in front of me. Here it was. Her letter.

So she'd been planning to do the right thing all along—to give the money to the victim, to truly help someone. She'd just never gotten the chance before she was killed. And no one had known about this, not until now. Maybe it always takes something big, something painful, to make us shift our perspective. In her case it was this terrible tragedy. In mine, it was finally understanding the mother I hadn't even known I'd lost.

I knew then that I had to call Tre and tell him to send the rest of our reward money to the Franklins. Leslie's money, the original money, was going back to the bank, but I had to make sure that my mom's final wishes were fulfilled.

All at once, I felt her presence—so powerful, it was as if she was in the room with me whispering into my ear. I understood exactly who she was and what she'd been trying to do.

And now I knew for sure who I was. Who I'd been all along, and it wasn't Sly Fox. It wasn't Willa Fox, either. Finally, I was ready to do the right thing and do it the right way.

I smiled to myself. Corbin would be coming back any moment now, and he'd have all the plans ready, all the documents for me to sign. I would sign them, but I would ask him if it would be all right to use my real name.

Maggie Siebert.

EPILOGUE

"**I WISH I** could get this damn thing to work," Leslie said, fumbling to adjust the angle of the beach umbrella, which seemed to have a mind of its own. "My last one got carried off by the wind."

"Why can't we just soak in the rays?" I said, lying down on my towel and stretching out lazily. "Forget the umbrella."

The sand was white and hot, and the water licked quietly at the beach, the edges of the teal waves barely foamy. I'd arrived yesterday at Leslie's place in Todos Santos on the Baja Peninsula. Today we were taking the day to relax and catch up. There was a lot to catch up on. Hostages, fake bombs, death-defying getaways. You know, the usual biz.

She chucked me a bottle of sunblock, SPF gazillion. "You can't just soak in the rays—you have Siebert skin. We got Mom's lovely porcelain complexion, so deal with it."

She was put off, at first, by the fact that I'd changed my name back to Maggie, since she was the one who had named me Willa. Then I pointed out that she was no longer going by Joanne, either. We were new/old people. And I also pointed out that it was only fair that this time I got to pick.

I squeezed out some lotion and started to apply it around the straps of the awesome red bandeau bikini I'd bought at the airport. Whatever possessions I had back in Paradise Valley were going to stay there until Cherise or Tre could get me a package through their contacts in the Sly Fox fan network. It was under the conditions of Corbin's deal that I was supposed to avoid contact with everyone in Paradise Valley, but there was no law against having a middleman. Besides, just because I'd promised to stop stealing and running away didn't mean I wasn't going to connect with my friends when I needed to. Some teeny-tiny rules still needed to be broken—when it came to people you cared about, at least.

"So you missed me all this time out here by your-self?"

She smiled. "If you want to know the truth it was nice to have a little me time for once."

"I'm glad it was so relaxing," I said, giving her the eye. "Next time I'll try to extend my stay on the road, maybe find a tougher case to crack so you can work on your downward dogs."

"Oh, come on. Of course, I thought about you

constantly. I worried a lot—I had no idea you'd skipped out on Corbin until he called me last week. I can only say thank God you didn't get killed by those psychopaths."

"Thank God I didn't," I repeated, shuddering away the memory of the trunk, the power plant, the gunfight. I could still hear those shots in my dreams and feel the panic of almost losing Aidan.

"So what did Granger say?"

I called him earlier that morning to let him know I'd arrived safely, and I had a few other things to report. "I told him the news. That Mom was planning to send the money to the Franklins. That she wasn't keeping it for herself in the end."

"How'd he take it?"

"He was emotional. I could hear his voice shaking a little bit. Guilty, I guess. Now he knows that she truly died for nothing. The case doesn't look good for him. The car DNA was a match. Chet hasn't confessed to anything yet, but they have Bailey's recordings that implicate him."

"So Granger'll probably be in for a while."

"Unless his legal team can do some magic, I guess. I gave him the other news, too. About the paternity test."

She leaned in. "And? He didn't have a heart attack right then and there?"

"He was happy," I said, defensive. "He said he'd been hoping it was true. But he said he would understand if I didn't want to call him 'Dad' or anything."

"What do you think? Will you keep in touch with him?"

"Maybe." He was screwed up—he'd let his ambition destroy lives—but he was my dad, after all. It seemed like he really wanted to change. Everyone deserved the benefit of the doubt, didn't they?

Leslie wouldn't want me to have contact with him—that much was clear—but she was no longer acting as my mom.

Whatever happened next, I wanted it to be on my own terms. And I wanted to do right by my mother and live by the lessons she'd taught me. Did that mean opening my heart and forgiving Granger? Possibly.

In any case, I couldn't think that far into the future. Right now all I could think about was the soft sand caking my toes. That me and Leslie were together again, building our home as we'd done so many times before. That I had no other obligation for the moment except to try not to get a sunburn. I had my life here. Weirdly enough, even though my mom was dead and my dad was in jail, I no longer felt like an orphan. I belonged somewhere. And after all my mistakes, I was getting another chance. I vowed I'd make the best of it, that I would stay true to my beliefs but also stay true to the people I loved.

Then, of course, Leslie, being my mom-like sister, had to go and break the spell with some practical nonsense. "So I looked into the school here and I think we can start you in the spring. You'll have to take some extra Spanish courses over the next few weeks to get ready for it. Forget French."

That was okay. I was ready to forget French. The language had done nothing for me, except provide me with an opportunity for my first heist. And we all know how that turned out.

A new school. Again. The truth was, I would miss Paradise Valley. As many bad memories as I had there, there were also plenty of happy ones. Aidan. Cherise. Tre.

I had no idea where Aidan was by now. He could be on the East Coast or he could be in Kansas. I prayed he was doing okay, that he was warm and not hungry, and that he was safe and well caffeinated. He would find his way, I was sure of that. It was hard to let him go and even harder to let him be alone out there. Still, I wanted him to be happy and he couldn't get that at home.

Cherise was always going to be my friend. We'd been through enough by now that I felt like I could count on that. We would keep in touch however we could and, who knew? Maybe someday I would even get back to Paradise Valley to visit—she'd spin some new records for me and we'd try on outfits in her room.

And Tre . . . somehow, I missed him the most. I kept hearing his laugh in my head at unexpected moments. Feeling the warmth of his gaze on me. Replaying the brush of his lips on my cheek. He'd always done what

325

he'd thought was best for me—not just going along with what I thought I wanted—and after those last few days in St. Louis, I finally understood what it meant. Now, I could honestly say I wanted the same for him. I wanted it for both of us, for us both to be right.

My brand-new phone buzzed. I reached into my beach bag and pulled it out.

It sucks here without you. Hope you're okay.
I checked and Christmas break starts the
20th. I think I can bring the bike with me.

I squinted at the words in the sunlight, smiling. It was like Tre had read my mind or something. Then I thumbed in my response.

All is fine. We'll pick you up at the airport.
It's do-over time. Xo

ACKNOWLEDGMENTS

WHEW! WILLA'S JOURNEY has come to an end, and what a journey it's been. I'm awed by the work Claudia Gabel, Melissa Miller, and Alexandra Arnold have put into this trilogy, keeping me in touch with the heart of the story and always redirecting the route when the road trip got off course. The glamorous and kind Katherine Tegen has always made me feel right at home at her imprint. The magnificent team at HarperCollins, including Barbara Fitzsimmons, Amy Ryan, Cara Petrus, Laura DiSiena, Melinda Weigel, Lauren Flower, Onalee Smith, and Casey McIntyre, have been a joy to work with. Grateful appreciation, too, to Leigh Feldman, Jean Garnett, and Henry Ginna from Writers House.

Whenever the final leg of Willa's expedition got too daunting, my dear friends were there to nudge me on. That includes fellow YA authors Kate Walton, Eugene Myers, Tiffany Schmidt, and Eve Mont, who all happen to live in Philly, which really makes me believe in geography as destiny. It also includes nonfiction author Abbott Kahler and civilians Steve Poses and Christina Sterner, Erin Small, Holly Mack-Ward, and Rebecca Goldner, who have each, in different but powerful ways, underwritten my efforts.

I'm so grateful to have family that support me through all the various stages, emotional and physical, of writing a book, and that now includes serious childcare hours. Thanks to my parents, Zella and Stephen Ludwig, my aunt Stelle Sheller, and my mother-in-law, Penny Bean, for enabling me to sit in front of a computer and mumble to myself. Thanks to my sister Susannah for making incredible video trailers for my books. Thanks to my sister Aubrey for making me feel like a superstar.

Thanks, as ever, to my incredible husband, Jesse, and my sweet son, Rainer, my very favorites.

BONNIE and CLYDE?
Try WILLA and AIDAN.

"A pretty twisted, modern-day Robin Hood story."
—Melissa de la Cruz, *New York Times* bestselling author